heart thief

taylor dean

TAYLOR DEAN

Heart Thief
Copyright © 2019 by Taylor Dean

Cover art: ©iStockphoto.com/svetikd]
Back cover art: ©iStockphoto.com/pepifoto]
Stamp design: ©iStockphoto.com/artag_lab]
Cover design: Jules Isaacs
Author photo: Jules Isaacs
Edited by: Charissa Stastny

PRINT ISBN: 9781691946280

Other titles in the *Love Under Wraps* standalone series:

December 2019
Rules are Made to be Broken
by Mylissa Demeyere

One rule: Don't fall in love with your best friend's brother. Should be easy, right?

January 2020
A Wrinkle in Forever
by Charissa Stastny

What do you do when forever unravels? Hold on tight.

TAYLOR DEAN

To Charissa and Mylissa,

The best author friends a girl could have!
I'm so thankful for your love and support.
It's been an honor to do this series with you.

TAYLOR DEAN

"Oh, I see," said the Tin Woodman. "But, after all, brains are not the best things in the world."

"Have you any?" enquired the Scarecrow.

"No, my head is quite empty," answered the Woodman. "But once I had brains, and a heart also, so having tried them both, I should much rather have a heart."

-L. Frank Baum, *The Wonderful Wizard of Oz*

chapter one

♡

"I HAVE AN important question for you this evening," Ryker says as he leans forward, his forearms resting on the edge of the table.

I press my lips together, hiding my smile, and pushing down my excitement. I'm not going to say *I know*, because I don't know for sure.

But I'm *hoping* that Ryker's about to propose. All the clues are there. Fancy restaurant, check. Candlelight dinner, check. Soft music in the background, check. Lingering for two hours over dinner and dessert while he appears nervous, check. Dressed to the nines, check. Bulge in his suitcoat pocket the size of a ring box, check. My family waiting by the phone to hear the official announcement, check.

This is it. My future. I never thought I'd meet someone like Ryker. It's taken me all of my twenty-nine years to find him. Nothing is as Disney-princess-perfect as I'd imagined it would be, but this is reality. So far, reality is surprisingly good.

"I hope you've enjoyed this evening. I love spoiling you," he says, his voice deep and smooth. His silver cufflinks catch my eyes as his sleeves peek out from his suitcoat.

If there's a word to describe Ryker, it would be . . . polished. I swear he was born with perfect manners.

"I've loved every minute. Thank you."

He grants me a warm smile, his eyes crinkling at the corners. I know he's as pleased as I am when it comes to our relationship.

The low murmur of conversation and the gentle tinkle of ice swirling in glasses surrounds us. Pleasant background noise for a momentous occasion.

Ryker's brown-eyed gaze sinks into mine, his mouth parts, and he inhales slightly, the words I want to hear about to drip from his lips.

His phone rings for the fifth time this evening, ruining the moment.

Okay, so maybe I haven't loved *every* minute of this evening.

"I'm so sorry, Mila." He runs one hand through his dark brown hair that's always styled to perfection, ruffling it slightly. A rare sign of frustration. "I wanted this night to be all about us, with no interruptions."

"It's okay. I know you have to take it. Go ahead."

He nods, his expression thankful. He brings his phone to his ear. "Ryker Martel."

Of course, I hate the interruption. But I do understand and I refuse to let it ruin the magic of our evening.

Ryker's father suffered a stroke a year ago, leaving Martel Investments in Ryker's capable, but swamped hands. I don't think the man ever stops working. I think he feels the need to prove himself by taking the company to new heights.

And he has.

For a price. I swear, the man doesn't sleep.

"No, that cannot happen, and I expect you to fix it immediately. Don't call me back until it's done," Ryker snaps.

When his phone call is complete, he holds up one finger. "I apologize, just one moment." He sends a text before turning his attention back to me, the woman he's been dating for the past ten months.

"Thanks for being patient with me, Mila. You're a gem." He takes a deep breath. "It never stops."

Ryker tries and succeeds at being attentive, so I don't allow myself to become upset. While he's inundated with phone calls day and night, he's never oblivious to the disturbance, often apologizing numerous times. Like I said, the man was born with manners. Toward me, anyway. I sure wouldn't want to be the person on the other end of some of his business phone calls. It gets quite heated at times. I'm glad I'm not part of the corporate world.

"I know you love it." He thrives on his fast-paced life. It animates him.

He shakes his head. "You get me. That's why we're perfect for each other."

"I think so too, Ryker. But don't be surprised if I hide your phone every now and again."

He stiffens. "You wouldn't do that to me, would you?"

Humor is always lost on him. He takes everything literally. "That was a joke."

He chuckles, even though he didn't find it remotely funny. "I was born without a funny bone. Don't give up on me, please."

"Never."

He reaches out to hold my hand across the table. Our fingers lace together.

There are so many reasons why I love this man, but his persistence at keeping our relationship alive amidst his crazy schedule takes top billing.

"Where were we?" he asks, focusing solely on me.

"You said you wanted to ask me a question." Hint, hint.

He taps one finger on the table like he's nervous. Not his usual behavior. "Ah, yes. I've been thinking a lot about our upcoming separation. It's going to be difficult to be apart from each other. Our relationship gets better every day. It's strange, I've never experienced anything like this before now."

He's leaving for Japan in two weeks. He'll be gone for three months, dealing with his father's foreign investments.

He continues after clearing his throat three times. I find his nerves endearing. "I know this is a tenuous time for us, when our love is still new and fragile. I'm sorry I have to leave."

"Me too." Ten months of dating is not exactly new, but I know what he means. We've taken things slow and easy, a pace we're both comfortable with.

"I can't imagine life without seeing your beautiful face every day."

My heart pitter-patters in my chest. "I feel the same. It's going to be tough without you."

He squeezes my hand, his eyes never wandering from mine, never distracted by the activity at the other tables. "I-I have to admit, I'm dreading it. Y-you've become a fixture in my life and I don't want that to change."

He's stumbling over his words. That *never* happens with my smooth-talking man. Here it comes. The question I've been waiting for all night.

"I don't want it to change either, Ryker."

Pleased with my reassurance, his eyes glitter. "The more I think about it, the more I realize it would be silly for my apartment to sit empty while I'm gone."

My smile falters at the change of subject. *What?*

"Your apartment?" He owns the top story penthouse in a luxury high rise. Yet, he calls it his apartment. I couldn't hide my surprise the first time I saw it. It's nothing short of amazing.

"That's what I'd like to talk to you about this evening. I have a proposition for you," he says with sudden confidence, his nerves a thing of the past.

My smile dies a quick death, exiting my face entirely. Proposition? Not a proposal?

"Why don't you stay there? It'd get you out of that quaint studio apartment you're living in and you'd be able to save a lot of money because you wouldn't have any rent to pay. Arthur loves you. He'd be much happier with you than the kennel. What do you think? It's the perfect arrangement, right?"

Wait. Is that his question?

Ryker doesn't seem to notice that all the blood left my

face. My mind is screaming *hashtag: relationship fail*. I misread his nerves, saw what I wanted to see.

He goes on, excited by his idea. "You're renting month to month. Give your two-week notice, and I'll send movers over to collect your belongings. All expenses paid. You wouldn't need to worry about a thing. Your baby grand piano would look stunning in my living room, don't you think?"

I nod, speechless. I mean, he's right. My baby grand would look stunning next to his gorgeous view of the Golden Gate Bridge. At night, the city lights are breathtaking from his floor-to-ceiling windows. It would be an amazing place to live. Absolutely. I would love it.

But that's not the issue.

I look down at my plate. Color me pale and call me blindsided. "Uh, that's a generous offer. Thank you, Ryker. I'm, uh, overwhelmed."

"I'd do anything for you, Mila Westerman. You know that."

Anything except propose. "I, um, I'm speechless. I'm not sure what to say." *Redundant thought, Mila. Pull yourself together.* I slip my hand away from his as my long black hair falls forward. I let it hang over one side of my face, a curtain of privacy while I compose myself. My heart's racing and I can't catch my breath. I inhale slowly, over and over. Deep, calming breaths.

I'm *that* girl. The one who thought she was about to be proposed to and couldn't have been more wrong. I've seen this scene in movies so many times, it has become cliché. How did I get here? I fell into the hope-for-marriage trap when I should've known better. I feel silly.

Slowly, I push my black hair aside and let my blue eyes travel up to his. I try to appear normal and fail miserably.

Realization slowly dawns on Ryker's handsome face. His eyes widen. "Oh. You thought I was going to propose, didn't you?"

I shrug away his perceptiveness. "It might've crossed

my mind." To my horror, my eyes well with tears.

He snakes his fingers through his brown hair. Very unlike him. "I'm so sorry, Mila." He leans in closer, his eyes direct. He holds out both hands, open palms resting on the table, an invitation for me to join him. "Hear me out. Please."

The subtle pleading in his voice makes me respond accordingly. Once again, our hands intertwine, his smooth skin warm against mine.

"I promise, this isn't the tragic dinner where the girl is disappointed that the man didn't propose."

Could've fooled me.

"My thoughts are there too. We're absolutely on the same page. I wanted to propose tonight. It was my plan. I've been debating over it for days now. In the end, I decided it wasn't fair to you to propose and then leave for three months. What kind of an engagement is that? I felt like I would be sending you the message that I just wanted to stake my claim, as though I was reserving you for myself while I was gone. I can't do that to you."

Oh. Okay. There's my smooth-talking man, spinning the situation enough to make me dizzy. I try to wipe the stunned expression off my face. That's a logical explanation and yet such a strange way to look upon an engagement. Again, I'm not sure what to say, so I say nothing.

Ryker releases my hands, reaches into his pocket, and pulls out the ring box.

At least I was right about one thing.

He hesitates, gathering his thoughts. "This is for you, a promise ring of sorts. I wanted to make my intentions clear this evening. I see a future for us, Mila. As a matter of fact, I'm counting on it. But I think we should wait to make it official until after I return from my trip." He maintains eye contact and grants me a tentative smile.

I'm a blank slate, still processing everything he said. I'm not being jilted. On the contrary. I'm being delayed, like a plane at an airport.

If you wait long enough, eventually every plane will arrive. I guess I need to wait a bit longer for my proposal.

I'm comforted by knowing I wasn't totally wrong about us. I hate to think I could be that clueless.

Ryker slips the ring on my left ring finger, making it look like we're engaged. The circle of diamonds catches the light and sparkles back at me.

Wow. Ryker never does anything by halves. I'm not sure I want to know how much he spent on it. This could be my actual wedding ring and I'd be thrilled. "It's gorgeous, I love it. Thank you," I whisper through a tight throat. I'm still reeling with emotions, my heart pounding painfully in my chest. For a moment, I thought I had given away my love foolishly.

"This is not the end, Mila. It's the beginning, I promise. Please be happy."

The beginning. The beginning. This is the beginning, I silently chant as I take a deep breath.

He's right. This is just the beginning of our life together. I force a smile. "I am. This ring will always remind me of you while you're gone."

Will it also represent that he wasn't sure about us? That he wasn't quite ready to fully commit?

Even though it's not what he's saying, it's the underlying message buried deep within a whole lot of sweet words.

I shake it off and remind myself to listen to his words and believe them. Don't let my inner doubts speak for him and say what he's not saying.

"You look beautiful this evening, Mila. Did I mention that already?" Ryker asks, interrupting my wandering thoughts.

"You did. Several times, in fact," I say, trying to appear unfazed by the evening's events.

"Would you like anything else or shall we go? I thought we could take a walk for a bit, enjoy the night air.

It's a beautiful evening."

Oh. I thought we were done. I was ready to escape. In all truth, I'd like to go home, curl up in my softest pajamas, and eat lots and lots of chocolate. Obscene amounts. Instead, I maintain a polite veneer. "That sounds lovely, thank you. Let's go."

Someday, I'll look back on this night and laugh at my naivety. But that day is not today.

For right now, it's labeled in the files of my brain as the longest night of my life.

And it's not over yet.

chapter two
♡

RYKER AND I lazily walk along the city streets hand in hand, a soft breeze licking our skin, the streetlights casting dim shadows across the pavement. He seems relaxed, or dare I say, relieved. As for me, I'm numb and still slightly dazed.

"Mila, I just want you to know that I won't stop thinking about you the entire time I'm gone. Not for a second. We have a connection, you and I, one I've never felt with anyone else." He squeezes my hand. "I feel like we're together for all the right reasons. Sometimes you just have to take a chance on love, and I'm willing to go on this journey with you."

It feels like he said all of this a moment ago. Nothing new. Shame on me, but my mind immediately wanders to my guilty pleasure, *The Bachelor*. He just repeated *Bachelor* rhetoric almost verbatim. I again force myself to listen to the heartfelt meaning behind his words.

"I feel the same," I say.

We share a warm smile, but my smile is a tad forced, maybe even a touch fake. I swallow my disappointment whole, in one gulp. It's now residing somewhere inside the cavernous recesses of my body. I'll push it down and keep it there for now.

Time to lighten the mood. "Ryker, have you been watching *The Bachelor*?"

He sends me a sidelong glance. "Excuse me?"

"Nothing, I'm sorry. Go on, bad joke." One he'd never get in a thousand years, even if he did get jokes. He's not a TV watcher.

He continues as though I never said anything. "You know I'm falling in love with you, Mila."

Falling.

Not *in* love.

More *Bachelor* rhetoric. *Stop it, Mila.*

It's simply a figure of speech, because he says it to me often. I've always taken it as *I love you, Mila*, and I'm positive that's what he means. It's just that, I feel a little knocked flat this evening.

"I'm in love with you too, Ryker," I say with no conviction whatsoever.

He glances at me, the corners of his mouth turned up in a pleased smile. "All right, then. Me and you. Are we good? Because I think we're perfect." There's a sweet tone in his voice. Soft, caring, yet firm and commanding. He could be a politician and do very well. If he wanted to, he could smooth talk the coat off a freezing man.

"We're good," I somehow choke out, as though my lips detect the lie and are trying to push them back down my throat.

I might lick a few wounds when I return to the privacy of my own home, but at least I know a proposal was on his mind. The knowledge that he plans to propose when he returns home will have to keep me warm for the next three months.

"Would you like to sit?" Ryker asks, motioning toward a bench.

I let out a sigh. The longest night ever might as well be even longer. I console myself with the thought that it can't get worse. "Okay." I feel like humming *This is the Song that Never Ends*, replacing song with night.

"Back to the subject of my apartment," Ryker says when we're situated. "I would love for you to live there. I'm serious. It would mean a lot to me."

I tilt my head to one side. "Just to be clear. Are you asking me to live with you or to live there while you're gone?"

"To live there while I'm gone. I know living with someone is not your style."

No, it isn't. "I appreciate the offer, I really do.

Apartment living is not for me, though. You know being a professional pianist means I have to practice the piano six hours a day. Can you imagine how annoyed your neighbors will be? Typically, I start at six in the morning. That's why I rented the studio I live in now. Do you know how hard it was to find a mother-in-law suite that was separated from the main house by a backyard in this city? Plus, the homeowners said my practicing wouldn't bother them, that they *loved* the arts. It's the perfect arrangement for me. I'd rather not lose the place."

"You probably won't need a new place. Have you thought about that?" he says quietly.

My eyes move up to his sharply, as my breath hitches. If he proposes when he gets home, then I suppose I might never leave his penthouse, because it will become my home too. The implication is there, I don't need him to spell it out for me.

Although if tonight is anything to go by, maybe I do.

Ryker goes on before I can object further. "As far as the piano goes, I've already thought this through. I live in an upscale high rise in the penthouse apartment at the top of the building. The soundproofing is amazing. The only wall I share with someone is the floor. The guy below me plays the electric guitar and has parties in his unit until the wee hours of the morning, and I never hear him. I'm not worried. Besides, I already checked with him. He's an early riser, works long hours, and said he's hardly home anyway. If he hears anything, it will be distant. It's not a problem."

I frown. "Are you sure? It's my second season performing with the Marin Symphony. It's an honor to be chosen to be a guest artist for a symphony. It's imperative that I'm able to practice every day."

"I wouldn't ask you to live there if I thought you wouldn't be able to practice. I know how important it is to you. I know your dream is to play with the San Francisco Symphony one day."

I love that he supports my goals in life. "I don't call it a dream, I call it a plan," I remind him.

He covers my hand with his and entwines our fingers. "I know you do, and I have no doubt you'll do it. Your talent is just waiting to be discovered."

"Thank you, Ryker."

"So, what do you say?"

Images of Ryker's penthouse apartment wander through my mind. Floor-to-ceiling windows, gleaming hardwood floors, and white. Lots and lots of white. The kitchen almost hurts my eyes with its white cabinetry, white tile, and white countertops. The white doesn't end there. His couches are white, his area rug is white, his sheer curtains are white. I'm scared to breathe, to touch anything, or to be human in any way, shape, or form. He keeps it pristine. I'm not a messy person, but I'm also not a squeaky-clean person either.

"What are you thinking?" he asks.

"I'm worried about making a mess in your home. Your apartment screams, *I'm going to need everyone to stop living here, please.*"

He stares at me blankly. Ryker and humor are not friends.

"I know you'll take excellent care of my home. I have no reservations on that front."

No pressure. "Yes, of course I will."

His head tilts back, his chin jutting forward, a sure sign of confidence. I'm glad he feels so sure of me. I wish I felt the same.

"So, you'll do it then? You can stay in my master bedroom. I think you'll find it very comfortable. I've spared no expense."

I sigh. His bedroom is whiter than the kitchen. I'll cause something to smudge simply by looking at it.

Should I do this? A list of pros wanders through my mind. First, no rent for three months. That would help my finances a lot. That's huge. Even though the symphony pays me well, rent in San Francisco is crazy high and I've been trying to build up a healthy savings account.

Second, I'd live in the lap of luxury. That one's a no brainer.

Which leads me to the third reason this would be good for me. It would be the ideal atmosphere for concentrating on my intense practice sessions.

I wrack my brain and try to think of any cons. Other than the color white, there are none.

It's an offer I can't refuse.

"Okay, I'll do it. Arthur will be my bodyguard and constant companion. How can I resist?"

Arthur is his teacup Yorkie Poo, a cross between a Yorkshire Terrier and a Poodle. He was chosen by Ryker, I'm sure, because the Poodle in him means he doesn't shed all over his furniture. He's the tiniest and sweetest dog I've ever seen. He's scared of his own shadow and is almost always shaking. I was in love with him the moment he walked toward me on wobbly legs, while I coaxed him with my voice. He placed his two front paws on my left shin, begging to be held. He's such a lightweight, I couldn't even feel the pressure of his paws on my leg.

When Ryker announced that his dog's name was Arthur, my heart melted in my chest. "Arthur," I'd said, "You're adorable."

I remember chuckling because Arthur is such an old man's name and here was this delicate creature looking up at me with literal puppy dog eyes. Once I picked him up and cuddled him in my arms, we were friends for life. He's my buddy.

"Arthur worships you."

"The feeling is mutual." I sort of want to add, "Too bad yours aren't." But I bite my tongue and keep my thoughts to myself. Bitterness is so ugly.

If Ryker can tolerate a dog in his white space, surely he can tolerate me. Either that or my future is destined to be an episode of *The Odd Couple*.

"You're going to love living there, Mila. And practicing with that view, it'll inspire you."

"I'm sure the acoustics are pretty amazing too." I'm starting to feel excited about living in Ryker's home. Although, at some point, we will need to have a serious discussion about color.

"I'll make all the arrangements first thing in the morning." He scoots closer and lines the back of the bench with his arm. He doesn't touch my back or shoulder. "The future looks bright for us, Mila."

"The future looks bright," I repeat, wondering about the luminosity of that statement.

He doesn't lean over and kiss me because he's not big on public displays of affection. But I wish he would. I wish he'd kiss me like he doesn't have a care in the world, like he'll never see me again in this lifetime and he can hardly stand it. A kiss filled with so much passion, I'll be swooning for days.

Strike one, no proposal.

Strike two, no kiss.

Disappointment swirls inside me.

Ryker is a careful man. Always a bit guarded, always overthinking his life, as evidenced by his proposition, and lack of a proposal, this evening. He's always thinking three steps ahead. Maybe four or five. I suppose that's why he excels in the business world.

"By the way, my mom wanted me to stop by this evening. Something about important paperwork she needs to give me. Will you come with me?"

Strike three, his mother.

Freddy.

Great. The never-ending night continues.

I try to force my lips into a smile, but it probably comes off more like a grimace. "Sure."

I've nicknamed his mother Freddy. She's a kind, gracious, loving person.

At first glance.

The first time I met her, I thought she was amazing. She told me I was beautiful, she told me I was lovely, she told me I must be so smart to play the piano so well and to have attended Juilliard.

I smiled and soaked it all in.

Then she bared her proverbial ugly teeth, reminding me of Freddy Fazbear on that creepy video game, *Five Nights at Freddy's.*

She turned to me and casually mentioned how being a pianist was such a sweet hobby. What did I do in real life?

"Real life?" I stuttered, taken aback.

"Yes, dear, what's your day job? Playing the piano will get you nowhere in life. Such a tedious instrument. It gives me a headache."

She went on with the conversation as though she hadn't insulted me and all of my hard work.

I soon learned it's her *modus operandi.*

My brother used to play *Five Nights at Freddy's.* By day, the characters are on stage, entertaining children, imitating a Chuck E. Cheese pizza parlor. Cute and sweet.

At night, they come to life, bare their creepy teeth, and terrorize the nighttime security guard.

That's Ryker's mom. So sweet—until she's not. She's scary, because you never know when she will bare her teeth and toss a barbed comment your way.

When I'm with her, I remind myself of the Eleanor Roosevelt quote: *No one can make you feel inferior without your consent.*

I refuse to let her mess with me. How she produced a wonderful man like Ryker, I will never know. I think it might be the love she smothers him with every day of his life. It's amazing he can breathe at all.

Time to fortify myself to face Freddy on this never-ending night.

chapter three
♥

DEBRA MARTEL OPENS the door of her ridiculously large home for only two people and greets us with a smile pasted on her face. It's only nine on this everlasting night and she's still dressed in a classy dress suit with her signature pearls at her neck, as though she's about to go to the office.

She doesn't work outside the home. She oversees the household. I have no idea why she dresses the way she does.

I wonder if sweats and a lazy night on the couch binge-watching Netflix are ever part of her agenda. I doubt it. Her bleach-blond hair is always perfectly coifed, her teeth so white, they hurt my eyes, and her forehead is clearly filled with so much Botox, her eyebrows can barely move. She's a woman desperately fighting the aging process.

"Ryker, you look so handsome." She air kisses each of his cheeks.

"And Myla, you're simply stunning this evening." I get one air kissed cheek.

"It's Mila." And she knows it.

She waves the air as though the pronunciation of my name doesn't really matter.

"What have you two lovebirds been up to this evening?"

Her smile says, *I love you*, her eyes say, *You're not good enough for my son.*

"Dinner at Acquerello," Ryker says.

"Such a lovely place. You have excellent taste, Ryker."

I doubt Debra believes I have a single smart thought in my head or enough class to choose such a place.

Debra turns and starts walking up the stairs with the assumption that we'll automatically follow like faithful subjects.

We do.

"Your father's not in bed yet. Come say hello."

It's tough to see James Martel, a once vibrant man, stuck in a wheelchair with half of his body paralyzed, and unable to speak intelligibly. His head leans to one side, dribble almost always resting on his chin. A result of a massive stroke.

His night nurse turns the TV off at our arrival. "I was just about to get him ready for bed, Mrs. Martel. I'll give you some privacy." She politely takes her leave.

Debra stands behind her husband, massaging his shoulders. "Sweetheart, it's Ryker. He's running Martel Investments and things are going as smooth as a lake on a clear day. If you could see him in action, you'd be so proud. As vice president, he's the best right-hand man you have."

With James incapacitated, the board of investors act as the president of the company, much to Ryker's dismay.

Ryker sits in the chair next to his father, holding one hand. "Hey, Dad. Great to see you. You're looking good. Don't worry about anything. I have everything under control. Just get better, okay?"

James grunts and tries to speak, but we can't understand him. It's obvious the man they once knew is no longer present. He's clearly frustrated with his limits. I feel for the poor man. It's been a year and he hasn't improved much, in spite of intense physical therapy.

I don't think he will ever recuperate, but Ryker and Debra always speak as though a full recovery is just around the corner. I wouldn't dare to be the one to discourage them and dash their hope.

"Come say hello, Mila," Debra says, a subtle command.

I walk forward and sit in the chair opposite Ryker. I place my hand on James' arm. "Hello, Mr. Martel. It's Mila. It's wonderful to see you. I hope you've had a good day."

He looks directly at me, his eyes droopy and sad. I

can't help but think it's a tender mercy that he's not all there anymore. I can't imagine how horrible it would be to be stuck in a body that's refusing to work. He tries to say my name, but it's garbled.

"Isn't she lovely, James? Mila and Ryker make such a beautiful couple."

I'm surprised to hear her say that, since I always feel like she thinks I'm not good enough for her son.

"Our son was always the kid who wanted to bring home the lost and broken puppy. So sweet."

There's the Freddy I've come to expect. I should've known a dig was coming next. She smiles, and all I see are Freddy Fazbear teeth. I hide a small shiver.

Ryker spends the next thirty minutes talking to his father, telling him about daily business dealings, as he often does. James calms down and doesn't seem as agitated as he did earlier. I doubt his father's peace comes from hearing about work, but rather the soothing sound of his son's voice.

The nurse returns to prepare James for bed, and we leave her to it.

Once the door is closed, Debra immediately launches into business mode. "A few items of paperwork arrived in an email today. I thought you might want to see them right away."

Or she could have simply forwarded the email, but I don't say that out loud.

We follow her to the office, where she hands Ryker a file folder.

"Thanks, Mom." He opens the folder, peruses the contents, scoffs, and snaps it shut. "By the way, Mila has agreed to be the caretaker of my apartment while I'm gone."

My mind reacts with a skidding halt.

Caretaker? Is that what I am? Earlier, he made it sound like he was doing me a favor by letting me stay in his apartment. Is it really the other way around?

I suppose it's mutually beneficial. I'm not crazy about being called the caretaker, though. I'm his girlfriend and future wife caring for our future home, a home that I will one day blast with some serious color.

"That's a relief. It's not good to leave a home unattended for a long period of time, and Mila will take good care of it. Besides, Mila needs a job."

Ah, Freddy makes an appearance again. Those teeth are sharp.

Ryker wraps an arm around my shoulder. "Mila has a job and has done quite well for herself, Mom."

"Oh, come now. Playing the piano is a hobby." Debra heads for the stairs.

"Playing with a symphony is hardly a hobby," Ryker says as we follow like lambs to the slaughter. He mouths the word *sorry* to me.

I'm glad he noticed. Most of the time he seems a tad oblivious to his mother's cutting remarks. Or maybe he's used to them and doesn't let her faze him. I'm not sure. I've never brought it up because I don't want to talk trash about his mother. Ryker adores her. He's a late bloomer when it comes to that horrible childhood moment when you realize your mother isn't perfect.

"I'm about to have some tea, would you join me?"

Again, Debra doesn't pause to hear our answer. She simply heads for the living room and takes a seat. In truth, it is *expected* that we join her.

She's a piece of work. I'm not sure how Ryker turned out remotely normal. As my future mother-in-law, Debra will be a permanent fixture in my life. But I'm marrying Ryker one day, not her. And he's pretty darn amazing in all of his polite, careful, and classy ways. I can put up with her, as long as I have Ryker by my side.

Even if I do have to explain jokes to him. Every time.

We take our seats on the couch and Ryker holds my hand. We share a small smile. Their private cook brings out a tray with three steaming mugs of herb tea.

Debra picks up her mug. "It's chamomile. Helps me sleep at night."

Maybe because she needs a break from her nagging conscience, the one that's trying to tell her to play nicely with others.

I take a sip. "It's soothing. Thank you."

She doesn't comment on the sparkly ring on my finger that makes me look like an engaged woman. I find that odd. She probably already knows it's a promise ring. Ryker discusses everything with his mother. I don't want to come between them, but when we marry, I hope he'll cleave unto me and me alone. Three's a crowd. I think that's a discussion we need to have in the near future. Long before marriage. Regardless, one of the things I love about him is how much he loves his mother. It says a lot about him.

Debra cuts to the chase. "Have you told her about Zane? She needs to know."

"Zane?" I say. "His brother. Yes, of course." I mean, I know he exists, but Ryker doesn't talk about him. Like ever.

"For some reason, Ryker thought it was a good idea to let Zane stay with him the last few times he was in town. Don't ask me why." Debra's face contorts into a mask of distaste.

Ryker speaks up. "Keep your friends close, keep your enemies closer. I liked knowing what he was up to."

"Your brother's your enemy?" I ask, surprised by his words. I hero-worship my older brother, Martin. He's always been my biggest champion.

"He's not trustworthy," Debra spouts, her face turning red. "Tell her, Ryker. Mila needs to be warned that he might show up at your penthouse uninvited and that she should never trust him."

"He will?" If I have to be warned, it doesn't sound like a good situation.

"He pops in every now and again. No worries. He

won't show up. He's overseas at the moment, traipsing the globe like the irresponsible person he is. He thinks he's out saving the world, but really he's just a nomad, never staying in one place for long, always restless and easily bored."

Debra adds her two cents. "He can't be trusted. He's always been jealous of Ryker and tries to undermine him every chance he gets. If he shows up, let me or Ryker know right away, Mila. We will take care of it. Don't try to deal with him yourself."

"Yes, let one of us know right away," Ryker confirms.

"He was at his father's side for about a month after his stroke." Debra sighs loudly. "Then he up and left him, going off to do whatever it is that he does." She waves her hand in the air, physically dismissing Zane's actions as insignificant. "He needs to come and see his father. It's shameful the way he ignores his family."

"Don't worry about it." Ryker squeezes my hand. "He won't show up. But if by some odd twist of fate he did, Mom's right, don't trust him. Never trust Zane. He's not a good person, but he makes a great first impression. That's why he's dangerous."

I nod. I actually feel a bit of sympathy for Zane. His mother and brother talk about him as if they don't like him. What did he do to make them feel this way? He must be bad news, the black sheep of the family. Honestly, he sounds suspiciously like his mother. This is a case of the pot calling the kettle black.

"Ryker tells me you don't have any family drama, that your childhood was quite normal."

Debra makes it sound like a crime. If so, I'm guilty. "Yeah, my parents are great."

"Aren't you lucky?" I detect anger, instead of praise. Debra downs her hot tea in a few gulps, reminding me of a drunk man drinking a shot in a bar. Her tongue and throat have to be scalded. Further proof that she's not really human. Just as I suspected.

My secure home life has given me the confidence I need to face the world and go after my dreams. The thing is, it's a myth that a career focused woman doesn't need or want love, or home and hearth. I want both. I've always felt like I have a team of people cheering me on in the background. I recognize how fortunate I am, but at the same time, I won't apologize for it.

"We'd better get going," I tell Ryker. "I have an early morning tomorrow." I cast Debra a sly glance, tempted to poke the beast. "My hobby keeps me busy."

"I'm sure it does," she returns, unfazed. "That's what hobbies are for, dear."

We stand, and Debra says, "You know, Mila, you really are a beautiful young woman. The combination of black hair and blue eyes is quite striking on you."

Surprised, I thank her, feeling touched by the sentiment.

"No, really. There's just something about you that screams beauty. I can't get over it."

I'm speechless. She's not usually so effusive. Maybe I'm all wrong about her. "Thank you, I appreciate that."

She puts her hands on her hips. "I mean, you're just not the pale, lifeless thing you were when I first met you. It's amazing how much Ryker has changed you."

Oh.

Freddy is alive and well. And in full attack mode.

Ryker clears his throat. "Well, that's what love will do for a person, right, Mila?"

I glance at Ryker's handsome face and force a smile. "Right." For an odd moment, I feel as though I'm standing with strangers, like I don't belong here. Like I'm in the enemy camp. I shift uncomfortably, ready to make my exit.

Sweet Debra returns on a dime. "Have a good night, you two. Thanks for stopping by. It means so much to your father."

"Have a good night, *Debbie*. Thanks for the tea." My

smile is saccharine sweet.

She immediately says, "It's Debra."

I know.

It's taken me a while to understand her, but now that I do, I'm up for the challenge.

Freddy: 10

Mila: 1

It's on.

chapter four
♡

ONCE WE'RE OUTSIDE amidst the perfectly landscaped and well-lit exterior of Ryker's childhood home, he takes me in his arms and holds me close. I love being held by him in this sweet and tender manner.

Soft classical music wafts down on us from his father's open bedroom window. It calms James as he sleeps.

Ryker backs up a little, cupping my cheek. He lowers his lips to mine and kisses me gently.

I again find myself wishing he'd lose control a smidge, kiss me hard and fast, like he can't get enough.

He's all about soft and slow, respectful, and don't get me wrong, I love it. But sometimes I want him to kiss me like he means it. Maybe delve into the throes of passion and not hang out in the lukewarm zone.

We have a quiet love. But it's love, all the same.

When it's over, he says, "C'mon, I'll take you home."

I grab his hand as he turns. "Wait, dance with me." It's the perfect setting to sneak in some romance. A moonlit night and unexpected music tinkling around us.

He shakes his head. "I don't dance. You know that, Mila."

I do, but it doesn't stop me from trying. "It's just us. No one's watching."

"I'm sorry, I don't dance whether someone is watching or not."

I place my hands on my hips. "Really? Look me in the eyes and tell me you don't dance around your penthouse in a button-up shirt, underwear, and socks while doing a perfect *Risky Business* slide across your glossy floors."

No smile. No reaction whatsoever. "A what?"

Ryker's not a movie watcher. He's too busy. "Okay, so I haven't seen the movie either, but haven't you ever seen a video clip of the iconic Tom Cruise slide across the floor while lip syncing to *Old Time Rock n' Roll* in his parents' house when they aren't home?"

"Can't say that I have. Is it . . . entertaining?"

My mind is boggled by his question. "Never mind, it's not important. But are you telling me you don't dance when no one is watching? C'mon, Ryker. It's the fun part of life. You don't know what you're missing," I tease.

"No. No, absolutely not. I draw the line here," he says with a raised voice. "I'm sorry, I don't dance. Please don't ask me to. As a matter of fact, don't ever ask again. My answer will always be no." His agitation reveals a crack in his polished exterior.

His reaction makes me take a step back. In all the time we've dated, he's never directed his sharp business tone at me. I don't like it.

"Excuse me?"

He rubs his temples in a circular motion. "Sorry, that came out wrong."

I can tell dancing is practically a phobia for him. My eyes blink heavily as this new knowledge sinks in.

He was out at strike three. This is strike four. His tone accounts for strike five.

I put my hands up in the air, a sign of peace. "I don't mean to pressure you. No big deal. Some people don't dance. I get it."

"Thank you. It's not something I'm comfortable doing. I would feel . . . silly," he says, returning to his smooth voice.

"No worries." Sometimes I wonder if he likes my playful side. I can't curb it. It's who I am. I often suspect he's simply putting up with me, while waiting for my serious side to return. I have both inside me. Does he realize I'm a package deal?

He walks me to the car while I try to swallow more disappointment. It gets stuck in my throat this time, refusing to budge.

This has been a tough night all around.

But I'm not dating Ryker for his dancing skills, or lack thereof. He has many more traits that I love. Like the fact that he opened the car door for me and held my hand as I lowered myself into my seat. Even though I'm perfectly capable of doing those things, I appreciate his thoughtfulness. In the dating world, a gentleman is a dying breed.

I predict he'll be a doting husband.

But . . . will he direct his sharp "business" tone at me when he's upset? Hmmm, something to consider.

As we drive through the dark streets, I begin to wonder about Ryker's mystery brother.

"Should I be worried about Zane?"

"I wish my mom hadn't mentioned him. I don't want you to stress over it. He rarely returns home anymore."

"Why don't you like him?" I ask.

"We've never had a good relationship. I guess you could say there's some serious sibling rivalry between us. Growing up, he was always trying to outshine me. If I mentioned that I love to swim, the next day Zane would be on the swim team. If I went outside to shoot some hoops, Zane would sign up for basketball camp. He's competitive, jealous, and plain unpleasant to be around. It's a long, dreary story and you don't need to worry about it."

Wow. I've never heard Ryker talk like that about someone. It's sad that he feels that way about his brother. Family members should love and accept each other, support each other, treat each other with tenderness. I don't know what I'd do without my family. They're extremely important to me. That's why I refuse to interfere with Ryker's relationship with his mother. I won't break up a mother and son.

Still, I hate feeling like he's blowing me off. Is he going to pat me on the head next? There's more to the story and I sense he doesn't want to talk about it.

"Is he your younger brother?"

"No, he's my older brother. By about two years."

Ryker's thirty. So that means Zane is thirty-two. That makes me the baby of the group at twenty-nine.

Brothers that close should be best friends. It makes me hurt for Ryker. "Someday when we have six or seven kids, I hope they'll be the best of friends." Like me and my brother. To this day, we talk on the phone often.

Ryker's quiet a heartbeat too long. "Six or seven?"

Is that his take away? We haven't discussed future family plans. I would love to have several children, not necessarily six or seven, but several. I hope that's not a problem. Now is not the time to whip out a heavy discussion, we've done enough of that already this evening. I blow off my remark as humor.

"That was a joke, Ryker. You know, something said to cause amusement or laughter."

"Oh, of course."

He was raised by Debra. Say no more. That explains everything. I doubt laughter was a thing in their house.

The car is silent as my thoughts review everything he just revealed. "Does Zane work for Martel Investments?"

"He did for a while, then he up and left. Abandoned his job at a moment's notice. Mom was relieved. She fears he'll try to usurp my place in the company. It's what he's always done all my life. Everything's a competition with him. Then my father had the stroke and life hasn't been the same since. Like my mom said, Zane stayed at my father's side for a while, before he took off again like he always does. I can't trust him."

"That's really sad."

Ryker pulls up next to my studio apartment. "Let's not talk about it anymore."

"All right."

He picks up the folder of paperwork off the seat between us, places it in his lap, and scoots over so we can be closer. He kisses me, whisper soft.

There's something niggling at me and I decide to be upfront. "Ryker, sometimes I feel like I don't really know you, the real you. I'm not sure why, I can't explain it. It's just a feeling. Please open up to me. I want to know everything about you."

His brow wrinkles. "What do you mean?"

"We've been dating for ten months and I just now learned about your brother." I feel like I should know him better than I do after that length of time.

"He's not part of my life. I don't like talking about him."

"I get that, but I wish you would've told me anyway."

"Sorry. I know I've been distracted by work lately. After my trip to Japan, things should calm down."

I think his life will always be about business. That's okay, I have a career that keeps me busy and it's extremely important to me as well.

He gets out of the car and comes around to my side to open my door, ever the gentleman.

After a few more soft hugs and kisses, he gets back in his car and drives away. I watch him leave from my doorway.

The longest night ever is finally over. I think I need a t-shirt announcing I survived it.

I'm not an engaged woman like I thought I'd be by night's end. Instead, I'm a promised woman. To quote Ryker, the future looks bright.

Minus dancing. And humor. And passion. And any other form of spontaneity.

Whoa. Where'd that come from?

My eyebrows knit. Disillusionment is a sneaky little fellow. If I let him in, he'll take over my mind.

I notice something strange on my driveway and go to investigate. It's Ryker's folder of important business papers, the one his mother gave him. It must've fallen off his lap when he exited the car.

I'll get it to him tomorrow. I go back inside and toss the

folder on my desk, my thoughts filled with Ryker and what our future will hold.

My phone rings and I grab it from my purse. I know who it will be.

"Hey, Mom."

"Mila! How'd it go? Should I start planning a wedding?"

My shoulders slump. "Not yet."

I hear my mother release her breath over the airwaves. "What? But you were so sure."

I hate dashing her hope. "He gave me a promise ring. He wants to wait to make it official until after his trip to Japan."

"Oh . . . well, perhaps that's a good idea. Maybe you both need some time apart to test the strength of your relationship."

"Maybe."

"Oh, Mila Are you terribly disappointed?"

"A little. I mean, he made it clear a proposal is still in the works. I guess I just . . . feel unsure of him now. The truth is, after tonight, it's like my eyes have been opened and I'm having a few doubts." There. I said it out loud. It's real now.

"Listen, no one is perfect. If you're looking for perfection, you'll never find it. The trick is to find the person who is perfect for you, the person you love so much, you can overlook their faults—the person who will do the same for you. That's love, true love, a love that will last. Always concentrate on the good, the reasons why you fell in love in the first place. Because the fact is, once you're married, faults have a way of becoming huge, blinking neon signs outside your bedroom window that won't let you sleep at night. You gotta close the curtains and ignore them."

Now there's a visual. "You're right. If he can overlook my faults, I can do the same."

"Yes, but at the same time, listen to your inner voice. If

it's telling you he's not right for you, then you need to stand up and pay attention. There's no reason to settle for something less than what you want simply because perfection doesn't exist. Now is the time to question your decision. Once you're married, it's a little too late."

I sigh. "I have three months to think it over, three months to be sure."

"Yes, you do. Time has a way of helping you see things clearly. If it's right, you'll know it, Mila. Don't force it. Just take it a day at a time."

"Thanks, Mom. Love you. You still make everything right in my life. I don't know how you do it."

It's like she kissed my scraped knee and all is right with the world now. I have a path forward and I shouldn't spend my time worrying about it. I don't have to decide right now.

I hate my misgivings. I was so sure and now that feeling is fading. "Sorry about upsetting your wedding plans."

"The only time I want to plan a wedding is when my baby girl is doing her happy dance that I love so much, jumping up and down because her man makes her so giddy she can't contain herself. That's when I'll plan a wedding to be proud of. Until that time, my subscription to *Bridal Guide* will be cancelled."

Giddy? Am I giddy around Ryker?

Not really. He's never made me feel like doing my happy dance. I can't think of a time a man has ever made me feel that way. Is that really how love should feel? Fluttery and crazy, wild and dizzy, light-headed and unsteady?

It sounds so impulsive, so thoughtless, like you're so wrapped up in emotion you can't see straight.

Is that what I want? I'm not so sure. When it comes to a life partner, maybe I don't know what I want.

I do know some things for sure, though. I want a man who loves me so much, he won't hesitate over asking me to marry him. It won't be an inner debate, it'll be a sure thing.

And if he loves me, he'll say it with so much confidence, I won't question it.

And when he kisses me, I'll feel his love in his passionate embrace.

On second thought, maybe I do know what I want.

chapter five
♥

I SIT AT my baby grand, prepared to start my warm-ups, but I'm distracted by the amazing view from Ryker's floor-to-ceiling windows.

I can hardly believe I live here, or that this could possibly be my home for a very long time.

It's early morning and the fog surrounding the Golden Gate Bridge is still lifting. The sun is starting to rise, painting a colorful picture across the sky. It's such a peaceful sight from Ryker's sky-high apartment. When I'm down amongst all the traffic, hustle, and bustle, it's crazy. It's an escape living up here. I see why Ryker loves it so much. I've been here two weeks now and I enjoy living here alone far too much. Not sure what that says about me.

The penthouse is modern and updated. It doesn't have the popular open concept everyone loves nowadays, though. The kitchen is tucked away to one side with its own breakfast table. But the large wall of windows and the balcony that extends almost the length of the penthouse makes it feel open and airy.

To my surprise, Ryker left his journal on his nightstand, a masculine leather-bound book, made to look old with roughened edges lining the pages. There was a note attached from Ryker stating he'd like me to read it, that it would help me to get to know him better. He said he didn't want any secrets between us.

I'm touched that he took me seriously when I said I felt like I didn't know him well. But I can't bring myself to read his journal. It feels like an invasion of his privacy.

No more wandering thoughts. Back to work. I have six hours of practice to get through before I have to be at the San Francisco Ballet Company for afternoon classes. Most traditional ballet schools still hire live pianists to play for classes and auditions. The pay is excellent, and it keeps me doing what I love.

Then I have practice with the Marin Symphony this evening. Our show will consist of highlights from various concertos, rather than focusing on one in particular for a change. It's been fun to concentrate on the favorite classical pieces, ones that most people recognize, even if they don't know their names.

My favorite is Rachmaninoff's *Rhapsody on a Theme of Paganini*. Everyone's favorite part isn't even until sixteen minutes into the piece. I feel like I'm cheating, but it's nice to cut to the chase and only play the most recognized portion. I'm also playing some Brahms, Vivaldi, Bach, Beethoven, and Mozart. All the classics.

I delve into my warm-ups and lose myself in the piano, disappearing into another place where only the perfect pitch and seamless notes exist. I feel the music and become one with it as it leaves my fingertips and escapes into the air, only to be captured by my ears and embraced by my heart. A continuous ebb and flow.

Two hours into my practice time, my phone rings. I'm ready for a short break, so I answer. It's Ryker, facetiming me through messenger.

"Hi, sweetheart. You are a sight for sore eyes," he says, smiling into the camera. "I needed to see your beautiful face and hear your sweet voice." He's still in his suit, sitting at the desk in his hotel room, looking mighty handsome with his brown eyes focused on me.

"Hey, Ryker." I study him closely. "You look tired. Are you okay?"

He loosens his tie and unbuttons his top button, relief evident in his features at the action. "Just a bit exhausted. Nothing a good night's sleep won't cure."

"What time is it there?"

"Eleven at night. If I calculated correctly, it's eight in the morning in San Francisco and you're right in the middle of practice. Am I right?"

"Spot on."

He's woken me up in the middle of the night a few times. I'm glad we're finally figuring this out.

"How's everything?" he asks.

"Just fine. But I have a confession."

"What's that?"

"There's a new love in my life."

Silence.

"Humor, Ryker. This is humor. Go with it."

He shakes his head, like I'm silly. "Okay, I'll bite. Who is the new love in your life?"

"It's not a who, it's a what. I'm totally and completely in love with your home. You now have competition."

He doesn't smile. "Not really. It's inanimate."

So, I'm not a comedian. But I wish I could make him laugh. Just a little. Even a small smile would be satisfying. I think he'd feel more relaxed if he could let loose.

That's not who he is though.

My gaze ping pongs from him to my lap. I'm unsure of his mood. "Are you sure you're okay?"

"Now that I see the face of the woman I'm falling in love with, I am."

There's that falling word again. I remind myself that it's his way of saying I love you and I let it warm my heart. I again attempt to keep the conversation light.

"Whoa, keep talking like that and I might hop on a plane and join you."

"Don't be ridiculous."

I feel myself deflate, releasing a long, low sigh. It's clear Ryker's not in a playful mood. He never is, but it's more pronounced when he's tired.

"Sorry, Mila. That was humor again, wasn't it?"

"A poor attempt, but yes."

"Thanks for putting up with me." His stony expression battles with his words, leaving me confused.

I watch my lips compress on the screen and I

deliberately relax them. "You know what, I'd better let you get some sleep. Thanks for calling. It's good to see your handsome face. Get some rest."

"Mila, wait. I'm sorry for being short." He runs one hand over his face. "I hit the ground running when I arrived, and I think I'm still fighting jet-lag. Can't seem to catch up."

I nod. "I understand."

"Miss you like crazy."

My heart bursts into a million tiny pieces at the crumb he's thrown me. I'll take it. "I miss you too."

His chest puffs out enough for me to notice his pleased response. "Before you go, will you flip the screen and show me your baby grand in my living room? I'd love to see it again."

"Arthur will be heartbroken, but okay." Of course, he never asks to speak with Artie. My little buddy is currently curled up on his dog bed, his ears perked at the sound of Ryker's voice.

I flip the screen and show him the view of my baby grand sitting in the corner of the living room, with only a wall of glass as its backdrop. It's an art gallery worthy picture.

He whistles. "That looks incredible."

"I think so too. It really is an amazing place to practice."

I flip the screen back to me.

"Hey, don't forget to put felt pads underneath the legs. I don't want the floor to get scratched. I ordered some for you on Amazon. Did they arrive?"

I lift a single eyebrow. "No, not yet."

Every phone call so far has included detailed remarks about how to take care of his home. *Wipe the faucets down after using them. Pour bleach down the drains once a week. Use a microfiber cloth to remove fingerprints on the stainless-steel refrigerator.* It dominates our conversation. If I'm being honest, I'm annoyed.

His eyes squint as he studies the screen. "Is that a blanket and pillow on the couch?"

I glance behind me, pretending I don't know they're there. My soda and popcorn bowl are still on the coffee table too. Should I announce there's a coaster under my soda can? I return to my piano bench, so the window is behind me. "Movie night last night. I fell asleep on the couch." My favorite way to relax at the end of the day.

"I don't usually sleep on my couch. Sounds, uh, fun."

His tone implies that it's anything but fun. More like the most distasteful thing he's ever heard.

Raised by Debra, I remind myself. Over and over. He needs someone to teach him how to relax.

"I'll put everything away. Don't worry. I promise not to trash the place like a rockstar in a fancy hotel." I immediately regret my words. There's not a chance he'll find them amusing, even if he found anything in life amusing.

His expression remains blank. "Of course not."

I take a deep breath and decide to be blunt. "I'm not a neat freak, Ryker. Is that a problem? If it is, please say so now."

"I trust you, Mila."

Somehow that answer makes me feel guilty, like he trusts me to keep his place as neat as he does. That's not going to happen.

He continues. "I wouldn't have asked you to live there if I didn't have faith in you."

"I guess that's all I can ask." I wish this conversation could start over.

He rubs the back of his neck. "I'm beat. Good night, Mila. I'll call again soon."

He's gone before I can say anything else.

"I love you too," I whisper in the silent room, sarcasm evident in my tone. I turn on the bench and catch my reflection in the window. My eyebrows are deeply furrowed, my lips turned into a frown.

That didn't go well. My heart is questioning my relationship with Ryker and wondering if we're really a good fit. The seeds of doubt planted inside me have become climbing vines, reaching up to strangle me.

I'm losing something, but I don't know what it is or how to define it. And I don't know how to catch it and bring it back, either.

Arthur whimpers from his dog bed, missing his daddy.

"Sorry, Artie. He'll be back, don't worry."

chapter six

♥

THE ELEVATOR DINGS as I rub my eyes. This day has lasted forever and I'm seeing double. I pull out my key with aching fingers and head for Ryker's penthouse, my steps slow. The classical pieces I practiced with the symphony are rolling through my head, granting me no mercy. I need a quiet evening to relax and de-stress. Clear my mind.

I received a text from Ryker, asking me to be sure to keep up with cleaning the floor-to ceiling-windows. I've been reminding myself all day that I'm getting free rent, so I won't feel irritated. He said a service comes and cleans the windows once every two weeks, but it's helpful if someone removes any built-up grime in between cleanings.

No I miss you. No I'm falling for you.

I let out a huge discouraged sigh. I wish I could go back in time and feel the same stirrings he created within me in the beginning. Even how I felt only a few weeks ago would suffice. I think my emotions are stuffed in a lost-and-found box somewhere far, far away.

The first thing that registers as I push open the door is loud music blasting from a music station on Ryker's big screen TV, Lady Antebellum's *Need You Now*. I wonder if I accidently left the TV on. Then I come face to face with a shirtless man standing in the doorway to the kitchen.

Adrenaline washes through my body, erasing fatigue and bringing me to life in an instant. Yet, I'm frozen in place, my hand rushing to my throat in a protective gesture.

He's barefoot, clothed in *only* a pair of torn-at-the-knees jeans. His short hair is damp, and a towel is hanging around his neck as though he just showered. He's holding a cereal bowl, and when he sees me, his spoon, dripping milk, pauses mid-air, like I told him to freeze with my imaginary magical powers and he obeyed.

For several moments too long, we stand there staring at each other, both in shock. It's as though we've turned into an artistic viewing of ice sculptures, a display for the public that captures this blip in time forever.

Frozen encounter.

I hear the music announce that I *need you now*, and I think to myself, I need someone right now. Someone to help me. Immediately. *Move, Mila.* Act. Do something. Someone has broken into Ryker's apartment and made themselves at home. It must be someone who knows he's out of town. Someone who thinks they can squat without being discovered.

He reacts first by reaching into his back pocket and pulling out the remote to the TV. He quickly mutes the music.

I spring to life, pull my phone out, and stumble backwards. My back hits the front door, latching it closed, effectively barring my escape. It's a heavy twenty-minute fire door. Can I turn and open it quickly? Nope. "Stay where you are, I'm calling 911 right now."

"Good. Tell them there's a strange woman who just busted into my apartment. She looks dangerous too. Tell them I'm scared for my life."

My trembling finger hovers over the keypad. Joke? Was that a joke? Have I been around Ryker so long that I can't recognize humor?

My breath comes in short spurts, and my eyes blink rapidly as I try to form a sentence. This man bears a slight resemblance to Ryker. He has the same dark brown hair, the same brown eyes. The similarities between them end there, though.

"W-wait. Are you Zane?"

"My reputation precedes me, I see."

This is the moment when I should laughingly say,

"Yes, I've heard of you. Don't worry, it's all good, though." But that's not the case. It's all bad. I have been *warned* about him. Told to never trust him.

"By the look on your face, I'm pretty sure that's not a good thing," he adds, taking another spoonful of cereal.

I don't confirm or deny.

Zane is slightly taller, more buff, and a bit rougher around the edges. Where Ryker's face is soft, Zane's is hardened, as though life has dealt him a few hard knocks. His bare bronzed chest and ripped abs are staring at me and they won't look away. Don't they know it's rude to stare?

Now that the shock of finding a man in the penthouse is wearing off, I'm wondering why I'm so terrified when he's not threatening in the least bit. What's he going to do, hit me with his cereal bowl? Douse me with milk? I know I should be wary of Ryker's mysterious brother, but instead I breathe out heavily with relief and attempt to calm my racing heart.

"You scared the life out of me."

"Sorry, I wasn't expecting anyone to barge in, either."

"Ryker felt sure you wouldn't show up on his doorstep."

He brings another spoonful of cereal to his mouth. "And yet, here I am."

"What are you doing here?"

"Gonna be home for a while." He shrugs nonchalantly, leaving me wondering at his evasive answer.

Ryker said he was a bit of a nomad, always wandering the globe. It appears he was right. I notice there's a pile of suitcases stacked in the middle of the living room. One is open, the contents spilling out onto the floor, as though he's been rummaging around in it.

"You can't stay here. I'm staying here." I point to myself. "I'm the caretaker of Ryker's apartment while he's gone." I hate being called the caretaker, but I guess that's what I am, essentially. Might as well accept it, earn my keep. And get busy cleaning the windows.

"Ryker's gone? Where is he?"

"In Japan for three months on business."

"Ah, I didn't realize he'd left already. Way to go, Ryker. He knows how to rep-re-sent. He's a shark when it comes to business. He'll do well for Dad."

My features squint, baffled by Zane's complimentary tone. Ryker does not return the favor toward him.

Ryker's voice is ringing in my ears saying, *Don't trust Zane, Don't trust Zane.* I straighten my shoulders to hide my wariness. "Like I said, you can't stay here."

"There's three bedrooms. Plenty of room."

"That's not the point. I live here."

His stance is wide, confident. But I notice the brief unsure glance he sends me. "Great. So do I. There's room for everyone."

I cover my face with my hands, exasperation quickly replacing caution. I've known Zane for five seconds and I already know he's nothing like Ryker. He's far too casual and unconcerned.

Arthur approaches on shaky legs, looking between us.

"Artie, you're supposed to be protecting me," I tell him. "Intruder alert. Sick 'em!"

"Really?" Zane says. "I'm shaking in my boots. If I was wearing any, that is."

Artie obeys me by approaching Zane and licking his bare feet.

"Help me. I'm so scared."

His deadpan tone makes me bite my lip to hide an emerging smile. "Hey, be careful. Dogs can sense fear. Just saying."

"I'd rather not suffer death by lick."

That breaks the ice. We both chuckle lightly.

Zane has a great smile, open and friendly. "I'm sorry I scared you."

"I apologize for the frosty reception. You took me by surprise, that's all. I'm Mila. Mila Westerman."

"Mila," he nods. "So, you're the caretaker while Ryker's gone, huh?"

Ugh. "Well, I mean, yes . . . but I'm also Ryker's . . . girlfriend." Why do those words bumble out of my mouth?

His head pulls back, like someone slapped him. He conceals his reaction quickly, but I know I surprised him and I wonder at his response.

He clears his throat. "Why the hesitation?" he asks coolly, acting as though he didn't react to my words.

Did I imagine his physical shock? Of course, I did.

He's perceptive and I'm far too transparent. Does everything I do and say scream uncertainty?

Because it's true. I'm uncertain of Ryker and I hate that the tiny seed of discontent is there, like grit in my eye.

"There was no hesitation. It's just a little complicated," I lie.

"May I ask why?"

"It's always complicated when a couple is talking marriage."

No physical reaction this time. As a matter of fact, he could be made of stone. "Is it?"

"Of course. It's a huge decision, one that effects the rest of your life." Why am I explaining myself?

His eyes drop to the sparkly ring on my finger. His eyebrows shoot into his forehead, a small pierce in his emotional armor. "Hold on. You're engaged? To Ryker?"

I let out my breath and it emerges as a bit of a huff. This has turned into a sore subject. So many people I work with have asked me if I'm engaged because my ring is sitting on my left ring finger, exactly where Ryker placed it. It's embarrassing to explain the details every single time. I've been thinking about changing it for days.

Now is the time.

I remove it and place it on my right ring finger. "It's a promise ring. We're not engaged yet," I say, subdued.

His eyes search mine, seeing far more than I want him

to see.

"Huh. A lot has happened while I've been gone. Regardless, Ryker's a lucky man."

I look down at the ground. "Thank you."

I feel like such a fraud representing myself as Ryker's girlfriend. I don't think I'll carry that title for much longer.

The thought has invaded my senses and it won't leave me alone.

chapter seven

♡

WHEN I LOOK back up at Zane, my cheeks pinken as I realize his eyes are unashamedly wandering up and down, checking me out. I'm wearing my skinny jeans, a flowy top, and cute ballet flats. I've felt cute and confident all day. But this is the first time I've felt *looked at*. The weight of his gaze flusters me.

His bare chest and abs are still blatantly staring at me. They have no manners whatsoever.

He seems to realize he's staring and turns his attention back to Arthur. "Articus, my main man, how's it going?" He leans down and picks Arthur up with one hand. "Hey, buddy. You gotta stop with the shaking. You'll never get yourself a girl this way." Zane glances my way. "Girls sense fear and will eat you alive. Just saying."

I cast him a smirk.

Zane kneels down, placing his cereal bowl on the floor. "Here you go, buddy. Go for it, get milk drunk. No regrets."

Artie goes to town, lapping like he's dying of thirst.

"I . . . I don't think he should have that. It might give him the runs and . . ."

"Add a bit of color to the blinding white carpet? Might be an improvement."

"Gross." But that merits a giggle.

"Yet, so true."

Now I know why Ryker doesn't have the sense of humor gene. Zane took it all, leaving Ryker with nothing.

I pull myself together quickly. I don't trust this man who has invaded my space. I have been warned about him. I take a deep breath, preparing to give him his marching orders, but I'm distracted when Zane continues to speak to Artie in a ridiculously mushy voice while he rubs his neck.

"Is that so good, Articus? So, so good, right, my little man? You're just so gosh darn cute, yes you are."

Ryker always talks to Arthur as though he's having a serious conversation with an adult. It drives me crazy.

Zane goes on. "Just a tiny hunk of cuteness, that's what you are." He picks him up, letting Arthur give him a lick-kiss on his lips.

I love seeing a grown man make a fool of himself.

I admit, I let Artie give me a lick-kiss every once in a while. But not while Ryker's watching. It grosses him out.

"Articus?" I ask.

"He doesn't look like an Arthur to me."

Not to me either. Ryker hates when I call his dog Artie. His head would explode if he heard Zane calling his dog Articus.

Both Zane and Arthur turn their attention on me. Zane says, "You gonna stand there all night?"

Zane is not exactly threatening. I'm feeling more comfortable by the moment. "Are you gonna prance around half naked all night?"

"I didn't know I'd be having company."

"No, let's get one thing straight. I'm the one having company. You are invading my home." I cover my eyes. "Can you put your abs away, please? We need to talk this out."

Zane laughs and removes the damp towel from around his neck, tossing it on the coffee table. That right there is enough to make Ryker have a heart attack. He grabs a white v-neck t-shirt that he left discarded on the couch and quickly dons it while juggling Arthur.

He studies me. "You know, you're not Ryker's usual type."

"Does Ryker have a type?"

"Yes, he does. Most of them are forever flirty, blond, spend their lives in pursuit of the perfect leather purse, and think weekly manicures are a necessity, not a want."

I cringe. Most of them? How many have there been? "Then, no. I'm not his type. My purse is genuine faux-leather. And I'm happy with it."

Zane laughs again. I don't join him. *I'm not Ryker's type.* A disturbing thought, and yet, I think I already knew it.

"Judging by your short nails, I'd say you're a pianist."

"What makes you say that?"

"That monstrosity over there in the corner does not belong to Ryker and he can't hold a tune if his life depended on it. It must be yours."

"Yes, it is." Good deductive skills. Or maybe it's obvious.

"All right, Miss Mila. Let's talk this out. What's the deal? Can I stay here? I promise you won't even notice I'm here. In spite of what you've more than likely heard about me, I'm not a serial killer and I won't rob you or attack you in your sleep. So, you can stop hugging the door and relax."

"I'm not . . ." Yeah, I am. I'm standing by the front door, ready to flee at the first sign of danger.

"Yes, you are."

He takes one step toward me and I instinctively back up, pressing against the door even harder.

"I rest my case," he says, his eyes locked with mine.

I feel like a wimp, so I take one step into the room, just to show him who's boss. I don't fool anyone. "Sorry, you're a stranger to me. And Ryker said . . ."

"Ryker said what?"

Not to trust him. But I won't say that out loud. "Like I said, that you wouldn't show up, that you were overseas. I didn't expect this."

"True. I was stationed at Baumholder Army Base in Germany, but my assignment has changed. I'm no longer deployed overseas. I wanted to be close to my father, so I did some finagling. Lucky me, my new assignment is right here in good old Fog City. I'm home to stay. I'm sure my family will be *thrilled*. I'll get myself a place to stay and be out of your hair in no time."

"Deployed? Are you military?" I was led to believe he was an irresponsible bum who traipsed the world at his whim. He's actually employed? Debra and Ryker left out a few important details when talking about Zane.

"Yes, Army. I now command the 108th Ordnance Detachment, EOD. We can be set up anywhere in the world where there's a need. Currently we're in a run-down abandoned fire station on the old presidio. My new office. I take over in a week."

"EOD?"

"Explosive Ordnance Disposal. The Army's bomb squad."

"That sounds dangerous."

"Not if you know what you're doing." He sighs. "Look, Mila, I'll leave and get myself a hotel. This isn't going to work. I'm clearly making you uncomfortable and I don't mean to. I'm sorry I scared you, I really am."

He looks at me directly, his eyes clear and bright. Honestly, he seems like a really nice, pleasant guy. He's given me no reason to fear him. Not one.

Ryker mentioned he made a good first impression. I would agree. Therefore, I should be wary, keep my guard up.

He goes on before I can respond. "Ryker gave me a key, said I was welcome anytime. I had no idea he was out of town already or that you were staying here."

He rakes one hand through his short hair, his biceps bulging. They have no manners either and have never learned not to stare.

He nods, his decision made. "I'll leave. It's for the best."

He sets Arthur down and kneels next to his suitcases. He gathers up his things and stuffs them inside his luggage. Soon the metallic sound of a zipper echoes through the space.

Arthur looks at me with sad eyes and whines like he's

distressed. He's a good judge of character and very particular about who touches him or holds him. Zane can't be all bad.

But I'm not about to decide whether or not to let a man stay here because of a dog's preferences.

Ryker said he likes to keep his enemy close. That's why he lets Zane live in his home. Perhaps keeping Zane here would be what Ryker would want. I should at least let Zane stay here until I speak with Ryker about the situation. Besides, this is his brother. His family.

"Wait," I say. "It's not my decision to make. This is your brother's home, not mine."

"The more I think about it, I doubt he'd want me to stay here with his . . . *almost* fiancé. I know what his answer will be. It's best if I go."

His tune changed quickly, and mine right along with it. Our roles have reversed. I sort of want to laugh aloud at the way we're dancing around each other.

"No, he opened his home up to you. You're welcome to stay."

He stills. "Are you sure?"

No, not entirely. But I think it's what Ryker would want. Besides, I'm suddenly overwhelmed with a ridiculous curiosity about Ryker's black sheep of a brother who doesn't appear to be at all the kind of man that was described to me.

I want him to stay. I want to know more about him.

"Yeah. It's only for a short time. It'll be fine."

He unfolds his body until he's upright. I feel like he's towering over me, every bronzed inch of him. Gulp.

"All right, then. Thank you. Only until I find housing, of course."

"But I should warn you, I'm a pianist, as you guessed. I practice piano six plus hours a day. Is that going to annoy you?"

He blinks heavily, his eyes guarded. "Not at all. I'd love to hear you play."

"Even at six in the morning?"

"I'm an early riser. Can't think of a better alarm clock."

He grants me a warm smile that does funny things to my insides. It's because he's a lot like Ryker and I miss him. That's all.

"You don't want to stay with your mother and father?" I ask.

"I'm not welcome there. Not on an overnight basis."

Wisps of fear wander through me. And yet, I'm intrigued. "May I ask why?"

"It's a long, complicated story with lots of family drama good enough for a daytime soap. If you're asking if I did something to hurt them, the answer is no. It's family dynamics and I'm on the outs."

I want to pepper him with more questions, but I don't. All in good time. "I'm sorry."

He shrugs like it's no big deal, but I swear I see a flash of pain cross his features. Subtle and fleeting. My curiosity is stoked. Who is this man I have been warned about?

He rubs his forehead. "I've been traveling all day and I'm beat. How 'bout pizza and a Netflix movie? A peace offering of sorts. My treat."

It's hard to keep up with my whirling emotions. One moment, I'm scared to death of him and telling him he must leave. The next, I'm telling him he can stay. Now we're going to be movie watching buddies. This is crazy. Wild. Dangerous.

And yet . . . I accept. "You just spoke to my soul. Deal."

"Pepperoni?"

"Double it."

"Miss Mila, you just spoke to my soul. But first you have to trust me and move away from the front door and see what happens next. I dare you." His eyes glitter at me.

"Challenge accepted," I tell him with attitude. I step away from the door and his lips curve into a taunting half smile. I face him head on even though my heart's beating wildly. "But I need to take Artie out for a walk or his bladder might explode."

"Already took him out earlier."

"Oh. Okay, thank you."

"No excuses now."

Ryker was right. Zane's first impression lulls me into thinking he's decent. A chill wanders up my spine. I shouldn't be doing this.

The thing is, I've never been okay with someone telling me how I should feel about another human being. I think that's my decision to make.

I walk into the living room and toss my lovely faux-leather purse on the couch, faking nonchalance. I follow, letting the soft cushions engulf my body. My earlier exhaustion is remembered.

"Living dangerously, huh?" he says.

We're like two predators circling around, unsure of what the other will do.

My stomach tightens from the thrill. "You have no idea."

chapter eight
♡

I RECEIVE A text from Ryker early the next morning, just as I'm about to begin practicing.

Ryker: ZANE IS THERE?

Me: Are you yelling at me?

Ryker: No.

Me: Yes, the devil is here. Did you feel him invading your space all the way from Japan?

Ryker: Mom told me.

Me: Is she spying on me?

That would be just like her. Making sure I'm faithful or something.

Ryker: No, she keeps an eye on Zane.

Me: Really? You know that's weird, right?

Ryker: Don't worry about it. I'll take care of it.

Me: It's no problem. He won't be here long.

My phone rings almost immediately after I send my last text.

"I'm so sorry, Mila. I didn't expect him to show up."

Apparently, no one did. "Neither did I. It gave me quite the surprise. I nearly called 911. Scared me to death."

"I'm sorry, sweetheart. I hope he hasn't been horrible to you."

"Not at all. Once everything was cleared up, we had pizza and watched a movie. It's fine."

Silence greets me for a full thirty seconds. "You and Zane watched a movie together?" he asks, alarm invading his voice.

"We did. He was very kind. He only tried to attack me twice."

"Don't trust him, Mila. It's all a show. Underneath his façade, he's a snake."

I don't see it, but I haven't even known him for twenty-four hours. Ryker has a lifetime on me. We sat on the couch last night, two feet apart, eating pizza and watching a movie for several hours. He didn't do anything untoward. He fell asleep and missed the ending of the movie, so I didn't exactly feel threatened. I tossed a throw blanket over him—or maybe at him—and went to bed in my own room with the door locked for good measure. I can't say I trust the guy, but a foundation has begun. If he keeps his distance, everything will be fine. My guard will be up whenever he's around, that's for sure.

"Duly warned. I'll draw a line down your floor. His side and my side. If he crosses it, I'll have him summarily executed by morning."

"Seriously, Mila. My mother proved that Zane was stealing from my father's business. He's a thief. The knowledge destroyed my dad. Don't leave anything of value out in the open."

"Those are some serious accusations." I know nothing about the circumstances and yet I find myself doubting it solely because Freddy "proved" it.

"They're not accusations. They're truth. My mother reported him to the police. An investigation is underway."

If that's true, then why hasn't Zane been arrested? He's innocent until proven guilty. In the eyes of the law . . . and in my eyes too. Freddy has the burden of proof.

"What's Zane doing there? Did he say?" Ryker asks.

"He's been stationed in San Francisco. He's looking for housing, so he won't be at your place for long. I figured you'd want me to let him stay. I mean, he is your brother. *Your family.* Was I wrong?"

Ryker scoffs. "I don't want him there while you're there," he growls. It sounds like he's speaking through gritted teeth as he hollers in that horrible business tone I don't appreciate.

Silence abounds as imaginary crickets chirp. "Ryker?"

"Sorry, I don't mean to take this out on you. I'm upset about his antics, as usual. He drives me crazy." His voice is polished again. I feel like I witnessed a *Jekyll and Hyde* moment.

I think Ryker has the Freddy gene. He clearly hides it well. I'm not okay with that.

"Look, I'm busy, he's busy. We'll hardly see each other. It'll be fine, really. He can stay, I don't mind. If you want to kick him out, that's up to you. But don't give him the boot on my account. I've been on my own for a long time and I can handle it." Gulp. Brave words. But this is my future brother-in-law—maybe—and it's high time peace prevailed in this family.

"I'll call him and we'll work it out. I'm so sorry this happened, Mila. Are you sure you're okay?" While his tone sounds forced, he's much calmer than earlier.

"I'm perfectly fine. Really."

"All right. Be safe, sweetheart. I'm falling more each day. More and more. Please know that. I've gotta go. Talk more later."

The connection is broken before I can say another word. He never plays the *You Hang Up First* game, thank goodness. But if he did, he'd always win.

I start my practice session with a conflicted heart.

Ryker Martel is telling me he loves me, even if he does use the term *falling* as his code word for *I love you*. I needed to hear it this morning to erase my growing doubts about us.

Hearing his worry over my safety helped to alleviate some of my concerns. I think he really does love me.

The thought should comfort me. It doesn't.

Instead, I feel uneasy. Why do I have the urge to flee? To run as fast as I can and never look back?

I think it's time to listen to my inner voice. It's trying to tell me something.

chapter nine
♥

A COUPLE HOURS later, Zane wanders into the room in his torn jeans and that's all once again. When I see him in my peripheral vision, I stop what I'm playing and break out into *The Entertainer*. I cast him a cheesy grin.

He laughs aloud, a pleasant, throaty sound. He manages an exaggerated bow. "I'm here all night. And all day. And all night. For a while anyway."

Yes, he is. I hope I don't regret the choice to let him stay. "I'm not going to ask you again. Please put your abs away. They like to stare and it's so rude."

He throws his head back and laughs as he disappears into his room.

He actually laughed at something I said. Huh.

I admit, I enjoy the sound of his laughter. It invigorates me. It's so easy and relaxed—and foreign. I guess I didn't realize how much I miss laughter with Ryker. But then, no one is perfect, as my mom reminded me.

He returns with his signature white t-shirt on, but this time his sunglasses are tucked into the vee of his neckline. "Better?"

"Thank you. Rule number one if you're going to live here. Be clothed at all times."

"Spoil sport."

There's this odd moment where we simply smile at each other for much too long. I lower my eyes and return to my piano.

"Did my practicing bother you this morning?" I ask.

"Not at all. I loved it and found it relaxing. You're . . . amazing, Mila. Really impressive."

My cheeks grow hot at the compliment. "Thank you. I'm playing with the Marin Symphony. You enjoy the piano?"

He plops down on the couch, propping his bare feet on the coffee table. An unforgiveable sin in Ryker's eyes. "I do. I associate it with happy times, time spent with my dad. My father used to take me and Ryker out on father-son outings. He took us to the usual stuff, ballgames and other sporting events. But he said he wanted us to be well-rounded, to appreciate the arts, so he also took us to the symphony on several occasions. There was almost always a pianist. It was my favorite part. Can you imagine that though? Two young boys with lots of energy sitting through a symphony?" Zane laughs to himself.

"Was it miserable?"

"No, actually. I fell in love with it. It fascinated me. To this day, I love it."

"Ryker must feel the same. That's how I met him. He attended one of my performances with the Marin Symphony. I met him during the meet and greet after the show."

Zane folds his arms across his chest. "Did you really? What a coinkydink."

"He asked me out to dinner right then and there. He gave me his business card so I wouldn't forget his name." I laugh aloud at the thought. "He missed Dating 101."

Zane leans his head back on the couch and releases a half smile, half scoff. "Interesting," he says slowly, then hops to his feet. "How about breakfast? I'm starving. Wanna join me?"

After what Ryker told me, I am feeling wary of Zane. I can't figure him out. He seems friendly, casual, relaxed, and pleasant. He must have another side he's not showing me. But, like last night, I don't feel threatened. He may not be an honest individual, but I don't think he bears any ill will toward me. Until he proves himself otherwise, I'm going to go with the flow. It's seems like the best course of action.

"I could use a short break."

"Sweet."

We make our way to the kitchen. Zane takes out two bowls, fills them with cold cereal to the brim, and adds milk. "Breakfast is ready, dear," he says with a wink.

"Quit impressing me, Zane."

"You ain't seen nothing yet."

"If you make me peanut butter and jelly for lunch, I won't be able to stop raving about you."

He chuckles as he opens the French doors that lead to the balcony and says, "Let's eat outside. The sun is calling my name."

I grab my bowl and follow. He's already sitting at the outdoor table, his bare feet once again propped up on the table as he basks in the morning sun. He takes a bite, dons his sunglasses, and leans his head back as he chews.

"Mmmmm, heaven."

Huh. I've never thought of a bowl of Lucky Charms combined with sunshine as heaven, but this is nice in a bohemian kind of way. "I didn't know we had Lucky Charms in the cupboard."

"We didn't. I picked them up yesterday. Stocked up. Ryker doesn't eat this crap."

No, he doesn't. He's into protein shakes and health food. Judging by Zane's physique, it's clear he doesn't eat junk all day either. Maybe this is his one vice. Scandalous.

"How are you and Ryker brothers?"

He shakes his head. "I don't know, it's an enigma."

"You're very different from each other," I remark slowly.

"Always have been. So, tell me about you, Mila. What's your story?"

That was a quick change of subject. The Martel men don't like to talk about their strange brotherly relationship.

"I grew up in the small town of Twin Falls, Idaho."

"Small town girl in the big city, huh?"

"Yeah. Not my first rodeo, though."

"Oh? Where else have you lived?"

"I attended Juilliard."

"Ah, New York City."

"Yes. I went on scholarship. My parents are hard-working middle-class people. They couldn't afford to send me there."

"What do your parents do?"

"My dad owned the local hardware store in downtown Twin. My mom was a stay-at-home mom, the kind that made homemade cookies for me after school. They're humble and sweet. They've sacrificed everything for their children. They're retired now, always wearing work out clothes and going to the gym every day to maintain their health. They're pretty wonderful."

"Siblings?" Zane asks.

"One older brother. He's still in Twin."

"Sounds like you had an ideal childhood."

I can't see his eyes with his sunglasses on, but I don't know him well enough to be able to read him anyway.

"Yeah, I did."

"What made you come to San Fran?"

"My father grew up here, so it felt like a piece of home. My dream is to play with the San Francisco Symphony one day. I'm hoping to be invited for an audition. I saw Daniil Trifonov play *Rachmaninoff's Third Piano Concerto* with them once. I was mesmerized."

"You have passion, Mila. It's refreshing. What else do you want in life?"

I tip my head to one side. "What else? That's not enough?"

"Sure it is. Just wondered if you wanted more."

"Not many people ask me that, like playing with the symphony is such a lofty goal, I can't possibly want more."

"*Do* you want more?"

"Yes, eventually I want a family, children. I have big dreams, but I also know what's most important in life."

He nods and turns to stare at the view, a brooding expression on his face. I have no idea what he's thinking after all I revealed.

I get to my feet. "I need to take Artie out for a short walk and restroom break, then get back to my practice session. Thanks for the cereal."

He stands as well. "Mind if I come with? I'd like to stretch my legs."

I hesitate. I can see where this is going. We're going to be friends and Ryker won't like it at all. It'll put me in an uncomfortable position and it will add to the strain on an already strained relationship.

Frankly, I can be friends with whomever I darn well please. And so far, I like Zane. I *should* be friends with Ryker's brother. Ryker *should* be friends with his brother.

"Sure. I'd like that."

I told Ryker that Zane and I would hardly see each other. Yet, so far we've enjoyed a movie and pizza together, breakfast together, and now we're about to embark upon a walk outside with Artie. I think I underestimated the relationship that might develop when living under the same roof. I think it's a good thing, though.

We're interrupted by Zane's phone. Of note, his ringtone is *Bad to the Bone*.

Somehow it suits him.

Zane mumbles, "Here it comes."

I don't understand until he answers. "Ryker, my man. How's it goin'?"

Zane holds the phone away from his ear. I can't make out everything Ryker is saying, but I can hear that he's yelling angrily at his brother at the top of his lungs. I don't even recognize his voice. He sounds like he's in a rage. I even hear a few choice expletives leave his lips, the kind of words I would never expect my smooth-talking man to say.

A scowl takes over my face. Ryker does have the Freddy gene and I'm not cool with that. There's another side to him that I don't know. Or like. I feel my disillusionment growing by leaps and bounds. I've heard about men who seem perfect during the dating timeframe, then become different people altogether when they're married. Will that happen with Ryker? I'm not sure I want to marry him and find out the hard way.

I shift from foot to foot, feeling extremely uncomfortable. Why is Ryker treating his brother like this? It seems completely uncalled for.

When the yelling stops, Zane calmly says, "Would you like me to leave?"

The yelling starts again. From my end it sounds very much like an adult on a *Charlie Brown* cartoon.

Zane sighs and waits for his chance to speak. "I can grab a hotel. No prob."

Ryker starts up again with his angry rant. It's so unlike the man I know. I mean, he's a hardheaded businessman with a reputation for being politely cutthroat. But I thought he had more tact, more diplomacy.

Zane sits back down and kicks his feet up, patiently waiting for a break in the tirade. "Yep, just until I find housing. In this market, won't take too long. I'm lookin' to buy."

Zane remains quiet while Ryker puts in his two cents. His voice is still raised, but he's settling down a bit.

"Okay. Sounds good," Zane says finally, ending the call.

"What was all that about?" I ask, incredulous.

"In a nutshell?"

"Yeah, I guess so."

"There was a lot of *How dare you show up at my apartment.* Even though he gave me a key, just sayin'. Then there was the *How dare you scare my girl. How dare you watch a movie with my girl. If you so much as look at her the wrong way, I'll have you drawn and quartered. You can't stay for long. Mila has a soft heart and doesn't think I should kick you out.* Thanks for that, by the way. That about sums it up."

"Are you serious?" Doesn't he trust me?

"That's putting it politely and leaving out a few choice words. I thought it best not to mention breakfast or that you were standing right next to me."

Zane has the audacity to wink at me.

I'm stunned for several moments, my mouth hanging open in, I'm sure, an unflattering manner. Once I regain my senses, I say, "I think that was a smart decision."

At that moment, something very odd happens, something very unexpected.

We both start to laugh. And once we start, we don't stop.

chapter ten
♥

AS WE WALK through the city streets, Artie does his business and wants to be held as usual. He's so teeny, a walk down the block exhausts him. One of our steps is five for him.

Zane holds Artie in his strong arms. He rests his head on Zane's chest and promptly falls asleep.

The sun, the bay breeze, and an invigorating walk is exactly what I needed. I should return to my piano, but today I feel like slacking off.

"This is not a dog. He's practically a cat," Zane says.

"More like a newborn baby."

"Seriously."

We walk in silence for a bit, enjoying a lazy gait.

Curiosity makes me say, "Can I ask you a question?"

"Sure. Shoot."

His fast response makes me feel like he's an open book. I like that. "What happened between you and Ryker?"

"He's never told you?"

"No, he doesn't talk about you much." I pause. "I'm sorry, that came out wrong."

He strokes Artie's head. "No worries. I'm well aware of how my brother feels about me."

"He told me about you, but not much more, other than there was a rift between you."

"You know, Mila, perhaps it's better if Ryker tells you. If you ask two different people about the same story, you'll get two different answers."

"I'd like to hear your side." He stops mid-stride and faces me. So I stop and do the same. "What? What's wrong?"

"Thank you."

"For what?"

"For wanting to hear my side."

I nod. "I'd like you and Ryker to have a relationship, so maybe it starts with us. You're probably going to be my brother-in-law, after all."

"Probably?"

A small sigh escapes. "Yes, probably. To be honest, I don't know for sure what will happen between me and Ryker. We're a work in progress." I'm still shaken by his angry voice as he yelled at Zane. Will he use that tone on me if I upset him? That's unacceptable to me.

"Fair enough."

"It kills me that he thinks of you as his enemy."

Zane stiffens. "He said that?"

"Sorry. I assumed you knew he felt that way."

"I guess I did." He shrugs and we resume walking.

"You know, Zane, no one will tell me the whole truth and it bothers me. Both Ryker and your mother talk around the state of affairs. I gotta say, it's tough to hear what your own mother has to say about the situation. If I can do something to mend fences, I'd like to help. Am I butting in where I'm not wanted? Tell me if I am."

"Here's the thing. You can't fix it, Mila. You should know that right now. You'll only be disappointed. And Debra's not my mother."

This time I stop in my tracks. "What?"

Zane faces me again. "My mother passed when I was only three months old. My father married Debra shortly thereafter and they had Ryker. I'm the barely tolerated stepson with the evil stepmother who pretty much hates my guts."

He says it casually, like it's no big deal. I know it must hurt much more than he's letting on.

"Oh, I didn't know that. I'm so sorry."

"It's been that way my whole life. I don't know anything different."

"What do you mean?"

Passersby stroll past us, ignoring the man and woman

having a deep conversation in the middle of the sidewalk, a small dog between them.

"I like to think of it like this. A king found his queen and he was enamored with her from the very beginning. He loved her more than he'd ever loved anyone in his life. They had a son to complete their happiness. But the queen was ill and the pregnancy took too much out of her. She died when her baby was only three months old. The king was devastated and couldn't be consoled. He poured all of his love onto his son, because he was a manifestation of the love between him and the love of his life. Then he found someone new, someone who could put a balm on his grief. He married her and she became the new queen. Unbeknownst to the king, she was evil. Soon, she had a son. But the evil queen could see that the king loved the child of his one true love more than he loved her son. She became jealous. She hated the firstborn son because he was heir to the king's kingdom. She wanted her son to be the heir and she'd do anything within her power to make it happen. Even if it meant turning the two half-brothers against each other." He pauses. "That was my life. It still is. But I took myself out of the equation."

"Wow. I wasn't expecting that. Everything makes sense now."

"It's complicated. I'm not sure Ryker understands it completely. He's been brainwashed by Debra."

"Why are you returning home? Why would you put yourself back into the situation?"

"I need to be with my dad. I don't think he has much time left. I have commitments to the Army. It took me a while, but I was finally able to get an assignment here."

My hand lifts toward him of its own accord, but I let it lower to my side. I can't offer physical comfort. It wouldn't be appropriate.

"I had no idea. Thanks for helping me understand the dynamics." I feel lied to by Debra and Ryker. The situation isn't quite what they made it out to be. Assuming Zane is telling me the truth, that is. I'm not sure why, but I feel inclined to believe Zane.

"Mila, keep in mind, Ryker's not the bad guy. He's a product of his mother."

The evil queen. How much of his mother is inside of him? I'm confused and unsure. "We'd better get back."

On the walk back home, my mind is reeling. I thought I was taking a walk with the bad guy, the villain, the rogue. The man I was supposed to be wary of, the man who should not be trusted.

Turns out, I'm walking with the prince.

The true prince.

chapter eleven

I ARRIVE HOME from practice with the symphony only to find music once again blasting through the penthouse. It's so loud, Zane doesn't hear me enter.

He's in the kitchen making dinner, wearing his usual at-home attire—torn-at-the-knees jeans and his signature white t-shirt. And of course, he's barefoot.

At least he's wearing a shirt. He's been here for three days and I've learned it's rare for him. If he has pants on, he considers himself dressed.

I observe him unnoticed for several moments. Adele is singing about sending her love to her ex's new lover and Zane is singing along, dancing around the kitchen as he cooks. The mess he's making causes my stomach to twist.

For a moment, my mind conjures up a vision of Ryker in the kitchen, plating expensive take-out he purchased for us. He's wearing a suit because he's always wearing a suit.

I wrack my brain, trying to remember if I've ever seen him in anything other than a suit.

If I have, I can't recall.

I like him in a suit. He's a clotheshorse and wears them well. I've always thought he looks like he walked off a magazine shoot wherein he was the lead model.

Every time I've ever visited Ryker, the penthouse has been silent. We eat formally at the dining room table and spend our time talking. The lights are always at full brightness. There's never candlelight.

The thing is, I enjoyed those evenings. I treasure the time we've spent together, even if it has been a tad formal.

Yet, I have to admit, this is more me. I like the relaxed atmosphere, the informality, the stress-free vibe. I immediately feel calm.

I could see Zane doing a *Risky Business* slide across the

floor while lip syncing to *Old Time Rock and Roll*. It would be as natural to him as breathing.

He spins around and freezes for a second when he notices me.

"Oh, hey Mila. I didn't hear you come in." He's completely unembarrassed, comfortable in his own skin. "I'm making chili. Want to join me?"

After I lift my jaw up off the floor, I toss my purse—which now reminds me that I'm a faux-leather purse kind of a gal—and music bag onto the dining table instead of putting them away. Somehow, the action feels scandalous.

"Sure. I'd love to."

"You like spicy? I'm all about spicy."

Shocker. "Spicy is fine with me."

"Wanna dice the bell pepper? I'll do the onion and suffer the consequences."

"Okay."

We stand side by side, our knives chopping away. Zane doesn't stop moving along with the music.

"C'mon, Mila. The rule of the kitchen is you have to dance while you cook. It makes the drudgery go by faster."

I'm Gonna Be starts to invade the airwaves. The beat begs to be danced to, so I move with the music as The Proclaimers sing about walking 500 miles to fall down at someone's door.

Zane adds the bell pepper and onion to a pan and gives them a good sauté before adding them to the pot he has brewing on the stovetop. I try not to notice the movement of his hips, but they've decided to stare at me because none of his body parts have any manners. The smell of tomatoes and spices are calling to me, making my stomach grumble. At least, I think hunger accounts for the strange feeling in my stomach.

Zane dances over to the sink, washes his hands and uses a paper towel to wipe the onion tears from his eyes.

"It just has to simmer for twenty minutes or so," he

says.

While the chili finishes up, we clean up the kitchen, dancing along with the music, laughing at ourselves here and there.

He leaves the cutting board on the countertop along with the salt and pepper shakers instead of tucking them away into the cupboards. "There, now it looks like someone lives here and this isn't a freakin' model home." He hangs the dishtowel on the oven handle, then messes it up so it's not perfectly folded. "Much better."

I can't help but giggle. We're acting like two kids who've been left home alone while our parents are out.

Zane grabs two bowls, ladles us each some chili, and covers the top with a generous amount of grated cheese.

"Hey, do you like Jeopardy?"

"The game show? Is that still on?"

"Yeah, you like it?"

"Sure."

He hands me a bowl as he heads for the couch. He switches the music off and flicks the TV channel to Jeopardy. He assumes his usual position with his feet propped up on the coffee table. I don't think the man has the ability to sit in any other way.

"C'mon, let's see who can get the most answers right. Your answer has to be in the form of a question, remember?"

"Yeah, I remember." I'm still standing in the living room, holding my bowl of chili, feeling dazed.

I'm not sure I've ever met a more unassuming man. This is Zane, like him or not. He is what he is and he doesn't apologize for it.

"You gonna sit?" he asks with his mouth full.

"What is letting the body rest while the buttocks and thighs hit the couch?"

He lets out a bark of laughter. "That was perfect. A true Jeopardy winner in the making."

I like this.

No, I love this. If this was a date, I'd call it the best date ever.

I take my seat on the other end of the couch.

He turns out the lights so we can watch the TV in darkness. Fog hangs in the air outside, but not enough to hide the city lights sparkling back at us from the large windows.

While the contestants are being introduced, Zane says, "Found a house today. It's an old Victorian fixer-upper. It's three stories, big on charm and authenticity. Big on the wallet too, but I fell in love with it. I'm gonna go for it. The seller's eager to get it off his hands. I should be out of your way soon."

He said he'd be out quickly and he's keeping his word. A flash of disappointment washes over me. I enjoy his company.

"But who will make me chili when you're gone?"

"No worries, I'll bring you some. Don't mind sharing."

His answer makes me smile.

chapter twelve
♡

I JUST PLAYED every piece I'm practicing for my upcoming symphony performance perfectly two times in a row. Not one single mistake, not one single slip up or hesitation. I'm so thrilled I stand next to my piano bench and do my silly happy dance.

It's always been my reward when I finally get a piece right. After all my hard work, it's my release, my own personal celebration. In truth, it's a great stress reliever. I jump up and down, my fist hitting the air several times in a row, my head bobbing from side to side.

My fellow musicians nicknamed my dance, Mila's Musical Moment. It became a joke at Juilliard, something I was known for.

Little did they know, I did it as a kid every time my strict piano teacher told me I'd passed off a song. It seemed to me as though it was a moment worth celebrating, no matter how brief.

Old habits die hard.

The front door slams and Zane walks in with his lazy swagger, his flip flops rhythmically hitting the floor. He removes his sunglasses and tucks them into the neckline of his t-shirt as he always does.

"What was that?"

I sit at my piano bench. "What?"

"That funny dance you were doing? I saw it. You can't deny it."

Fine, I might as well fess up. "It's my victory dance for whenever I get something right on the piano."

"It's cute."

"It was cute when I was five and proud of myself for playing *Row, Row, Row Your Boat*. Now it's triumphant."

He chuckles. "Do it again."

"No, it's reserved for winning moments. Doing it now would be blasphemous."

He points at me. "Gonna be watching for it. Got my eyes on you, Westerman."

"Whatever." He's been easy to live with over the past week. Nothing seems to bother him and he's never in a hurry. He's a go with the flow kind of guy. I haven't seen his "unpleasant" side. Instead I find him affable and easy going.

"I have news," he announces.

I turn on my bench and face him.

"We have been summoned by the queen mother to dinner at the palace promptly at six this evening, along with a reminder that being late is completely unacceptable. We shall therefore show up at six-fifteen. No Jeopardy for us tonight. No worries, I'll DVR it and we'll catch it later."

Jeopardy has become our evening pastime and stiff competition. "Hold up. We?"

"Yes, Debra's spies found out I was in town and that I'm living here with you. I imagine her head is spinning on her neck right about now. Watch out for projectile pea soup."

Gross. "Why do I have to go?" I ask, sounding like a petulant child.

"It's not a death sentence."

"It feels like one."

"My thoughts exactly," he mumbles under his breath. "Because she asked that we both attend. And because I don't want to go alone." He cups his hands close to his chest. "Please don't make me. Please, please, please."

I roll my eyes. "I've known you for one week and I consort with your arch nemesis. What makes you think I'll be any help?"

"She'll be outnumbered and we can gang up on her."

We exchange a fist bump. "You have no idea how appealing that sounds."

His expression grows serious. "And I want to see my dad. She keeps telling me it's not a good time, that he's having a hard day, or that he's sleeping. She's blowing me off."

"That's not right. Can't you insist upon it?"

"I could. I have a key and . . . actually the house is in my name."

"What? That huge house is yours?"

He makes a funny face. "Technically."

"I bet Debra hates that so much."

"I'm not sure she knows."

"The plot thickens."

"I have every right to be there. But I'd rather not upset my father by getting ugly."

"It's too late for that, Zane. It's been ugly all of your life and Debra made it that way."

I asked Ryker to explain the rift between himself and Zane in detail. He told me there was no actual rift, that Zane was simply an unpleasant person who causes problems everywhere he goes.

His answer was most unsatisfying, and I told him so. He had to go and told me he'd explain more later.

I expect the truth. I need to know his side of the story and what I could be potentially marrying into.

"Don't feel sorry for me, Mila. I'm not asking for sympathy. I got this."

"You got this, but you don't want to go alone to have dinner with your stepmother in your childhood home?"

He pretends like he's making a jump shot. "Two points for Mila."

He lands and his entire body stills, observing me. His large brown eyes blink heavily as he stands before me. "Come with?" he says quietly, the most vulnerable I've ever seen him.

How can I resist?

It's Friday night and I have a rare free weekend ahead of me. I've played for ballet classes and practiced with the symphony all week. A break would be nice.

If Debra wants me there too, I should at least make an appearance. "Okay," I whisper. "I'll come with you."

We both retire to our rooms to get ready for the evening. When we exit and find that we're dressed alike in jeans and t-shirts, him in flip flops and me in sandals, it gives us a good chuckle.

"You're wearing that on purpose, aren't you?" I ask.

"Just bein' myself."

As we leave, he adds, "I can't help it if my clothing irritates the queen mother."

His choice of vehicle is as casual as his choice of clothing. He drives an older Jeep, the top unattached. I climb in and find it rustic in a charming way. It's not terribly neat, but it's not filthy either. My mom's motto was, "*Clean enough to be healthy and dirty enough to be happy.*" That describes Zane's Jeep. I put my long hair into a quick braid to keep it from becoming a snarly mess during the drive. Zane flips on his music and it's too loud, but once we're driving in the open Jeep with the rushing wind, it's perfect.

I close my eyes, letting the wind hit my face and the music envelop me. I feel myself relax and de-stress after the busy week I've had.

All too soon, we're in front of the Martel mansion.

Zane checks the time on his phone. "Six-twenty. Perfect timing."

I suppress a smile right along with him. "We're horrible people."

"If we're horrible, Debra's a monster."

"It had to be said."

"Mila, I want you on my team," Zane says with a laugh.

We approach the door and I love the two-against-one feeling. It's the most confident I've ever felt when facing Freddy. I follow Zane's lead to see if we ring the doorbell or just enter.

He rings the doorbell. But Ryker does too when he visits.

If I'm visiting my parents, I always enter without even knocking. They're always happy to see me barge in.

Visiting Debra is a different beast.

Speaking of beasts, Debra answers the door and grants us her "baring her teeth" smile. It makes me shiver.

"Oh, I didn't know you'd be arriving together. How sweet." She glances at her watch with dramatic flair.

"We're coming from the same place. Seemed easier," Zane says.

"Too bad it couldn't have been sooner."

"Didn't you say six-thirty?" he asks innocently.

What a stinker. Yet, I'm enjoying every minute.

"No, Zane, I said six and you know it," Debra says, her face sour.

He doesn't apologize. He doesn't get a hug or any air kisses either. She simply looks down her nose at him as though he's something disgusting. "So glad you're home, Zane. Your father will so be pleased."

Her words are not believable. At all. I'm rethinking the authenticity of every single one of her compliments.

I get one air kiss. "Mila, so good to see you, dear."

I doubt that very much.

Zane folds his arms, looking uncomfortable. I can't say he necessarily looks sad to the average onlooker. But to me, he looks troubled. I think his humor covers up a world of hurt. It makes me feel a flash of pure hatred toward this woman who has rejected Zane so fully during his lifetime. How do you reject an innocent baby?

"Ryker says he misses you terribly, Mila."

"I miss him too." It's the truth. I miss what we had.

"I know how hard it must be for you two lovebirds to be separated. You must be pining for each other. Don't worry, you'll be back in each other's arms soon."

I nod because I don't know what to say to that. I know she's not thrilled about Ryker dating me. I feel like she's making comments about us only for Zane's benefit, like she feels the need to mark Ryker's territory for him.

My thoughts are confirmed when she directs her next comment to Zane. "Those two. They can't keep their hands off each other. It's quite adorable."

Not true. Ryker is not big on PDA. In public or private.

Debra looks me up and down. "Where have you two just come from?"

Zane answers. "A wrestling match. They were about to start the female mud fights when we had to leave. Sorry to miss it. Do we smell like smoke?"

Oh, he's good. He knows how to poke the beast just right.

Debra's face turns red. "Don't be ridiculous, Zane. You're such a smart aleck." To me, she adds, "He always has been."

"I think he's funny."

"Oh, he is," she says with a flutter. "Such an *interesting* personality, our Zane." She hands a wrapped gift to Zane. "I bought you something. A welcome home gift."

Zane accepts the present. "For me, huh? How do I rate?"

He unwraps it quickly. It's a twelve-pack package of department store socks.

Wow. Debra has a cruel streak inside of her that scares me. I can't play in her league.

Zane slaps his thigh. "Look at that. Amazing invention. Did you know these existed, Mila?"

"Something called shirts exist too," I tell him quietly, so Freddy can't hear.

"Who knew?" He tosses the package on a foyer table and pounds his flip flops harder against the tile floor.

"Just a gentle reminder, Zane. Some occasions require shoes and socks," Debra says as we follow her toward the dining room.

Our dear, sweet Freddy is at her best this evening.

Look out.

I cast Zane a glance as we cross the threshold. But his eyes are elsewhere.

James Martel is sitting in his wheelchair next to the table, hunched and defeated. His normally blank face alters when he sees Zane. A wave of recognition crosses his features, animating him in a way I've never seen before. His back straightens, his expression brightens, and his eyes widen.

Zane rushes to his father, engulfing him in a bear hug. "Dad."

A strange sound emanates from James, a sort of wail and grunt combined. He does it over and over again, clearly expressing happiness in the best way he knows how.

I have to hold back tears at the sight of the reunion of father and son. All this time, I thought James wasn't "there" at all. I was mistaken. Something inside of him absolutely knows Zane.

When I glance at Debra, her face is a mask of anger. She can barely conceal her feelings.

I don't need to confirm the truth of what Zane told me about his life. It's more than obvious.

"That's enough, Zane. I don't want him to get over excited."

She's such a killjoy. Something tells me it's going to be another one of those long evenings.

TAYLOR DEAN

chapter thirteen

♡

ZANE TAKES THE seat next to his father, gripping one of his hands tightly in his own.

But James has other plans. The long, throaty noises continue to emanate from him, almost as though he's trying to tell Zane something. I see it as a great expression of love for his son. I have to hold back tears. The two of them clearly have a strong connection.

"It's all right, Dad, I'm home. Everything's okay. I'm home and I'm not leaving. I'm stationed right here in San Francisco now. I'll be here everyday to see you. That's a promise."

"All right, then. Let's eat, shall we?" Debra claps her hands twice like she's in a "clap on" commercial.

The lights don't respond, but their private cook appears bearing plates of food.

James' nurse quietly sits next to him, holding several small bowls of pureed foods on a plate.

"Let me feed him." Zane takes the plate from the nurse. "Take a break, I can do it."

"Zane, that's good of you, but that's why we have a nurse." Debra stops the nurse from leaving.

"I want to do it."

Zane doesn't wait for Debra's permission. He begins to spoon-feed his father, moving slowly, wiping his chin with a napkin in between mouthfuls.

Debra nods at the nurse, and she quietly exits the room. I see why Zane calls her the queen mother. She truly rules over her domain.

Debra and I begin to eat our dinner, while we watch Zane feed his father. There's so much tension in the room, my stomach starts to hurt. Zane completely ignores Debra and concentrates on his father.

Debra chews her food slowly, her eyes burning holes in the walls. Every few moments, she remarks on the food.

"The asparagus is delicious."

"The chicken is so tender."

"The homemade rolls are divine."

I nod and smile, agreeing with each comment. Mostly, I keep my head down and eat my dinner.

"Thank you for taking such good care of Ryker's penthouse, Mila. You know how much that place means to him. It's his pride and joy."

"Yes, it is." He isn't *falling* in love with it, he *is* in love with it. Hmmmm, that was a bitter thought.

"Thank goodness, you have so much time on your hands."

That grabs Zane's attention. "Mila's very busy and works hard. Just because she practices at home doesn't mean she has time on her hands."

Whoa. I like Zane as my great defender. Go team Mila and Zane.

Debra smooths her perfect hair. "I simply meant it's really . . . nice of her."

"I know what you meant," Zane says, his tone firm.

That's when I notice the tears dripping down James' cheeks. Zane gently wipes them away with a napkin without commenting.

Is his emotion about seeing Zane or his inability to communicate properly? Or because he can hear the thinly veiled venom in his wife's words?

Either way, James Martel is feeling and comprehending more than we realize.

Even though I want Zane to have time with his father, I'm relieved when the nurse comes to take James upstairs to rest. He's nearly falling asleep while sitting up. The poor man can't keep his eyes open, even though he's fighting it as hard as he can.

Zane stares down at his plate, his forearms resting on the edge of the table. He doesn't take a bite. "He hasn't improved. Is he still undergoing therapy?"

"Every day. I take good care of him, I assure you. Some of us have been here the entire time and have never left him."

Zane stills. "I couldn't stay. The Army doesn't look too kindly on their soldiers going AWOL."

Another tidbit Ryker and Debra fail to mention when they speak of Zane.

"Of course not. Don't worry about it. Ryker's been here the entire time. He visits nearly every day. He's a devoted son. Your father hasn't been alone."

The look on Zane's face nearly kills me. His expression is the very definition of devastation.

He hides it quickly. "I'll be here every day as well. Take some of the load off of you."

"There's no need, Zane. I have plenty of help."

"I'll be here because I want to be here and for no other reason than that."

"If you must," Debra says with her fluttery wave.

I've never seen anyone run roughshod over Debra. I'm rooting for Zane. I like the way he stands up to her. He's not rude, but he's firm.

Zane grabs his fork and stabs a bite of chicken. He takes a few more bites in quick succession, a sour expression on his face. He doesn't look like he's enjoying his meal. More like he's eating cardboard. I think he's eating only because he feels obligated.

"I suppose you're wondering why I asked the two of you to dinner this evening." Debra fingers the pearls at her neck as she often does.

"Does there have to be a reason?" Zane asks. "I'm your stepson and I wanted to see my father. Isn't that enough?"

Debra laughs nervously. Zane knows how to push her buttons and make her flustered. It's a beautiful thing.

"Ryker has asked me to bring the two of you together and discuss the current situation with you."

Excuse me? Heat rises to my cheeks. Ryker asked his

mother to speak to us for him? Uncool, very uncool.

"What exactly is the current situation, Debra?" Zane asks.

I notice he doesn't call her mother. Interesting.

Debra rolls her eyes. "The two of you."

Zane stills again, like a predator about to strike. "What about us?"

"Ryker's very worried about the two of you living under the same roof. He feels it's not appropriate and I agree. Something needs to be done."

"He hasn't expressed that to me," I say. I mean, he did at first. But in the end, he's the one who decided it was okay for Zane to stay, not me.

"My son is a trusting man, much more so than me. He's not worried about you, though, Mila."

Wow. There's nothing subtle about the implications she left hanging in the air. She doesn't trust me, even though her son supposedly does, and she certainly doesn't trust Zane.

"Meaning?" Zane pushes.

"Come now, Zane. Do I have to spell it out?"

"Yes, please do."

"You've always wanted what Ryker has. And we know you'll do anything to get what you want. *Anything*."

Zane stares her down, then shoves his unfinished plate away from him. "I won't be at Ryker's home for long. I've already found a place I'm interested in. I made an offer two days ago."

I'm bothered that Zane doesn't defend himself.

Debra gathers her thoughts. "That's fine and good, but until the deal goes through, I think it's time to discuss the alternatives."

Zane's face is deadpan. "What might those be?"

"Find other living arrangements immediately. This is the woman your brother wants to marry, Zane. Show a little respect."

"Wait a minute," I say, standing up so quickly my chair

scrapes the floor. I'm so upset, I'm about to explode. "Zane's been the perfect gentleman. It isn't fair to imply otherwise. If Ryker doesn't trust me, then we have issues between us that far outweigh jealousy."

Debra scoffs. "Oh, Mila. Ryker isn't jealous of Zane."

Zane slowly stands, his eyes on me.

Maybe he should be. The thought hits me like lightning hitting a chimney, shocking the entire house.

I return his heated gaze. "It sure sounds like he is. If it walks like a chicken, and talks like a chicken, it's a chicken. Zane hasn't done anything wrong. Don't make it sound like he has."

Zane's chest rises and falls. He holds me captive with his eyes. I don't know what he's thinking, but I wish I did.

"I didn't say that he had." Debra stands as well.

I turn my attention to Debra. "If Ryker has an issue with this situation, he should talk to me about it. I don't appreciate him calling in a third party. We can solve this between us and we don't need any help." I look back at Zane, who's still watching me with intense eyes. "I think we should call it a night. Shall we drive home together?" I glance at Debra again. "Or is that unacceptable too, Debbie?"

"It's Debra."

Out of everything I said, I can't believe that's her response.

I head for the door. Behind me, I hear Zane say, "I'll be here tomorrow morning to see Dad."

"Call first to make sure it's convenient," Debra spouts.

"Nine AM. I'll be here," Zane announces, brooking no argument.

Zane catches up to me and we leave the house together. We climb into his Jeep and he takes off like the devil is on our heels. It's still not fast enough.

Zane laughs into the wind. "Oh snap, that was fun. When you called the queen mother Debbie, I thought she was gonna blow a gasket."

When I don't laugh, he takes a deep breath and says, "I'm sorry, Mila. I don't want to cause problems between you and Ryker."

"It's not your fault. Clearly, Ryker and I have several issues to iron out. My relationship is about me and him. Not me, him, and his mother. I'm so mad, I could spit."

"I'd like to see that."

I turn in the open Jeep and spit into the wind. Zane laughs harder than I thought he would at my actions.

"Why aren't you upset?" I ask.

"I am. But this is the norm. I don't expect any different."

"You didn't defend yourself. Why not?"

"It would be the same as spitting into the wind. Useless and it never ends up where you intend."

He has a point. "I'm sorry you grew up facing that every day of your life."

"I always had my father. I was never alone."

"Still, it had to be hard."

"I don't think I realized what I was missing until I was a teenager. Before that, it was just my normal. I had no idea how dysfunctional we were."

"You're not dysfunctional. Debra is."

When we arrive at Ryker's penthouse, Zane finds an open spot on the street, parks his Jeep, and cuts the engine. Neither one of us bother to remove our seatbelts. We sit in the crisp night air, cooling off and breathing deeply.

"Hey, Mila."

"Hmmmm?"

"Without Dad at full capacity, it's not often that someone stands up for me. Thanks for that."

"She's a bully. My future mother-in-law probably hates me now. And if she hates me . . . Ryker . . ."

"Ryker's a big boy. He'll make his own decisions."

"Will he?" I have my doubts.

"I'd like to think so."

I rub my eyes, feeling bone weary. "It's his mother and

he loves her. I get it. But he doesn't see her for what she is."

"No, he doesn't. But he will one day. I'd venture to say it'll be sooner rather than later. And it won't be pretty."

The sounds of horns honking and engines rumbling waft through the air. If I listen carefully, I can hear seagulls squawking in the distance. Fog is setting in, making me shiver.

"I'm glad I have the weekend off," I mumble. "I need time to recover from that fiasco. Time to think things through." The unsaid hangs in the air between us. I need time to sort out my relationship with Ryker. I feel like we're a sinking ship filled with red flags.

"Thanks for going with me," Zane says. "I'm sorry it didn't turn out well."

"It never does. Not once. It doesn't bode well for me."

"You can handle Debra, no problem. She just wants Ryker to be happy. If he's happy, she's happy."

"I don't understand why Ryker didn't talk to me about it. It doesn't sound like he's happy with me right now."

"Ryker will always be happy if he has you. He's a lucky man."

We both turn our heads, cushioned by the head rests, and look at each other.

I purse my lips. "I know I shouldn't be telling you this, but I'm unsure of Ryker."

"What do you mean?"

"I'm not positive we're a match," I say quietly. "I have a lot of doubts and I don't know what to do about it."

"Sometimes a separation helps you to see things clearly. Give it time."

"Ever since he's been gone, I've felt uneasy. It grows stronger every day."

"Hey, it's not the end of the world." His voice is as quiet as mine, almost a whisper. "Everything will work itself out."

"Yes, I suppose it will."

"How about I take you out tomorrow? I think it's time for some serious cheering up. Call it a thank you for not making me face the queen mother by myself. I loved having you by my side."

Team Mila and Zane wanders through my mind again. I ignore the flutter it causes in my stomach.

A day out with Zane? We're friends. Why not? "Actually, that sounds nice."

"We'll hop onto a cable car and ride off into the sunset. We'll forget everything and everyone. Just me and you."

I like the sound of that. More than I should. Our eyes study each other for several moments too long. I swear there's a subtle shift in the air between us. "Okay. I'd like that," I whisper. I love this lazy way of having a conversation.

"Where shall we go?" he asks.

"Into the sunset sounded good. I'm down with that." Sounds like a nice escape.

"All right then. After the sunset. Where to?"

"I don't know. You know the area. You tell me."

"How about Chinatown? Have you been yet?"

"No, I haven't."

"It's one of my favorite places to explore. We'll grab dim sum while we're there."

"What's dim sum?"

"Say what?"

"What's dim sum?" I ask again.

He releases air between his lips. "We can't be friends now."

I do like he did earlier. I cup my hands to my chest and say, "Please, please, please?"

"You talked me into it."

I mock sigh with relief.

He sends me his sexy half smile. "Dim sum is the best food in the world. You'll love it."

I'm skeptical. "I don't want to eat anything weird."

"This is not a *Survivor* challenge. It's lunch. Dim sum

isn't weird. It's a variety of steamed buns, rice noodle rolls, and dumplings, all served in steamer baskets. You choose what you want from a cart and everyone at the table eats family style. You haven't lived until you've tried it."

"I guess I haven't lived then."

"Nope. Not until now."

He makes me feel like I haven't lived until I met him. Something about his enthusiasm for life, his way of living on his own terms, his casual, relaxed lifestyle.

"Okay, I'll ride off into the sunset with you. But when it comes to dim sum, I make no promises."

"Deal." He holds out his hand so we can shake on it.

I watch our hands clasp together as if it's happening in slow motion. He holds my hand in his long after we shake.

My eyes travel up to meet his as I wonder what's happening. A chill wanders through me, from the tips of my toes to the top of my head.

Zane frowns and releases my hand. "Aw man, I'm so mad."

"What? Why?"

"I forgot the new socks Debra gave me. I need them. I don't even know where to buy them."

We laugh and the sound wafts up to the sky, getting lost in the night air.

I run my fingers through my long hair and mimic him. "Aw man, I'm so mad."

That merits a smile. "Pray tell."

"I forgot to braid my hair for the trip home. It's a rat's nest." I pull my brush out of my purse and attempt to tackle the mess.

Zane grabs the brush. "Hey, I got it. Turn around."

Our eyes meet again, and I hesitate for a few seconds. Having Zane brush my hair somehow feels highly intimate. "You want to . . . brush my hair for me?"

"I'll be gentle, I promise."

"The wind has made it all snarly."

"I can get them out for you."

"Um . . ."

"Don't overthink it, Mila."

I look deep into his eyes and see sincerity. "Okay, thank you."

I turn in my seat, my back facing him. He sections off a piece of hair, starts at the bottom and works until he reaches the top. He runs his hand over the section of hair several times, smoothing it out, before moving on to the next piece.

"How do you know how to brush a woman's hair?"

"I've had a few girlfriends in my time."

A flash of jealousy takes me by surprise. I don't know where it came from and I brush it aside. He's thirty-two. Of course he's had relationships in his life. "Any of them serious?"

"Not enough to want marriage."

"Do you want marriage and children one day?"

"I do. I'd love a houseful of little urchins that get crumbs everywhere and call me dad."

I hide a smile, close my eyes and enjoy his ministrations. I've always loved when someone brushes my hair for me. Of course, it has always been my mother who did it in the past.

This is entirely different.

His touch is so gentle, I never even feel a tug from the snarls. He takes his time, in no hurry at all.

"You have beautiful hair. I love it long. I hope you never cut it."

"I don't plan to." I cringe. My voice came out ridiculously high. How embarrassing. I might as well have announced that his touch does something to me, that it affects me in ways I can't control.

And I think to myself, *I like Zane. I like him a lot.*

That's as far as I allow my thoughts to go.

chapter fourteen

♡

AFTER ZANE RETURNS from visiting his father, we catch the cable car at the corner of Powell and Market.

"Hop on," Zane says, holding out his hand.

I grasp onto his hand, his warmth invading me. He helps me step up into the iconic cable car San Francisco is known for. All at once, we're face to face, and there's nowhere else to go, no way to step backward.

He looks down at me, his eyes half shuttered. "We can get off anywhere between Bush and Jackson," he says, his face close to mine, the closest it's ever been.

I hold onto his hand tighter as the cable car starts to move, trying to keep my balance.

"From there we walk downhill one block and we'll be in Chinatown on Stockton Street. It's filled with produce markets. The next block is Grant Avenue. That's where you find the gift shops."

"Okay." I feel his breath on my face and it makes me dizzy. Nothing he said has registered. "I take it you've been there many times," I say, my voice breathy.

"Oh yeah. The perks of growing up in Fog City."

He turns and moves into the cable car. We forego the bench seats and stand on the sideboards, hanging onto the poles. Zane leans out as far as he can, letting the wind rush on his face.

He's sort of crazy, maybe even reckless.

Today, all I want to do is join him, to feel wild with him. I lean sideways, my hand gripping the pole tightly. I let out a little scream, feeling free and easy. Letting loose never felt so good.

Shame on me, I've only taken a cable car ride three or four times since I moved here. Now I'm wondering why I haven't done it every day. But it wouldn't be the same without Zane. I wouldn't be leaning out of a cable car without him.

I don't want to think about my text exchange with Ryker this morning. But it's seared into my mind.

Ryker: What happened last night? You upset my mom.

Me: She insinuated you don't trust me.

Ryker: It's Zane I don't trust.

Me: If you have something to say, please talk to me about it.

Ryker: Can't talk now. Will call later. Please apologize to Mom.

I hesitated over my response. There were so many nasty retorts popping into my mind. I decided against all of them and settled for a simple NO WAY.

I haven't heard back from him since. I guess this is our first fight.

I let out another scream, releasing all of my stress, releasing all of my thoughts about Ryker. I'm glad I'm not at home moping around. Zane turns, flashing me a cheesy grin. I guess he approves of my decision to let it all hang out.

When we finally arrive in Chinatown, it's crowded with throngs of tourists. Zane takes my hand in his, leading as we weave through the masses.

We're not holding hands like a couple. He's simply ensuring we don't get separated.

But when the crowds thin, neither one of us lets go of each other's hand. I try not to read too much into our actions. I only know that I don't want the connection to be broken.

I like my hand in his. I like the way he's leading me on this adventure, a huge smile on his face. I feel free and easy, like I'm escaping some sort of doom looming behind me.

When Zane realizes we're not in a crowd anymore, he deliberately releases my hand. I notice his lowered brows as he looks at me, the worry that crosses his features. He's backing up, reinstating the invisible line between us.

It had to be done. I feel bad that I wasn't the one to insist upon it. It should've been me. I'm promised to Ryker. What must Zane think of me?

A friendship is developing between us. Nothing more, I tell myself over and over. He was holding my hand so we wouldn't be separated in the crowds. That's all.

Don't overthink it, Mila. That's what he told me last night. I need to listen.

And yet, I want to explore this newfound friendship. I'm looking at Zane with new eyes and my mind is filled with dangerous thoughts.

If my feelings for Ryker are not strong enough to keep me from falling for someone else, then he's not the right man for me. It's as simple as that.

It's not simple for Zane, though. It's all kinds of complicated. His relationship is already tense with his brother. I'm sure he doesn't want to make it worse.

Wisps of guilt are floating through me and nagging at my conscience. But this is my life and I have to explore all of my options. The fact is, I'm not married, or even engaged. I'm a free agent.

We wander around, enjoying the Chinese architecture, lamp posts, and red lanterns. The smell of strange herbs and seafood invades the air. It's as though we have left the U.S. and stepped into mainland China. Everything surrounding us feels foreign, yet captivating. After rambling around the kitschy Grant Avenue, we leave the main street and explore the side alleys. There, we observe a glimpse into the authentic Chinese way of life.

"There's so much to see, it's overwhelming."

Zane bumps my shoulder like a buddy does to a good friend. "Enjoying yourself, though?"

"Yes, I love it. Thanks for showing me around."

We pass through the infamous Dragon gate, and we watch Chinese ladies deftly making fortune cookies.

"Ready to go eat?" Zane asks after we enjoy a few

freshly made fortune cookies.

Actually, I'm filled with trepidation. "Okay," I say anyway.

Zane takes me to the City View restaurant. It boasts white tablecloths, elaborate Chinese décor, Chinese music playing softly in the background, and small carts holding the much talked about dim sum Zane is so crazy about.

It's unlike anything I've ever experienced. "This is seriously amazing." I'm having a hard time containing my smile.

He mimics celebratory dance moves from his seated position. "Score. I made Mila happy."

His casual nature makes me laugh. I'm trying not to stare too deeply into his eyes. I'm drawn to them, like they're magnets. Does he feel something between us? Or is he simply being nice to his possible future sister-in-law?

The thought is akin to pouring cold water over my head. Especially when he breaks our eye contact. Every time.

We're just friends. That's all, I remind myself.

"My dad used to take me here. While we ate, he'd tell me stories about my mom. I loved it."

"Tell me one. I'd love to hear more about your mother."

His eyes brighten, pleased with my interest. "They met in college. Every day during lunch hour, she would be sitting on a bench reading a book. He noticed her for weeks before he gathered up the courage to approach her. He said he knew she was *the one* after speaking with her for five minutes. That's all it took, and he knew. Just like that."

"That's beautiful. I wish it were that easy."

"Maybe it is."

Help me, every time he looks at me, I feel like I'm drowning in his chocolate eyes. After last night, I can still imagine the sensation of his hands gently running through my hair. And I want him to do it again. "It isn't."

"You must've known Ryker was the right one, enough to move in with him."

Stunned, I correct him. "Ryker and I don't live together. I moved in after he left for Japan because he asked me to be his caretaker. I'm a wait-for-marriage kind of girl. It's how I was raised and those beliefs have become a part of who I am." I press my lips together, unsure why I'm sharing such personal information. All at once, it's important that he knows my relationship with Ryker didn't progress that far. Not sure if I want to examine my feelings over the matter too closely.

His expression softens. "Oh, I apologize. I didn't know."

Zane looks down and doesn't comment further. To do so would be traveling into uncomfortable territory, a place called Rykerland. I don't want to talk about him, either. I'm not positive I know where we stand right now. Everything feels wrong between us. After investing ten months into our relationship, I hate that we're falling apart.

But we are. Crumbling at the foundation. I've felt it for a while now, ever since the non-proposal.

Zane is spontaneous and fun and . . . I'm so confused. My stomach is tingling, my heart's beating on double time, and my cheeks are permanently flushed. I'm not sure what I'm feeling, but I like it. I don't want this day to end.

Zane returns to the subject of his mother. "Dad told me my mom had the softest heart of anyone he'd ever known. When she loved someone, she loved them fiercely and unconditionally."

"She sounds lovely. I wish I could've met her."

"Physically, she had a weak heart. She had to limit her activities or the stress on her heart would be too much. The doctors advised against pregnancy, but she wanted a child, so she decided to do it anyway."

Wow. He's a product of the most selfless love known to mankind. "She gave her life for you."

"She did. I don't remember her but somehow, I've always felt loved by her. The sacrifice she made for me, it . . . changes me every day of my life."

Underneath his casual exterior, Zane is deep. After expecting him to be the unpleasant, untrustworthy thief, it's a nice discovery. "I get that."

"She died of heart failure in her sleep."

"I'm sorry."

"Dad says she loved too much. That's what killed her."

"I don't believe that. You can never love too much."

"He always told me her heart was overworked because she gave away so much love. He said so much love passed through the walls of her heart, it made it burst."

So sweet in a tragic way. "Your dad's a romantic."

"He is. As a kid, I believed him. Of course, I now know he simply wanted me to know how much my mother loved me."

"I like the romantic version."

"I do too."

chapter fifteen
♡

THE CART LOADED with dim sum choices slides up next to our table. A young Chinese girl offers a delicate flourish of her hand toward the cart. "You pick."

"Please choose for me, Zane. I have no idea what anything is."

Zane makes his selections and the food is placed on the table.

He takes his time to explain what each one is. "These are dumplings with either shrimp or pork in them. This is *char siu bao*. It's barbecued pork inside a steamed bun. This is *cheung fun*. It's rice noodle sheets filled with shrimp, pork, or beef, folded over and pan fried. This one is *wu gok*. It's an intricately made lattice work of fried batter with a ball of mashed taro root, pork, and mushroom inside. *Lo mai gai* is lotus leaf wrapped sticky rice with chicken, sweet sausage, mushrooms, and scallops on the inside. Choose your poison. They're all delish."

Are they? I swallow hard and hope I won't be sick after experimenting with new foods. I decide to be daring and choose one of each.

Slowly, I take a small bite of each one while Zane watches my expression.

"Well?"

"They're all really good, but the barbecued pork in the steamed bun is to die for." To my surprise, I have a taste for this kind of food.

"Yes! I knew I'd make you a believer. Soon, you'll be addicted like me."

"Do they sell take out?"

He guffaws. "That's my girl."

I take another huge bite. "I'm hooked."

"Sure, you can order take out. But they don't deliver.

You want some, you gotta come down here."

I close my eyes as I chew. Amazing. "This is dangerous stuff."

"Right?"

We're silent for a while as we make fast work of our food.

I wipe my mouth with my napkin. "Can I ask you a question?"

"Sure. Anything."

"Why don't you call Debra mother? I mean, you were a baby when she married your father. She's the only mother you've ever known."

Zane sets down his chopsticks. "My memories are vague, but I remember moments of calling her mom, like Ryker did. She always corrected me and told me to call her Debra. I always knew there was a division between Ryker and me. Ryker was her son and I was not."

"But she raised you, right?"

"No. She was Ryker's mom and she took care of him. I always had a nanny. My father more than made up for it though. He poured all of his attention on me."

"And that upset Debra."

"Yep. She was always annoyed with me. As a kid, I was well aware of it."

My heart hurts for him. "I'm sorry."

"Hey, I'm fine. Stop worrying about me."

"Why'd you leave the family business? If you don't mind my asking."

"I was away from the situation for quite some time when I went off to college. Got my MBA. I had every intention of working with my father, taking my rightful place in the business. It was what my father wanted, and it was what I wanted too. So, I pushed forward and I did it. But the state of affairs with Debra and Ryker . . . got out of hand. Debra was always trying to thwart me in some way." He stares into space and lets out his breath. "She couldn't really influence the workplace, but she made

Dad's life miserable by constantly complaining about me. She made Ryker watch my every step. If I took an hour lunch or was ten minutes late in the morning, my dad got an earful. It was a constant barrage. It got worse and worse, the accusations more and more serious. Leaving was the right thing to do."

He doesn't mention being accused of stealing from the company. I imagine it's a sensitive subject. I'll leave it alone for right now.

"So, you joined the Army?"

"I did. Specialized in explosive ordnance disposal and I've never looked back."

"Do you plan to return to the business one day?"

"Yes, I do. When the time is right."

"What makes the time right?"

"When the queen mother isn't screaming *off with his head*."

My entire body goes still. "Zane, the way she treats you isn't right. Don't let her control your life."

"I didn't do it for her. All of my choices were made with my father in mind. Too much stress over the situation was making his blood pressure shoot through the roof. Like I said, it was the right thing to do."

I'm not so sure about that. I hate that Debra chased him out of the family business. It makes my blood boil. "Why did your father stay with Debra?"

"Good question. He was always a shrewd businessman. But when it came to family, he was the one who always tried to keep the peace. He couldn't bring himself to give up on Debra and Ryker."

"Even though it chased you away?"

"We made the decision together. It was something I had always wanted to do. Dad loved my Army stories and lived his adventures vicariously through me. It all worked out in the end."

I know he's feeding me a positive slant. But it's more than that. He really believes the rhetoric he's fed himself over the years. He's convinced he did the right thing.

Maybe he did. Maybe the situation was intolerable. It probably has been his entire life and escaping was a relief. I can't blame him. He needed to get away.

He looks down at the table. "Why am I talking about my father in the past tense? He's not gone yet. He's a fighter."

I observe him as he continues to eat. I wonder who this man really is. Is he the unpleasant and competitive man Ryker and Debra accuse him of being? Is he a thief? Or is he the laid back, easy-going man I see? Is he putting on a show just for me? If he was as competitive as Ryker says he is, wouldn't he be trying to steal his brother's girl? I feel his friendliness, his interest, but then I feel the brick wall he slams between us. Like when he released my hand earlier. Or the way he won't hold eye contact with me right now. Little nuances that scream NO, nothing can happen between us.

Okay, message received. Loud and clear. He's just being friendly. He's not trying to pick me up and he's not being forward.

I'm a horrible person for entertaining the possibilities with Zane. I'm human and he's . . . gorgeous. Shame on me.

It's just that . . . a voice inside me is persuading me to end things with Ryker. My crazy interest in Zane is proof that my feelings for Ryker are not as strong as I'd once believed.

A sobering thought.

A group of college students begin to couple up in the small open area in the middle of the restaurant, deciding to make it their dance floor. They steal our attention as they laugh and goof around with silly dance moves to the beat of the lively Chinese music now playing over the restaurant speakers. Until this moment, the traditional music has been soft and soulful, emotion evoking.

Now the music is light and energetic, almost parade-like with its heavy downbeat, inspiring the rowdy group to get up and dance.

All at once, Zane's hand is in front of my face. "C'mon, Mila. Let's dance."

I look up at him and I'm met with his huge smile. How can I resist? Zane is all about fun. There's nothing intense and brooding about him.

Hand in hand, we join the group. Other customers join in the fun too as we attempt to interpret the music into physical movement. We receive odd looks from the staff, but we ignore them. I'm sure they think we're all crazy.

We're breathing hard and laughing as we jump up and down with the music. It's exhilarating to let loose with Zane. He simply doesn't have any social anxiety. I love how relaxed I feel with him.

When the song ends, we clap for ourselves. The music changes to the soft and slow poignant tunes once again.

Couples join together for a slow dance and Zane follows suit, taking me in his arms without hesitation. No big deal, simply going along with the crowd.

I tell myself it means nothing and follow his lead.

His arms wrap around my waist and we start to sway to the music.

At first, we're stiff and it's more than obvious we're not a couple who are familiar with each other.

The sounds of the stringed instruments used in traditional Chinese music meets my ears. The erhu, pipa, and guzheng combine with the dizi flutes, taking me away to another time and place.

I move closer and rest my head on his chest. I can't hear his heartbeat above the music, but I can feel it pounding against my ear in a steady rhythm, like it's about to break free and burst out.

I feel his arms tighten around me, bringing me even closer. We were so uncomfortable at first, but now our bodies meld together naturally. We're a perfect fit. He feels natural and right, like I'm where I belong.

I let my hands leave their awkward position on his biceps. They travel up his arms, to his shoulders, and slowly wrap around his neck.

He hugs me even tighter and I do the same until I don't think a breath of air could fit between us.

I've danced many times in my life. Never this close. Never this intimate. I could stay in his embrace forever. Nothing has ever felt so right to me, so mind blowingly perfect. It hits me then. I've never felt so attracted to a man. The strength of my attraction takes me by complete surprise. I mean, his biceps, abs, and chest have no manners and like to stare at me, but I'm guilty of staring right back.

The truth is I've been attracted to him from the get-go, but didn't want to admit it. I've been fighting my feelings, trying to remain true to Ryker.

Now I let those feelings take over and consume me. I hold him close and realize this is what I've been missing, what I've been craving. Zane has the magical ingredient I want. This is it. I've found it. I gently rub his neck.

With no warning whatsoever, Zane pulls away and takes a step backward. Surprised by his actions, I meet his troubled gaze.

I feel slightly mortified at my behavior. He must be wondering about my intentions.

I am too. What am I doing?

At the same time, I see the intensity in his eyes, the powerful concentrated stare he's sending me, filled with uncertainty and doubt. It's clear he's shaken to his very core. His eyes tell me his emotions are wild and uncontained.

I take a step back, my reaction primal. I was wrong to think he didn't have an intense bone in his body. He's bursting with raw emotion.

Yet I have no idea what he's thinking. Have I shocked him? Probably.

"We should go," he says.

Consumed with guilt, I nod. "Okay."

He's right, we can't do this.

Until I figure out my relationship with Ryker, I'm not really a free agent.

This can't happen.

chapter sixteen
♥

NOTHING HAPPENED BETWEEN Zane and me. Not really. But my mind went there and I can't ignore that fact. A mental betrayal is still a betrayal.

I bang on the piano keys harder than necessary, releasing my anxiety. The end has been brewing between Ryker and me. It's time to face it head on. I have to talk to him.

It leaves me in an awkward position. I wish I hadn't left my perfect studio apartment. I checked. It's already been rented. That door is closed to me.

It's Monday morning and Zane starts work today. He hasn't made an appearance yet. I'm sure my practicing woke him up when I started at five am, earlier than usual. I couldn't sleep.

When he finally walks out, owning his swagger, dressed in ACUs (Army Camouflage Uniform) and looking so handsome, I miss my fingering and an awful jarring sound emanates from the piano. Artie whines from his bed.

"Sorry I disturbed you," he says, rubbing his ears. "Ouch."

I smooth my palms over my thighs. "Hard to cover up a mistake on the piano. It happens, though. All the time."

"It makes getting it right all the more impressive."

Small talk. Ignore the elephant in the room. Pretend like nothing happened between us. It's what we've been doing since Chinatown on Saturday. Keeping up a light banter.

Technically, nothing did happen between us.

I wish I could convince my mind of it.

I keep things light. "First day on a new job. Shall I make you a sack lunch? I'll even write *have a great day* on your napkin."

"Do it and I'll frame it in my office."

"Nah, the element of surprise is gone. Maybe next time."

He leans down to tighten the laces on his boots. "Fine. Ruin my day at only six-thirty in the morning."

"Hey, you lied to me."

"Excuse me?"

"You do know what socks are."

He laughs aloud as he stands. "Guilty. Join me for breakfast?"

I want to, therefore I shouldn't. "No, thanks. I think I'll keep practicing."

He mock stabs his heart. "You're far too dedicated, Mila. Especially at this hour."

"This hour is the best time of the day," I holler as he retreats to the kitchen.

"For sleeping," he hollers back.

I smile as I return to my piano. My safe place. I'll hide here whenever he's home. Ignore the spark between us.

Zane returns with his bowl of cereal and parks himself on the couch, watching me intently. I keep playing as though I'm in front of an audience. Total concentration. I let nothing distract me. It's the place I have to enter when I perform. Or I'd blank every time.

When I'm done, I realize Zane is now standing next to the piano, his finished cereal bowl on the coffee table. His aftershave pricks my senses.

"I could sit and listen to you play all day," he says.

That was the best I've ever played that Mozart number. I wanted it to be perfect for Zane. Crowds often applaud me. But hearing Zane's compliment makes my heart soar.

"And you did. Several times last week."

"My private performances. Lucky me."

I tear my eyes away from his and start to play again, hiding in my piano. "Enjoy your day," I return lightly.

"You too. See you for a Jeopardy rematch tonight. I will

prevail."

Not if I come home late after symphony practice. Which I have every intention of doing.

It's for the best. I don't want to spend more time with him. I like him too much and it can't go anywhere.

Dead end.

Besides, I hardly know the guy. My feelings are silly, surface level stuff. Physical attraction only.

When Zane leaves, I don't acknowledge his departure.

When Ryker's ringtone blasts through the air, I jump. It's time to have a serious talk and I'm dreading it.

"Good morning, Mila. I trust you had a good weekend." It's the end of the day for him, yet he's still in his suit, not a hair out of place, looking fresh and handsome.

"I did. Yes. Thank you. It was good. Fun. Relaxing." TMI. *Stop, Mila.* I almost added the words *eye opening* and *breathtaking.*

"Good. I'm so glad you enjoyed yourself. You deserve a break. You work so hard to achieve your dreams."

Has he always spoken so stiffly, so formally? I suppose he has. I'm comparing him to Zane and I don't want to go down that road. They're two very different people and that's okay.

"Thank you."

"May I apologize for Friday night? I'm so sorry my mother upset you."

I let my breath out heavily. It's time to get real. "I was more upset with you, Ryker."

He rubs his neck. "I know. I probably shouldn't have asked my mother to get involved."

Probably? "No, you shouldn't have. If you have an issue, bring it to my attention. Communication is key in a relationship."

"I hate that Zane is living there with you. I hate it," he blurts with an angry raised voice. "I don't trust that jerk. He tries to take everything that's mine and I won't stand for it!"

His nostrils flare, his expression turning into a fiery mask of rage.

And then it's gone, as quickly as it appeared. He rubs his five 'o clock shadow as he visibly calms himself down.

"I'm sorry, Mila. Zane always upsets me."

I'm so taken aback by what I witnessed, I'm speechless. Does Ryker have a temper? Does it flare up on occasion? How has he hidden this from me for so long? Do I really know him?

"I don't understand. Then why did you let him stay?"

"I told you, I like knowing where he is and what he's up to. It's already been a week. Has he really found a house?"

"He has. And he put an offer on it." If he's paying attention to what Zane is up to, shouldn't he know that already?

Something is niggling at me and I realize what it is. Ryker allows his distrust of Zane to take precedence over his fear of Zane living with me. There's something wrong with that logic. If he's so worried about Zane's behavior with me, he shouldn't have let him stay.

"Good. He should be outta there soon."

Not the issue. It's time for me to be totally honest with him. "Ryker, I think we need to talk."

"I apologized. I'm sorry. It was wrong of me to include my mother. But she's there and she can see what's going on. I can't. She has to be my eyes."

He doesn't trust me, but then, maybe he's right not to. My heart has been easily swayed. He must've sensed my wavering long before I did.

I'm just going to blurt out how I'm feeling. It has to be said. "Ryker, it's not only that. We have bigger issues and I think it's time to face them. I've thought a lot about this and I've realized there's something missing between us. I'm not positive we're right for each other. You must've felt it too. That's why you didn't make things official before you left."

He's silent for much too long, his face rigid, his jawline tense. Do my words make him feel anything? He breathes in deeply before he speaks. "Please don't give up on us. I know this separation is hard. All I ask is that you wait until I return home and give us one more chance before you make any decisions about us. Please, Mila. We owe it to ourselves to at least give this more time."

I do still have love for him left in my heart. A little sliver. I thought I wanted to marry him. Those feelings are still there, but I feel them slipping away. I was so sure. Now I'm very unsure.

I decide to say how I'm feeling directly to his face. "I'm very unsure of us, Ryker. I feel like I need to be totally honest with you. I love you, but I don't think we're a match. I think we're meant to be friends, but I don't think we're meant to be married." I pause. "I don't think we should see each other anymore in that context." There. I said it. To my surprise, I feel so much relief.

His face flashes red as his eyes widen. Then his reaction once again disappears, like I imagined it. "I understand. It's a huge decision. I've felt myself wavering too."

Whoa. Wait, he did? Maybe that shouldn't come as a shock. I think I knew that the moment he didn't propose. Turns out, he was right. I'm glad we're not engaged.

"Okay, then. I think I should move out. It doesn't feel right to live here anymore. I feel like I'm taking advantage of you."

He frowns, this time not bothering to cover up his feelings. "Please don't do that, Mila. If you leave, I'll have to make other arrangements. I'll need to find another caretaker; I'll need to find someone who can take care of Arthur. It'll be a huge headache." He places his hand on his forehead. "I really need someone to take care of my home."

Huh. He seems more upset about having to find a new

caretaker than losing me. That's telling.

I guess if there's honesty between us, I don't mind being his caretaker. It does make life a lot easier for me.

"Are you sure?"

"Yes, of course I'm sure."

I struggle with my feelings, a tug of war on my heart. On one hand, I want out. On the other, I don't want to leave him in the lurch. It's on the tip of my tongue to suggest that Zane could be his caretaker, but I bite my tongue before that atrocity can be mumbled out loud. "All right then, I'll stay."

He breathes a deep sigh of relief. "Thank you." He pauses, gathering his thoughts. "Mila, let me reiterate this one more time. I don't want to give up on us. I want to continue with our relationship when I return home. I want to see where it takes us. We have something between us, there's no denying it. Please, promise me you'll give us another chance. That's all I'm asking for."

I don't owe him anything. I've already given him so much of my time. I can't think of another way to say *it's over* without being cruel. I hate this. "Ryker . . . of course I'll see you when you return. But I can't promise anything else. I'm sorry. I really don't see a future for us."

His eyes narrow slightly and a flash of anger crosses his features before he covers it up. It was there, I know it was. I didn't imagine it.

"You know I'm falling for you. More and more each day."

Is he? He sounds insincere to me now. Like it's a last-ditch effort to sway me.

I don't say I love you back. I can no longer say it aloud and feel like I'm telling the truth. I nod a few times instead. He still can't out and out say I love you. I feel like a fool to have held onto this relationship for so long. I should've known better.

"We'll work this out, Mila. I know we will."

"Ryker, I just said . . ."

"I know, I know. I heard you. But I still have hope." He studies the screen. "Is that a bowl and a spoon on the coffee table?"

I don't even bother turning around. I know Zane's cereal bowl is still sitting there. I don't clean up after him. He gets around to it on his own time. "I'll take care of it."

"See that you do," he says firmly. "Goodbye."

I hang up, wondering if I made things worse or better. Did I give him hope?

I have no idea. One thing I do know is that I let go of a future I thought was my path in life. It wasn't and I feel that loss keenly. I feel restless, like I don't know what to do with myself. I wander through the penthouse, walking back and forth enough times to carve out a path in the floor.

What now?

I don't like the present situation I'm in. It doesn't feel right. It's only temporary, though.

Ryker's journal, still sitting untouched on the nightstand, calls to me. I haven't wanted to read it, feeling as though I would somehow be trespassing.

But today of all days, I need to know him, to understand him, to feel what he's feeling.

I plop down on the bed and open the book smack dab in the middle.

Woke up.
Worked out.
Had protein shake.
Sent emails.
Drove to work.
Productive day.
Ate a clean lunch.
Saw Dad.
Visited with Mom.
Grabbed a burger.
Went home.
Watched the news.

Went to bed.

Well, that wasn't a very exciting day. I flip through the pages looking for an actual entry.

I can't find one.

Each day is the same—a general laundry list of what he did with little variance. He asked me to read this, feeling it would help me get to know him better.

It does.

It tells me more about him than he can ever imagine. This can't be right. I search every page and it's more of the same. I search out some of the pages marked with the dates when I know we went out together. It never says anything more than *Went out with Mila.*

There are no feelings, no emotions bleeding onto the page. This is who Ryker is. He lives his life and does what is expected of him. Like a robot.

I can't do this.

I slam the book closed and toss it onto the nightstand. I pull off Ryker's promise ring and place it in his top drawer where he keeps his watches.

I am no longer promised to him. I need to rethink my life. It feels oddly like starting over again and I feel lost.

When Ryker returns, I will end things with him again, face to face. Not through the phone.

In my heart, I know I want more.

Much, much more.

chapter seventeen
♥

ZANE WALKS IN looking bone weary. "Hey."

"Hey." I glance at my watch. It's two in the morning. "Late night, huh?"

I told myself I wasn't waiting up for him, but who am I kidding? I push my blanket and pillow aside, but I don't flick the lights on. The TV illuminates the room, giving off a soft glow. Artie moans at the disturbance, walks over to my pillow, and curls up on it, promptly falling back to sleep.

Zane and I have settled into a routine. We often have Lucky Charms together in the morning for breakfast. Each evening, we collapse onto the couch when I get home from practice and he gets home from visiting his father. We veg in front of the TV, eating dinner and watching Jeopardy, each of us trying to answer the most questions correctly. With our schedules, it's really the only time we see each other. I stopped fighting the inevitable interaction and now I look forward to it.

Zane flops onto the couch and sighs heavily. "Saved the world today."

"I'm eternally grateful. I did not save the world today, but I did make baked chicken thighs, potatoes, and fresh green beans for dinner. Hungry?"

"I am. But I don't think I can get up. I'm beat."

"I'll get it for you."

"I'm eternally grateful," he throws back at me.

I bring him a plate stacked high with food just as he finishes removing his boots.

He has also removed his ACU jacket and is now wearing his tan t-shirt, tucked smoothly into his ACU pants, along with a belt. He looks trim and fit. It's true what they say about a man in uniform. Gets me every time.

"Thanks, Mila. You're a lifesaver."

"You're welcome. But don't get used to it." I join him on the couch. "So, tell me how you saved the world today."

Zane has been here another week now. He closed on his new home, but renovations are being done before he can move in. Ryker's not happy about it, but once again, he didn't ask Zane to leave.

I'm certainly not going to ask him to leave. I enjoy his company. But we do keep our distance from one another. No more hand holding or hair brushing. No more intimate dancing.

"Got a call for an emergency response to render safe a chemical agent in a small town in northern California."

"A chemical agent? That sounds scary."

"Yep. Technically, it was a nerve agent."

"Even scarier."

Zane takes a bite of chicken. "Me and my team responded by helicopter. We get there and the whole place is crawling with cop cars and fire trucks, their lights blazing. A deputy sheriff greeted us, and I couldn't help but notice we were standing in a high school football field."

"A high school? Strange place for a nerve agent."

"That's what I thought," he says, spearing green beans onto his fork. "He explained that a high school chemistry teacher had been doing a class project where the students made G-series nerve agent in an enclosure and tested it on rats."

"That's crazy."

"Right? It killed the rats and . . . let's just say, they didn't die a happy or peaceful death. Once they'd completed their experiment, they couldn't get the desensitizing chemical to the agent inside the enclosure because it had accidentally fallen over in the wrong part of the maze. The teacher panicked when he realized he now had a deadly nerve agent in a classroom full of students with no way to desensitize it without opening the enclosure and exposing everyone to it."

"Oh my gosh. So, they called you guys?"

"First, the teacher dismissed all the students. Then he called the principal, who called the fire department, who called the police. Each, in turn, looked inside the room, saw all the dead rats in the enclosure, and refused to enter a second time, knowing it was beyond their scope. They evacuated the high school, cordoned off the area, and called the State Emergency Operations Center for help. They called the FBI, and the FBI called the Army, and the Army called us."

"What did you do?"

"After calculating the downwind hazards, we directed everyone to get farther away from the building. A lot farther away."

"Smart move."

"We donned our protective gear and went inside the lab. We found the huge plexiglass enclosure glued to the surface of a table in the middle of the room. This thing was elaborate. It had all kinds of controls and levers so you could move things around inside the maze. The problem was, it was huge and not easy to move. So, the usual fix for this would be a three-to-one ratio of high explosives to nerve agent and blow that sucker in place. Problem solved."

"But you couldn't do that?" I ask.

"It would've blown up a huge portion of the school. We figured that wouldn't be appreciated by the community."

"I think they would've been relieved to have the nerve agent gone."

"Maybe so. But we really didn't want to blow up the school. We took a break and discussed our options. Moving the table with the enclosure presented a problem because it wouldn't fit through the door. We didn't want to turn it sideways and risk any nerve agent escaping into the air."

"I'm nervous just listening to this dilemma. What did you do?"

"We decided our best course of action would be to move the table out onto the football field and blow it in place."

"But, how did you get it out the door?" My stomach feels sick thinking of Zane in this situation, risking his life to save the lives of others.

"We asked the firemen to widen the door opening. They politely declined and lent us their rescue saw. Don't blame them one bit, that nerve agent is nasty stuff. We're equipped with protective gear to handle it, they're not. So, we cut the doorway to widen it. Then we cut the legs off the table and placed the enclosure on an audio/visual cart. We very slowly walked that baby outside until it was in the center of the football field, as far away from any buildings as possible. But then we were faced with another issue."

"What was that?"

"As soon as we fired the shot, it would break all the glass in the surrounding buildings."

"Oh wow."

"Something had to be done so people wouldn't get hurt. So, they evacuated all the nearby houses. I felt bad for the residents."

"Why not move it someplace else to blow it up?"

"G-series nerve agent is nothing to fool around with. Moving it is a dangerous task and we'd already moved it as far as I was willing to move it. The amount in that enclosure could've killed every student in the school and everyone who came to render aid. By blowing it in place, the problem is over quickly. Then, all they would have to deal with is broken glass." He casts me a knowing glance. "In the end, they were happy to deal with broken glass."

"I imagine so."

"We set to work. We laid a bed of explosives in a slight depression and put the enclosure on top of them. Then we added more on top, rigging them all so they'd blow at the exact same time. When we fired the shot, the whole thing disappeared in one bright flash. As did all of the aforementioned windows."

"Fair trade."

"Exactly. Once the shot area cooled down, we tested to ensure that the nerve agent was completely gone. It was and our work there was done. We hopped back onto our helicopter and had the pilot make a pit stop at McDonald's on the way home. Had myself a couple of breakfast burritos. So good. But not as good as a proper dinner. Thanks, Mila."

"Hold on. You went to McDonald's via helicopter?"

"I did. It was way too much fun."

"You guys are crazy. But, wow. You really did save the world today. Or at least one community."

"Yep. Felt good too. I love this job."

Zane polishes off the rest of his dinner. "That really hit the spot. I think I'll grab a shower and hopefully I won't fall asleep standing up. If you hear a loud thunck, it'll be me hitting the shower floor. Please save me so I don't drown."

I'm glad the lights are low, because I know my face turns bright red at the thought of seeing him in the shower in all his glory.

I shake my head to erase the visual.

"Mila?"

I move my hair away from my face. "Yeah, okay. No worries, I'll save you."

His eyes follow the movement of my hand. He flips on the light and I squint at the brightness.

"Where's your ring?" he asks.

I look down at my hand. He finally noticed. "I took it off. I'm giving it back to Ryker."

"Why?"

"We had a talk. I told him I didn't think we were going to work out."

"What did he say?" Zane is wide awake now.

"He asked me to give us a chance when he returns home. I couldn't make that promise, though. Other than that, we're pretty much over."

He's silent for so long, I think he's not going to respond. "I'm sorry. That must've been hard."

It should've been hard. I'm sad that it wasn't. "Don't be. There's something missing between us. I'm not sure what it is, I just know we don't have it."

"Will you be leaving the penthouse?"

"No, Ryker asked me to stay and continue to be the caretaker. It makes life awkward, but I'll survive."

"Oh. Okay." Zane stands there staring at me with a strange look on his face. He nods. "I'll be in the shower."

I sit on the couch, staring at the TV. I tell my thoughts they're not allowed to join Zane in the shower.

They don't listen.

chapter eighteen
♥

IT'S EIGHT AM. Still no sign of Zane. I've been waiting to start my practice session. Zane was so exhausted last night. I don't want to disturb his sleep this morning.

I've already mopped the floors, dusted every surface in sight, wiped windows until my wrists ached, and cleaned the kitchen from top to bottom. The Roomba is quietly wandering around the room. When it bumps into Arthur's dog bed, he growls, but doesn't bother to move. It's my only entertainment in the too silent penthouse.

The room smells of lemon dusting spray and not one single thing is out of place. Ryker would be pleased.

Ryker still calls me nearly every day. He acts as though nothing has changed between us. He likes to talk about what we'll do together when he gets home.

I know I need to say something more to him. Instead, I haven't answered the phone for the last three days. Maybe I can let that do my talking for me. I know I was clear with him. I'm not sure there's anything else I can say without feeling like I'm being mean. It's weighing on me heavily.

I wander into my bedroom, Ryker's master bedroom, and throw open the closet door. There's a stack of boxes in there that have been begging me to clean them out. It seems like a good time to tackle them.

Soon I have a large pile of old bills and receipts that are ready to be shredded. That's when I come across a folder I don't recognize. I open it and stare at the contents with a frown.

I know what it is. This is the "important" folder Debra gave Ryker on the night of his non-proposal. Ryker accidentally dropped it on my driveway. I meant to give it to him, but I forgot about it.

If I remember correctly, Ryker looked at the contents,

scoffed as if he was disgusted, and closed the folder.

Now I'm staring at what he saw and anger is building inside of me.

There are several random pictures of Zane in his uniform, all printed on regular pieces of printer paper. It's obvious the pictures were taken without his knowledge. The pictures have caught him in the middle of mundane tasks. One is of him crossing a street, one is of him exiting a grocery store, and one is of him sitting in a restaurant by himself, to name a few.

At the bottom of the first page it says, ZANE MARTEL. Whereabouts: Westrich, Germany. And then the times and dates are listed. The other pages follow the same pattern.

Debra and Ryker actually spy on Zane? They have him watched so they can be aware of his whereabouts?

Is Zane really that much of a threat to Ryker? Ryker's willing to sacrifice his jealousy to allow Zane to stay in his apartment, just so he'll know where he is. Still, it strikes me as excessive and paranoid. Maybe a little crazy.

I stare at each picture, at the firm set of Zane's mouth, the troubled gaze of his eyes, and the slight hunch of his shoulders. The way he looks when he thinks no one is watching.

The banished prince.

It bothers me more than I care to admit.

When nine AM strikes, I decide to go ahead and start practicing. It's Saturday and Zane's used to me waking him up on most days. I start with scales. Such a lovely sound. He'll be up in no time.

As I predicted, it forces him out of bed. He enters the living room looking sleepy-eyed. In my peripheral vision, I can tell he's only in jeans.

"Hey, you're late today. I overslept."

"Sorry," I say, concentrating.

"What happened in here? Did the cleaning fairies attack?"

I glance at him, missing the correct keys. "Clothes,

Martel. Please." Him and his ill-mannered body parts. They can't help but gape.

He retreats to the bathroom. I hear water running as he bangs around, getting ready for the day.

When he returns, he slowly approaches my piano. I don't look up. I only know he's there because his aftershave precedes him.

The keylid cover on the piano slowly begins to close, nearly covering my fingers. I look up at him as I pull my hands away.

"What are you doing?"

"Saving you from yourself."

"I need to practice."

"It's Saturday. Take the day off." He sends me an eyebrow raise, challenging me.

"I have a performance this week."

"And you'll be amazing."

"Not if I don't practice."

"You've practiced every single day this week. You've played for ballet classes every day this week. You've practiced with the symphony every single night this week. You'll do better if you take a break."

"I . . ." He's right. I'd planned on taking today off. "Nervous energy is building inside me and I have to do something or I'm going to go crazy. I always get this way before performances."

"Go crazy with me."

If he's trying to shock me, he did. We stare at each other as Ryker's fancy wall clock ticks loudly in the room, making me aware that time is passing while we're lost in each other's eyes.

I look down at my lap. "What do you want, Zane?"

"I want you to relax. Look at this place. It doesn't look like anyone lives here."

"I'm the caretaker." I've never been the girlfriend/almost wife enjoying free rent for a few months. This has never been about me. It's been about Ryker's needs. A sobering thought. "That means I'm doing my job."

"Hey, you live here. So do I. For now, anyway."

"We don't belong here."

"Sure we do. Ryker gave us permission to be here. He could ask us to leave at any time."

True.

"Let's get outta here, get some fresh air. Let's do something crazy, like shop for things to add color to this place. Ryker will appreciate it, he just doesn't know it yet."

"Ryker will hate it."

"You don't know that for sure."

I study him, worry evident in my features. "Why do you stay here, Zane? When you know how Ryker feels about you?"

He retreats into himself, enough that I notice. "He's my brother. Shocked me when he offered, I admit. I thought it was a breakthrough. I guess I'm always hoping we can somehow be friends, mend our ways. We'll never be best friends, but at least we can try to like each other."

I feel for him because I don't think that will ever happen. "Zane . . ."

"I know Ryker has ulterior motives when he lets me stay here, Mila. I know they keep track of my whereabouts. Joke's on them. I have nothing to hide. Guess I figure some good might come of me staying here. Might change our relationship. You never know."

"He's not here right now."

"That's true."

"So why stay here?"

"Because you're here."

"You want to be here because I'm here?"

"Yes. Does that scare you?"

"It terrifies me. In a good way." I swallow. Hard. "Are you the good guy or the bad guy?"

"You have to decide that for yourself." He holds out his hand. "Come with me and find out."

I look down at his hand. If I reach out and take his hand, I'm making a conscious decision to be with Zane. This is a turning point and we both know it.

I could ignore him. I could spend my day practicing, like I should. I could turn away and never go down this forbidden path.

But I don't. Deliberately, I reach out and join our hands.

He smiles, slow and delicious. "Let's get the heck outta here. Ryker's ghost is haunting us."

It does feel like Ryker's always with us when we're in the penthouse. We need to escape.

chapter nineteen

♡

WE SET OFF on foot. First stop—a little hole in the wall breakfast place where we eat chocolate covered croissants with fresh cantaloupe and honeydew melon.

"I dream of these when I'm out of town," Zane tells me. "Seriously, I wake up with my mouth watering."

"I can see why."

Next, we wander in and out of shops, choosing bright-colored trinkets and various throw pillows, the brighter, the better.

We laugh as we choose each item. We grab vases, ceramic geckos, an owl, a fish, even an elephant. Each one is expertly painted with bold colors and designs. We choose trays and flowers and candle holders, each one a daring statement.

I love each item and would decorate my own home with them. I doubt any of it will remain in Ryker's apartment, but we'll enjoy it while we're there.

Still, each item makes us dissolve into laughter, simply because we both know Ryker will hate them. Stiff, no humor Ryker will not even find them amusing.

We drop off our purchases and pick up Artie. Then we hop into Zane's Jeep and grab lunch items at the grocery store. After that, we head for Golden Gate Park, where we spend the afternoon at Stow Lake, wandering the wooded pathways, riding the pedal boats, and talking non-stop. Artie loves it, even if he does want to be held nearly the entire time.

As we sit in the sun on a small dock, eating our lunch with our feet soaking in the cool lake water, our jeans rolled up to our knees, Zane says, "This has been a perfect day."

I finish off our last strawberry. "Yes, it has. Thanks for

getting me out of the house."

"You needed an intervention. But I also love your dedication."

I let my head fall back as I bask in the sunshine. We chose various fruits and cheeses, along with a baguette for lunch. Our rather European dining choices make me feel as though I'm on an outing in the French countryside.

I sit up and stare at the sun's reflection on the rippling water. My lips part as I let out a deep sigh. Zane has a calming effect on me.

Unexpectedly, Zane reaches out and takes my hand in his, slowly and carefully lacing our fingers together. Our united hands sit between us on the dock, a question and an answer, waiting to be acknowledged.

While Artie is curled up on his lap, I stare at our clasped hands. I knew we were headed in this direction. I think I knew from the first moment I saw him. Perhaps this was inevitable. With his actions, he's asking me to recognize it, to say it out loud.

My eyes travel up to his. He doesn't say anything at first. He simply runs his thumb over my skin, back and forth.

"Don't freak out," he whispers.

His words are true to who Zane is and I love it. "I'm not."

"Yes, you are. I can see it in your eyes."

"I don't want to be the cause of more family drama."

"Mila, family drama will exist whether you're in the picture or not."

"But your relationship with Ryker, this could ruin everything."

"You can't ruin something that doesn't exist."

"I don't want to come between the two of you."

"Don't look now, but you already are."

"No . . ."

"You can walk away. We don't have to do this. It's your choice." He pauses. "Just know . . . I want this."

I squeeze his hand, unable to stop myself from a non-verbal response. There's something about Zane that makes me happy, makes me feel alive. I can't walk away. I want to find out where this will lead. I want to explore that magical ingredient he has that makes my heart race in weird ways.

"I'm not going anywhere."

He nods, his eyes flashing. I wonder if anyone has ever stuck by him, other than his father.

He surprises me by scooting closer, so our hips and thighs are touching and our arms and hands are entwined in a way that feels intimate, like the time we danced on the makeshift dance floor in Chinatown.

Only this time, there's nothing to stop us.

Artie looks up at us, then licks Zane's arm. "Articus approves of us."

Us, I think to myself. Zane and me are an us. I rest my head on his shoulder, testing how it feels to be close to him. I don't have questions and I don't have doubts. Oddly, it just feels right.

It always has. He makes me feel like I'm ready to dive into the deep end headfirst, like I'm ready to go for it, no reservations.

"Are you ready for this? For us?" Zane asks.

My insides quiver at the thought. "I am. This is exactly what I want."

"I'll try to move slow, but it won't be easy."

I close my eyes to calm the adrenaline racing through me. "I don't want slow."

He squeezes my hand. "Noted." He kisses the top of my head, letting his lips remain for longer than necessary. "I think I can handle that request."

I love the smile in his voice. I want to pour so much love on this man, so much that he won't have room to receive it.

Zane rests his head on mine, and we simply sit there like that, snuggled up and entwined with each other. I wonder if he'll kiss me, but he doesn't, even though I announced I don't want him to move slow. Instead, he seems content with simply holding me for the time being. I lose track of how long we sit there like that, not talking or feeling the need to fill the silence with useless chatter. We both allow the instant in time to be exactly what it is—our first moment together as an official couple. It's an experiment in the feeling of just being us and I think we both want to prolong it, to make it last.

I love this. I feel close to him, like we're one. I feel his strength and his confidence seep inside me and become a part of me.

When the sun lowers in the horizon, Zane says, "I guess we should head home."

"Yeah, I guess we should."

We take our time about it, leisurely walking to his Jeep, hand in hand. I breathe in deeply. I'm not sure I've ever felt so relaxed, so at ease.

Once in the Jeep, Zane surprises me when he asks, "Do you want to see my new home?"

"I'd love to."

The sight of his home is unexpected. It's a rambling three-story Victorian in need of a lot of TLC. Zane takes me on a tour, his enthusiasm for the house evident in everything he says. The house smells strongly of sawdust and lots of other unpleasant renovation odors. I see why Zane hasn't moved in yet. The floors are stripped down to the joints and new hardwood floors will be put in at some point.

"Zane, you can't move in here soon. It's not livable like this."

He shrugs. "The renovation will take two or three months. I figure I can shack up in one of the bedrooms in the meantime, after all the demo is done."

"Or just stay with me. No one needs to know."

"Oh, they'll know. They know everything. They probably knew about us before we did."

My mind wanders to the pictures I found this morning. Have pictures been taken of me and Zane? Does Ryker already know about us? I feel like I'm living in a surreal spy movie.

"Hey, don't worry about it. We haven't done anything wrong. We won't let them make us feel like we have."

"Maybe we should keep this on the downlow," I suggest.

He walks toward me until we're face to face, his eyes on mine. I'm not sure how I ever thought he wasn't an intense man. His penetrating gaze leaves my knees weak and my lips quivering.

Artie is tucked into one arm. He rests his other arm above me, leaning on the wall I'm standing against. "On the downlow?" he says, his voice raspy.

"Yeah. Just between me and you." I can feel every inch of him longing to close the distance between us.

But he doesn't. He lets us both want it, yearn for it.

"A secret love affair? Is that what you're suggesting?" he asks.

Love? Me and Zane? He's not holding back at all. "Yes, I guess I am. For a while anyway. I don't want anything to ruin us before we've even begun."

"By anything, you mean Ryker and Debra." It's a statement, not a question.

"If they find out, they'll interfere. I have no doubt of that."

"You're right. They will." He breathes in deeply. "Okay, I'm in. I like the idea of this being ours and no one else's."

"Just me and you. For as long as we can have it that way."

"I like the sound of that," he says quietly. "It won't last for long, though. They're always watching."

"Maybe not. But we'll enjoy it while it's ours."

"Yes, we will." His lips wander over my forehead, a whisper on my skin.

My breath is ragged as it makes its way through my windpipe. We haven't even shared a kiss yet, and we're talking about our love as though it's a very real tangible thing.

He lowers his face, pressing his forehead to mine. I can feel his breath on my face and as I look up at him, I again wonder if he's about to kiss me. His eyes drop to my lips, then travel back up and meet my gaze once again. He licks his lips and I swear he does it in slow motion.

"Okay," he says. "We're a secret. For now. Just long enough to make us secure as a couple, ready to face whatever life throws our way. Deal?"

"Deal."

"Not for too long, though. Not being able to kiss you in public is going to kill me. Not being able to hold you or touch you whenever I want will drive me wild."

Technically, we haven't done any of those things yet. Speaking about them before they've happened is making my chest rise and fall as though I can't catch my breath. My insides have turned to jelly and I'm about to melt into a puddle on the floor.

I can't speak. I simply nod. I think we have a lot to look forward to while we explore our new relationship.

Zane backs away. I'm tempted to grab his shirt by the collar and pull him back. Kiss him until he can't breathe.

But I don't. I like when the man makes the first move.

"Let's get outta here," he says.

On the way home, I ponder over our day together and I reach a conclusion. Even though Zane's lips have not so much as touched mine and I really have no idea if we're physically compatible, I think I know what Ryker and I were missing.

Chemistry. Both mental and physical.

It's that simple.

chapter twenty

WHEN WE ARRIVE home, we place an assortment of bright yellow, red, and teal pillows on the couch. They look amazing against the white couch.

We place a gray and white striped tray on the coffee table, with a red vase and yellow flowers on top. We put teal candle holders on the dining table. We add a few more vases with flowers to the sparse shelving unit along the living room wall. We also add the ceramic animals, interspersing them with Ryker's books. It makes the room come alive. The colors pop out and grab you.

We stand back to study our efforts. Zane wraps one arm around me. "What do you think?"

"I love it," I tell him.

"Vast improvement."

"And Ryker can easily remove it all if he hates it."

"Annnnnnnd he will."

For some reason, the thought makes us giggle like kids.

We add the painted geckos to Ryker's nightstands, one on each side. They're so silly and lighthearted, my eyes are drawn to them immediately.

"I can guarantee I'll be taking them with me when I leave."

"I'll fight you for them," Zane says, and we laugh a little more.

Zane grabs my hands. "C'mon, jump with me. It'll mess up the covers and make this place look lived in." He pulls me toward the bed.

"No, we can't."

Well, we could, actually. My white comforter is on the bed. I placed Ryker's expensive white bedspread in his closet, folded neatly. I was scared I'd mess it up.

"We can and we will. It's the finishing touch to add

some life to this place."

Zane pulls me up onto the bed and he starts jumping up and down. With my hands in his, I almost have no choice but to join him.

"Higher!" he says, laughing.

I jump a little harder, going higher with each bounce. I'm laughing so hard, I can hardly catch my breath. He props me up with his hands and I almost feel like I'm flying.

Artie enters the room and barks at us, I'm sure wondering if we're going crazy.

I am. I'm going crazy with Zane. And I love it.

We collapse onto the bed, out of breath, laying on our backs, and breathing hard.

"I don't know about you, but that felt great," Zane says.

"It did. But everything feels good with you."

"Everything?"

"Everything so far and everything I imagine doing with you."

He faces me, so I turn and face him too. He reaches out and moves my hair out of my eyes. Gently, he cups my cheek. His simple touch makes my blood rush through my veins at an accelerated rate.

"You're beautiful, Mila."

My mind races as I ask in an uncertain tone. "What are we doing?" I'm very aware that we're in Ryker's bed, of all places. We're alone, but it doesn't feel like we are.

"What do you want us to be doing?"

I scoff. "That's a dangerous question."

"Now I gotta know the answer. Will it make me blush?"

I grab a pillow and hit him over the head with it a few times. He doesn't fight back. He just laughs in response.

My phone rings, startling us. We both sober quickly as I pull it out of my pocket like it's a ticking time bomb.

"It's Ryker."

"Don't answer," he says.

I slide my finger across my screen, turning it off. "I haven't answered his calls for several days."

"You haven't?"

"No. He's calling as though nothing has changed and I don't know what to say to him."

"Have things changed?" he asks, his Adam's apple bobbing as he swallows.

I guess he needs to hear me say it. "Yes. There's someone new in my life."

He raises his eyebrows in a flirty manner. "Who might that be?"

"The garbage man. Haven't you noticed? He's really cute with his bulging stomach and wifebeater t-shirts. I'm in love."

He remains deadpan. "Hmm. I'm so jealous."

"You should be."

"It's all right. Full disclosure here. I have another secret love too."

"Who?"

"That gray-haired lady in apartment 2B. She's always out walking her dog in the morning, wearing her flannel robe and fuzzy slippers, rollers in her hair, a ciggy between her fingers. Man, she gets me going every time."

I hit him with the pillow again and he dissolves into laughter, holding his stomach as he rolls around on the bed. I can't help but join him. What a goofball.

When we calm down, we face each other again. Our smiles slowly die. The air in the room feels heavy, like it's pushing down on me, pushing us toward each other.

"It's you, Zane. It's you." I whisper my words because I feel like I uttered something sacred.

He nods, discerning my meaning.

After a few moments, he says quietly, "We're alone. No one watching, no one disapproving."

I push thoughts of Ryker out of my mind. I want this moment to be all about Zane. "Just us."

"No ghosts?"

All at once, I can't think of anyone but Zane. I'm not even sure I could utter my own name. "There's only you."

He scoots closer, again cupping my cheek. His eyes blink heavily, almost in slow motion. "Is this what you want, Mila?"

"Yes," I whisper.

As the word leaves my mouth, his lips touch mine in the softest, sweetest manner. They move against mine with a caress so light, I nearly shiver. He massages his lips against mine, the touch tender. He takes my bottom lip in between his and holds it gently. Then he moves to my top lip, doing the same, savoring each move and holding it for several moments.

Even though it's a slow kiss and I've been craving a deep kiss, I wouldn't change a thing. This is the perfect first kiss. So unhurried, it's tantalizing. Each touch is designed to entice—and the desired effect is achieved. He takes his time, kissing me so leisurely that when he pulls away for a micro-second, it feels like an eternity and I can hardly wait for his parted lips to return to mine, to feel his lips exploring mine. The world around me disappears and only Zane exists.

When it's over, he backs away. We stare at one another for several moments.

"Wow," he says, his voice gritty. "That was unexpected."

It was better than I could've imagined. "For me too."

"I have no idea where this is going, but I want to find out."

"Me too." It's all I can say. I'm speechless.

"Okay, c'mon, we have a Jeopardy rematch waiting for us." He pulls me up and off the bed, changing the atmosphere abruptly.

Good decision. The moment was entirely too intense for a first kiss.

"Are you okay?" he asks.

I think I must look as stunned as I feel. In true Jeopardy style, I form my answer into a question. "What is thunderstruck?"

Zane throws his head back and laughs heartily.

As for me, I stand there and stare, soaking him in. I sort of feel like doing my happy dance, jumping up and down and giggling. Is this the giddy feeling my mom thought I should have over my man?

If so, I'm there.

While Zane retrieves the next Jeopardy recording in our line-up, I go to the kitchen to throw together a light dinner. Just some sandwiches and fruit.

I can't help myself. I do actually feel giddy. I break into my happy dance, even though it's not a Mila's Musical Moment. It's still one of the most important moments of my life. I know it, I feel it. Mom was right. I need a man who makes me feel like I can't contain myself.

I jump up and down and the most ridiculous giggling sounds escape my lips. I don't care. I'm a grown woman who has finally found love. I know it because there's no comparison to how I felt with Ryker. This is completely different, and I'm smitten. I don't know how I know, but I do. I just know. Zane's The One.

The sound of Zane clearing his throat interrupts me.

I swing around, my face as red as an apple.

"I didn't hear any piano playing." I can tell he's trying really hard to hide his smile.

I bite my lip, caught in the act of swooning over a man. Like a teenager. "No."

"Does that mean that cute little dance you just did was for . . . *me*?"

My mind rehearses lots of snappy comebacks. *I'll never tell. A girl's gotta have a few secrets. That's for me to know and you to find out. There was a bee.*

Instead, I just say, "Yes."

His face breaks out into the biggest smile I've seen to date.

chapter twenty-one
♥

ON MONDAY NIGHT, we're both home in time to watch Jeopardy live and our stiff competition is in full swing.

Except we're cuddled up on the couch, holding hands, and congratulating each other when we get one right. Maybe it's not exactly a stiff competition.

"What is Bonanza?" Zane hollers in response to the classic TV show category-answer about a man who has three sons and lives on a ranch in Nevada.

He gets it right and I give him a high five.

"Who is Alf?" I shout. It was another TV classics answer about a character who likes to eat cats from the planet Melmac.

"Good one, Mila," he says.

All at once, our show is interrupted with breaking news.

The scene is of the Golden Gate Bridge. Traffic is backed up in both directions due to some sort of accident.

"Must be a bad accident to stop traffic," Zane remarks.

We get to our feet and look out the window. Sure enough, we can see a long line of headlights fanning out into the distance.

Then Jeopardy is back on and we sprint back to the couch so we don't miss anything, chuckling at our priorities.

Several minutes later, the news interrupts again. This time a reporter is live at Fort Point, speaking about the situation at the Golden Gate Bridge. Cameras are pointed to the underside of the huge bridge.

"The Golden Gate Bridge is officially closed to both northbound and southbound traffic. Police have discovered an unidentified object suspended underneath the bridge. The object is described as a large can suspended by a rope. Speculation says it could be a bomb, therefore precautions are in place. However, experts are saying if it is a bomb, it's too far down to damage the bridge."

Zane sits up, leaning closer to the TV, his attention immediately piqued. "That's not true. Depends on what kind of bomb it is. The right bomb could easily take out the entire bridge."

On the heels of his words, his phone rings. I think we both know what will happen next.

No. My stomach clenches painfully.

Concern marring his features, Zane answers. "Captain Martel." He listens for a second. "I can be there in fifteen." He listens again. "I'll be there."

He hangs up, his eyes flying to mine. "I have to go. They've called my team to take care of the situation at the bridge."

He rushes to his room to change his clothes.

Paralyzed with fear, I stare at the TV. The strange object dangling from the bridge. The possibility of a bomb that could go off at any moment. Zane rushing into the situation, putting himself in danger. A fall from that height is almost a guaranteed death. Only a handful of people have survived such a plunge. So many things could go wrong.

I could lose Zane. The magnitude of his job hasn't hit me yet. Not until this very moment.

I don't like it. Not one bit.

He's out and ready to go in two minutes flat. He gives me a quick hug, his mind on his mission.

"Zane, wait. Are you going to the bridge?" Dumb question. Of course he is. But I don't want him to.

"Yes."

"Do you think there's a bomb?" I ask. Another dumb question he can't answer.

"I won't know until I look."

How? How is he going to look? It's suspended from the Golden Gate Bridge.

"I have to go, Mila. Everything will be fine."

He's close to the door and I'm standing in the middle of the living room with ice running through my veins. "Zane, wait!"

He turns and looks at me. And before I even know what's happening, he's running to me and I'm running to him. We smack into each other in the middle and his lips are on mine, hard, fast, and demanding. It's a wild kiss, the kind of kiss I've been wanting, the kind that says *I'm crazy for you*. The kind that says *I can hardly stand to be away from you*. The kind of kiss that tells me he has feelings for me, out of control feelings. Nothing lukewarm here. No, quite the opposite . . . and I love it.

He pulls away and holds me by my shoulders. "I love you, Mila. I'm sorry if it's too soon to say that, but there it is. I love you. I've loved you since the first moment I saw you. That's just the way it is. I love you."

No falling. He's in love with me.

He kisses me one more time, another rough kiss filled with more emotion than I suspected he felt for me.

And then he's off, heading for the door with fast footsteps.

"Zane!"

He pauses.

"I love you too. I do. Please come back."

He turns, his eyes so intense I take a step backward.

"Make no mistake, I'll be back for you."

And then he's gone.

I stand there, unable to move, frozen in place. Fear is coursing through me, along with high doses of adrenaline.

I reach up and touch my tender lips. He kissed me like I've always wanted to be kissed. Like he means it.

I rush to the TV and find a news channel that is covering the situation live and non-stop.

I'm glued to it as they announce the Army bomb squad

has arrived.

This is Zane. This is his job. Ryker said he was irresponsible, a nomad who wanders the earth. That's so unfair. He's a modern-day hero. A man who goes out and does his job without asking for accolades or attention. If I ever hear Ryker lambast him again, he'll get an earful from me.

The camera is too far away. I can't really tell what is going on. I can only see a group of people standing on the bridge above the suspended can, huge lights trained on them, and a light trained on the can below them. They lower something down to the can, but the wind is whipping at it, making it difficult.

A reporter keeps saying the same things over and over. A possible bomb is suspended under the Golden Gate Bridge. The bridge is closed to all thru traffic. The Army bomb squad has arrived and has the matter in hand.

Nothing new. He knows nothing. He's a spectator like all the rest of us, waiting on tenterhooks to see what will happen.

Next, my heart is in my throat as I watch a figure rappel off the side of the bridge, the wind making him sway dangerously.

Is that Zane? I close my eyes. *Please don't let it be Zane.*

The reporter narrates what he's seeing, what we're all seeing. A man risking his life to see what's inside the suspended can.

New video footage appears on the screen. The reporter says, "This just in. Video footage of the can being placed on the Golden Gate Bridge. A man, reportedly acting suspiciously, was sighted on the bridge, attaching the rope and lowering the can. He climbed onto the rope in an attempt to lower himself down to the can. However, he lost his grip, and slid down, hitting the can on his way to the water below. His body has not yet been recovered. We have no further information as to why the can has been placed on the bridge or why the man made an attempt to get to it."

I feel sick when I see the man slip and fall to the cold water below.

The image on the TV switches back to the present. I can't tell what's happening and the suspense is killing me. I walk back and forth, nervous energy consuming me.

Zane is there. In the thick of the danger. Possibly standing above a bomb. Possibly dangling next to one.

I could lose him. But then, anyone could lose their loved ones at any given moment. None of us know when our time is up. That's why you don't spend your life falling. No, if you love someone you say it. Become the fallen. Zane knew there was a chance he wouldn't return home. He knew it, and he did something about it. He pronounced his love for me. Perhaps earlier than he might have under normal circumstances. But I'm so glad he did. I loved hearing those words from his lips.

I've finally found love. And I don't want to lose it.

I hear the reporter say, "This just in. The Army bomb squad has ruled out the threat of a bomb. It's unclear exactly what is in the can, but I repeat, the threat of a bomb on the Golden Gate Bridge no longer exists. Travel across the bridge will reopen shortly."

I collapse on the couch, feeling like I can finally breathe normally.

No bomb.

The live broadcast ends and I no longer have the minute by minute view of Zane's team working on the bridge.

I look out the window, knowing he's out there somewhere, still on the bridge, still risking his life.

I can't stand the tension, the waiting, the anxiety. I have to do something. I leave the TV on, in case any new updates are broadcast.

Then I sit at my piano and I play my heart out. I transfer all of my stress into hitting the keys with much more force than necessary. Forte all the way.

And I wait. And wait. And wait.

chapter twenty-two
♥

I FEEL ZANE'S lips on mine. His soft, sweet kiss. It feels so real. I want it to be real. Am I dreaming? *Wake up, Mila.*

"Wake up, Mila."

It's Zane's voice. He's here, he's home.

I open my eyes and see him hovering above me. He kisses me again. "Hey, sleepyhead."

A weird sound escapes my throat, half squeal, half croak. I throw my arms around him, making him lose his balance and fall onto me. "You're back."

I kiss his cheeks, his chin, his nose, his forehead, his lips, his neck, whatever part of him I can reach in my frenzy. I repeat, "You're back," over and over in between kisses.

He goes with it, kissing me back when he can. When I finally calm down, he mumbles, "I'm gonna leave more often."

I hold his head in my hands, I touch his shoulders, his back, his arms. "Are you okay? All in one piece?"

He grabs my hands, putting an end to my exploration, and holds them on either side of my head. "Hey, calm down. I'm fine."

He kisses me like he did last night, a deep, penetrating kiss. A little wild, a bit out of control. A kiss that makes me feel like I have been kissed. And thoroughly.

He takes his time, in no hurry for our embrace to end. My hands ache to hold him, but I'm trapped, at his mercy—exactly where I want to be. I relax in his arms and enjoy the feeling of being loved by Zane.

He stops before things get out of hand. He lifts himself up and pulls me up with him. He's still dressed in his uniform and he looks beat.

But he's alive and perfect.

Holding my hands, he says, "Look at you. Fully dressed and crashed on the couch. Please tell me you didn't stay up all night."

"I did. I couldn't sleep. I had to know you were okay."

He pulls me into his arms and hugs me close. "I'm okay. Everything's okay. This is my job. You can't worry like this every time I get a call. You won't survive it."

"I know, I know. This one hit very close to home."

He holds me in his arms, gently rocking back and forth. I could stay here all day. I don't know how long he holds me, but it's a long time. So perfect. He smells like the ocean, salty and fresh.

It comes to an end when Zane backs up and holds my face in his hands. "Okay now?"

I nod and we sit on the couch holding hands. "Tell me what happened. Every detail."

He scrubs one hand over his face. He hasn't slept and I can tell he's exhausted.

"Never mind," I amend. "Sleep first. Have you eaten?"

"No."

"I'll make breakfast. Eggs and toast sound good?"

"That sounds amazing."

He sits at the breakfast table while I cook. I don't need to prompt him any further. He starts telling me about the events of last night all on his own.

"Once I arrived on site with my team, the first thing we needed to do was rule out a radiological threat."

"Radiological?"

"A nuke."

"A nuclear bomb? They can be small enough to fit in that can?" I ask as I break the eggs into a bowl.

"Absolutely. We attached a portable radiation detector to a line and dropped it down. The winds were blowing like crazy, so we had to drop a second line to hold it in place. We slowly moved it all around the can until we verified it wasn't a nuke."

"But it still could've been a bomb?"

"Yep. We lowered down other diagnostic equipment to try and figure out what we were dealing with and to see if a person could safely approach. The wind was our enemy and it took a long time. But we finally determined it wasn't a bomb."

"Thank goodness."

"So, I put on my gear and rappelled off the side of the bridge. The can was about sixty feet down."

I freeze, ice running through my veins. "That was you?"

"Yep." He points to himself. "Team leader. Gotta go."

"They caught it on camera. Scared the life out of me. I hoped it wasn't you."

He shakes his head. "It was me. Once I was stable, I had to determine if it was safe to remove the lid. The can was a thirty-three-gallon plastic garbage can being blown around by the wind as though it was a kid's toy. Once I verified it was safe to open the lid, I took a look inside. It was filled with survival-type stuff. A CB radio, a couple of jugs of water, food, clothing, a blanket, a flashlight, a life vest, and a handful of political pamphlets."

"What the heck?"

"Turns out, the jobless guy who did it planned to live in the flimsy can for at least a week. Some kind of bizarre protest to bring attention to the plight of the aged and infirm. Makes no sense."

"But he fell when he tried to climb down to the can."

"He did. They found him this morning, clinging to a rock near Point Diablo."

"Wait, he's alive?" I move the spatula around the pan as I cook the eggs.

"Miraculously, he survived. It's a two-hundred-and twenty-foot drop to the frigid water below. That's like falling twenty stories. He has two collapsed lungs and some broken ribs. He was nearly swept out to sea. Amazing he's alive."

"So, what did you do next?"

"Put the contents of the can into a satchel and sent it up. It's evidence. Once back on the bridge, I asked the police if I should bring the can up."

"What'd they say?" I ask as I butter the hot toast.

"They said, nope. Cut the line and let it drop into the bay. They had the evidence they needed, and they were eager to open up traffic to the bridge as soon as possible. So that's what we did. After that, the rest of the night was clean up and paperwork."

I bring our plates to the table and sit across from him. "Your job scares me."

"It should. Complacency is what kills people. A healthy amount of fear and respect is in order to survive."

"How long will you stay in this job?"

"I owe the military another year. Then I have a decision to make."

"Stay in the Army or go back to your father's business?"

"Yes. And once I make the switch, I won't be leaving again."

Zane starts to eat. I can tell he's in a hurry because he's ready to crash. I'm relieved that he won't be in the Army bomb squad forever. Only one more year. I think that's about all I can handle.

A wisp of fear enters my soul at the thought of him returning to Martel Investments though. More fear than the bomb squad inspires. It's the enemy camp and he'll be deep within the trenches. Right along with Ryker and Debra.

Should I be worried for him?

I don't know. I'm distracted because my heart is still beating on double time after that crazy kiss on the couch. We're definitely compatible. I want to beg him for a repeat performance.

"About last night," he says.

We look at each other and smile like two kids who just stole cookies from the cookie jar.

"I guess I'm just like my father. Once I know, I know. I guess it runs in the family. Have I scared you? Do you wanna run away and never look back?"

Um, no. If he knew my thoughts, he'd be blushing. "No, not at all. But I'd be happy to run away *with* you."

He offers me a fist bump. "Deal."

In spite of his light response, the glimmer in his eyes tells me he's more pleased than he's letting on.

Me too.

chapter twenty-three
♥

MY PHONE RINGS and I know I need to answer it this time. It's Tuesday, nearly a week since I last spoke to Ryker.

Zane pauses our show. "You'd better answer. He's not gonna give up. I think this is something we have to face and not hide from."

I love that he says we. We're in this together. "Yeah, I guess I better talk to him."

It's late evening for us. I think Ryker's calling during his lunch hour in Japan. I stand, feeling bereft after leaving Zane's warm embrace. I miss having my head nestled on his chest. Our time together in the evening is my favorite part of the day.

At least Ryker's call is not a video call this time. He won't see Zane in the background, waiting for me to return to him on the couch. It's not like he'll see that my hair is askew. Or the soft candlelight on the coffee table. All evidence of a romantic evening.

"Hello."

"Hello, Mila. It's been a while."

"Yes, it has. I'm sorry. My performance season starts this week. I'm so busy."

"I just bet you are."

His tone gives me pause. "Excuse me?"

"I imagine you are one crazy lady right now. I know how you get before a performance. You have a one-track mind."

"It's true." My guilty conscience is hearing things he's not saying. I pace the floor and Zane watches me with troubled eyes. He knows the thought of Ryker floods me with uncomfortable emotions. My relationship with him feels unresolved. The thing is, I've already moved on.

"So, what else have you been up to?"

Besides making out with your brother? Not much. I'm obsessed with him. "Oh, I'm pretty focused on my practice sessions right now. Hard to fit much else in."

"I'm sure you'll find a way."

Do I detect a bit of sarcasm? "Maybe when the season is over."

"Where's Zane? Do you see much of him? I hope he's not bothering you."

Oh, he's bothering me all right—in the hot and bothered way. I stop pacing and meet eyes with Zane. He's watching me with intense eyes.

I maintain eye contact with him. "No, Zane's not bothering me at all. With work and renovations on his new home, our paths don't cross often."

Which is true. I wish we had more time together.

"I hope you've taken what I said to heart. He can't be trusted. Don't let your guard down for a second."

Irritated, I tell him, "He's given me no reason not to trust him." I turn around and pace the floor once again. "Look, Ryker, did you call to talk about Zane or call to talk to me?"

"I called to hear your voice, of course. I miss you, Mila."

"Ryker, I . . ."

"I know, I know. No need to say it all again. But I still look forward to seeing you when I return home."

"I look forward to your return as well." So I can officially end things face to face. I hope that sounded Switzerland enough. It's the most I can give him.

Honestly, I look forward to Ryker's return because then I can move out and not feel obligated to stay here. For the sake of my relationship with Zane, I need to sever all connections with Ryker. Until I move out, that won't happen.

I look back at Zane. He hasn't moved an inch. He's still watching me, his expression brooding.

"Is *he* there right now?" Ryker asks, his voice low.

"Yes, he's here. Would you like to talk to him?"

He doesn't answer. Instead he says, "Where is he?"

"He's watching TV." I run my fingers through my thick mane, massaging my scalp. I think a headache is coming on.

"Are you watching TV together?" he spits.

I breathe in and out deeply in an attempt to remain calm. I feel guilty about ending things with Ryker, but that feeling is quickly fading. "Yes, we're watching TV together." I refuse to say more. It's none of his business. I'm really beginning to hate this awkward situation I find myself in. At least Ryker hasn't mentioned the word *falling* again during this uncomfortable phone call.

"Be careful, Mila. I can't stress it enough. Zane is bad news."

No, he's not. He's the best news I've ever had. The headline of my life.

"I'm only thinking of you. I have to go. Talk again later."

The click of the phone seems loud in my ear. Ryker and his abrupt phone endings. When he's done, he's done.

I'm done too.

I let my hand fall to my side, feeling troubled.

I'm not uneasy about me and Zane. I'm uncomfortable with the location of our budding romance. I wish it wasn't unfolding right here in Ryker's penthouse. It makes me feel like he's watching us, like I'm doing something wrong, engaging in forbidden love.

"That was awkward," I say, my voice echoing around the room.

"Eventually, he's going to find out about us."

"I know."

"Tell him."

It's not a challenge or a dare. He's as calm as he always is. But I sense underlying tension. "I don't think that's wise. Your entire family will . . . explode."

"My family exploded a long time ago. Nothing we do will make it worse or better."

"I want more time with you." My voice holds a pleading tone.

"You have it."

"Time without family drama."

"It will never happen."

"It's happening right now. I want it to stay like this."

He's quiet for several moments, thinking it over. "Tell him, Mila. Tell him everything. Diffuse the situation."

"I don't want to." Am I hurting him by keeping us a secret? We haven't necessarily been careful or secretive. We just haven't announced it to Ryker and Debra.

"Why?"

"It's our secret. And I like it that way."

"What are you worried about?"

"Once they know about us, I'm scared it will somehow ruin us."

"Never in a million years. I won't let them."

My chest rises and falls. I want to run to him and throw my arms around him. Hold him close, never let him go. If I hang on tight enough, I won't be able to lose him. Is he underestimating his crazy family?

I think he is.

"Are you scared to tell him?" he asks.

"No. And I don't think I owe it to him, either."

Zane looks down at his hands. "Okay. Fair enough."

I know I need to say more. "As long as we're both living in Ryker's home, it's weird that I'm seeing you. It makes me feel like Ryker and Debra have a say in our lives—and I don't want them to have that kind of power over us."

He nods slowly. "Well said."

"Are you upset with me?"

"Nope." He grabs the remote and switches the TV to a music station. An instrumental version of *Unchained Melody* fills the air.

He walks toward me, exaggerating each step, making me wait when I'm anxious to be in his arms. "If Ryker and Debra are going to mess with us, and make no mistake, they will mess with us, then I'm going to take advantage of every moment I have with you while I have it," he says softly.

He takes me in his arms and holds me close as we begin to sway to the music. "They can't touch us," I say vehemently.

"They can and they will. Expect it."

"Don't say that. We won't let them."

"And yet we're hiding from them."

"I thought you agreed it was for the best right now."

"I do. We're fortifying the ranks while we're not under attack."

"What does that mean?" I ask.

"It means, we need this time, me and you. Time to build our relationship before family interferes. It's a smart move, Mila. I see the wisdom in it. I'm not upset with you. But one day soon, I'm gonna tell the world you're my girl. I'm gonna shout it from the rooftops. So be prepared."

"I'll shout with you."

"Deal." His arms run up and down my back.

"Team Mila and Zane."

"Team Mila and Zane," he repeats with a smile in his voice.

His arms wrap around me tightly and I do the same, melting into him. I burrow my head against his chest and let the beautiful music envelop me. We hold each other long after the first song ends. And many, many songs later.

Gently, he cups my chin and brings my face up to his for a kiss, the soft, slow intimate kind I know Zane loves.

Eventually, it turns into the hard and fast kiss Zane is an expert at. Somewhere in the midst of the kiss, we stop dancing. Somehow, he walks me backwards without me even realizing we've moved. Somehow, I end up pressed against the wall, kissing him with as much enthusiasm as he is kissing me.

And somewhere along the line, I know without a doubt that I'm deeply and madly in love with Zane Martel. More so than I ever thought possible.

This. This is what I've wanted. For a man to kiss me in a way that expresses everything he's feeling inside. I feel his love, his desire, his longing. It's more than that, though. I feel his emotions like they're right there on the surface, displayed for me to see. He's not holding back. He's giving himself to me, heart and soul. No falling. He's the fallen. I'm right there with him. His kiss says he can't get enough, like he wants to consume me.

There's no going back now.

Zane's wrong. Debra and Ryker can't touch us. Not when we're building such a strong foundation.

We're solid. They can't break us.

chapter twenty-four
♥

AFTER FRESHENING UP in my dressing room, I make my way to the meet and greet. I'm still in my black evening gown, my hair in a perfect up-do, soft tendrils curling on my neck and cheeks.

My first performance of the season went off without a hitch. I was in the zone and played my best yet. There was something about knowing Zane was in the audience, his eyes on me, that made me feel different, more alive, more animated than I've ever felt before.

I feel his love. I feel it emanating across a crowded performance hall and landing on me. And I absorb every molecule like a starving woman at her last meal.

As I visit with patrons, I finally find Zane in the crowd. He's across the room, his eyes on me every time I glance his way. We share a few small smiles, strangely satisfying smiles that say we have a secret that's ours and ours alone.

I've never understood the meaningful glances between loving couples, the looks in their eyes, the silent messages they send each other. Now I do. Yet, it's only a glimpse of the bond that awaits us as our relationship progresses. I look forward to every moment, each new development.

This is torture. I have a crazy desire for the evening to be over so I can be with Zane and kiss him until he begs for mercy.

Besides, I have the most amazing news to share with him. I'm about to burst if I don't blurt it out soon.

My step is light as I make my way through the crowd, stopping here and there to chat with patrons. I appreciate the kind words, the praise, but I'm eager to speak with my man.

There he is. I see him, leaning against a wall as he waits, doing nothing except watching me, his eyes doing things to me we've never done before. The sight of him makes my breath hitch in my chest. I now know what breathless truly means.

He's holding a dozen beautifully wrapped red roses.

For me.

It's the first time I've ever seen him dressed in a suit. He does it justice, but I much prefer him in his ripped-at-the-knees jeans and white v-neck t-shirt. That's the Zane I fell in love with.

But the dark gray suit he's wearing this evening fits him like a second skin. I didn't even know he owned a suit. He's wearing a burgundy dress shirt, open at the neck, no tie—a slight snub at convention. He looks casually sleek, like he walked off the pages of a glossy magazine.

Wow.

As I approach, one of the ushers, an older man, momentarily steals Zane's attention.

"Zane, how you doing, buddy? Good to see you. It's been a while." He slaps his back a few times. "There was a time when you never missed a show. Good to see you again."

That's my symphony loving man. It's a unique preference, and I'm glad his father passed it along to him when he was young. It gives us common ground, a place where he understands me and my passion.

Zane's eyes find me again and his expression changes. He goes completely still and blinks heavily. I love the slight smile curving his full lips. It's like he's captivated.

By me.

As long as I live, I'll never forget that face, his countenance. The way his chest slowly rises and falls with exaggeration. Like I do something to him.

I know he does something to me. I've never felt anything like this. Not even close.

I walk a little closer. So does he.

"Miss Westerman, incredible performance this evening.

You were amazing," the usher says.

"Thank you," I say, my eyes never leaving Zane's.

Zane closes the distance between us and hugs me tightly. "You were breathtaking."

He hands me the bouquet of roses. "For you."

"Thank you. And thank you for coming this evening. It means the world to me."

"Are you kidding? I'm not going to miss a single performance. If you're playing, I'll be there."

I can't contain my smile. I'm brimming with excitement. "Guess what?"

"What?"

"A man from the San Francisco Symphony attended this evening. He knocked on my dressing room door after the performance."

"And?"

"He asked me to audition."

"What? A personal invite to audition to play with the San Francisco Symphony. Mila, that's amazing."

"I know." I smile so big, it hurts. "I'm so excited."

Zane holds my shoulders as though he's keeping me down. "I know you want to, but don't do it here."

"I might. I can't help myself."

"Restraint, Miss Westerman. A happy dance is probably considered unbecoming for a serious musician like yourself. Wait until we're home."

"Find me a place. I can't wait. It might happen right here and I'll blow my cover. Everyone will know underneath it all, I'm just a silly little girl."

Zane chuckles. "Nah, it's obvious you're a full-grown woman, my dear." His eyes twinkle. "I think I can help you. Come with me." He grabs my hand and weaves through the crowd, stealing me away.

We break through the doors and into the fresh night air. We run down the street, him in his suit and me in my evening gown, laughing as we go. It's such a perfect moment. I imagine we're running in slow motion, unseen wind in our hair and on our faces.

He finds a dark storefront and pulls me into it.

"Okay, go!"

I don't do it alone.

He joins me in my wacky happy dance, my Mila's Musical Moment. He jumps up and down with me and pumps his fist in the air, moving his head at silly angles as he tries to mimic me. I laugh so hard at the sight, my stomach hurts.

He picks me up and twirls me around. "I'm so freakin' proud of you, Mila Westerman. You did it, you did it." I slide down his body as he lowers me down, still holding me in his arms. "I'm gonna kiss your face off."

It's the kind of thing I expect Zane to say. "Well, there you have it. That's quite possibly the most romantic thing you've ever said to me. Romance is definitely not dead." I don't wait for him to initiate the kiss. I initiate it this time, practically attacking him.

He doesn't seem to mind.

chapter twenty-five
♥

THE ELEVATOR DOORS open, and as I enter the hallway, my step has a bounce to it. The thought of Zane makes me want to skip like a little kid. It's only been a few days since that amazing kiss in the dark storefront and we've already shared similar moments several times.

Kissing Zane is my new favorite thing in the world. I'm so happy, I might burst. If I do, rainbows and sprinkles will fall out of me. Life is that good.

My parents are coming this weekend to hear me play with the symphony. I can't wait for them to meet Zane. I've told my mom so much about him, I imagine she thinks he deserves sainthood.

I hope Zane is already home from visiting his father. I just finished playing for ballet classes and I have the evening off. I can't wait to spend it with him.

Instead of the usual music blasting through the penthouse, a loud voice meets my ears. Angry. Gruff.

My steps falter. Is that . . . is that . . . Ryker? He's home?

I walk slowly toward the wide-open door of the penthouse. I linger in the hallway, listening to the words the livid voice is saying.

"Did you really think you could get away with this? Seriously, Zane. Who do you think you are?"

It *is* Ryker. He's home, and he's giving Zane a piece of his mind. Guess our secret has become public knowledge.

I move to the doorway. For the first time in my life I lay eyes on the two brothers together, side by side.

Ryker's in his usual suit, looking refined and polished.

Okay, stuffy. Why didn't I notice that before?

Zane's in his signature jeans and t-shirt. Barefoot.

I know where my heart stands. No contest.

This turn of events doesn't matter, I tell myself. Me and

Zane are good. Nothing will change that. The two of us together, we're strong. *Team Mila and Zane.* Ryker can't hurt us.

Ryker is walking around the room as he talks, gathering up every single colorful item Zane and I placed in his penthouse. He's making a pile on the floor, like he's collecting the garbage so it can be taken out. I suppose that was expected.

"Did you think I wouldn't find out? Did you really think you could take what's mine? How dare you!"

Is he referring to me when he says you can't take what is mine? I've got news for him.

Turns out, Ryker is not a smooth-talking man. That was a façade. He's an angry, ill-tempered jerk. If I'd married him, I would've seen this side of him, no doubt directed at me often. I'm glad I saw it long before I tied myself to him for life. Thank goodness I found Zane, otherwise I would be questioning my judgement with every man I meet from here on out.

Ryker's handsome features are contorted with rage, making him ugly. I don't recognize this man. After all the time I spent with him, I truly never knew him. He didn't reveal himself to me. Conversely, I've known Zane for a short period of time, and I feel like I know him inside and out. He's shown me who he is, and I love him.

Zane's acting cool and unfazed, leaning his back against the wall, arms folded across his chest. He's doing what he usually does when he faces Ryker's temper—calmly waiting for the storm to pass. I adore my diplomatic man.

"All my life, Zane. All my life. You've always wanted what I have. You've always tried to take what's mine. I'm sick of it."

Zane says nothing. He could be passing the time on a sailboat on a lazy summer day and he'd look no different.

"I have proof, don't bother denying it. You should know by now, Zane, you can't use the bathroom without me knowing about it. I will always be watching you. I won't let you take what's mine or interfere with my life."

Ryker grabs his briefcase, flips it open angrily, and pulls out a large envelope. He rips it open and removes large glossy eight-by-tens. He tosses them on the dining room table.

"I have eyes everywhere."

Zane pushes away from the wall and studies the pictures on the table. I can't see what they are, so I step into the room.

Both men notice me then. Ryker whirls around, his eyes fierce and glaring. "Mila. Good. You're here. You need to hear this."

That's his greeting? Okay, then. The lines are drawn.

"What are you doing home?" I ask.

"I'm here to save you from yourself."

He came all this way to save me? Seriously? "I don't need saving."

He sends me a *shame on you* look. "You don't even realize what you've gotten yourself into, do you?"

Zane's eyes land on me. With my entrance, his expression has changed into a mask of concern and worry. He shakes his head slightly in the negative, like he's telling me he doesn't want me to be here. He's protective of me, but I can handle Ryker, especially now that I see him for what he is.

Arthur whines in the corner, approaching Ryker on shaky legs.

"Shut up, Arthur. Back to your bed. Now!" Ryker roars.

Whoa. That was mean. My sweet Artie retreats silently to his bed and curls into a ball. Is this how Ryker always treats him? If so, his fear and shaking all make sense now.

At this point, my feelings toward Ryker are not anywhere near kind or caring. They're on the opposite end of the spectrum. A four-letter word that begins with H.

Ryker grabs the pictures on the table and throws them

at my feet. "Don't bother denying a thing."

I look down and see a picture of Zane brushing my hair while we sit in his Jeep. There's another one of me and Zane walking through Chinatown, hand in hand. Yet another one shows us dancing—very close—in a Chinatown restaurant. One is of us sitting on the dock at Stow Lake, my head on his shoulder, his head resting on mine, the sun beginning to set in the background. Another one is of us escaping after my first symphony performance, holding hands as we run down the street, my roses dangling in one hand. We look so happy, so carefree. Of course, the photographer also caught the passionate kiss we shared as we stood in the dark storefront.

When it comes to the nature of my relationship with Zane, the pictures say it all. Am I supposed to feel guilty? Does he expect me to apologize, to act like I have been caught doing something horribly wrong?

Not going to happen.

Instead, I want to ask if I can have the pictures to frame for my wall. I don't have any pictures of us, other than the occasional random selfie. Most are silly. I know that query won't go over well. Yet, I'm so tempted.

I look up at Zane, suppressing my smile. I want to say, *look at these great pictures of us*. But, again, I notice that his calm exterior has turned to blatant worry upon my arrival. I wish I could reassure him that everything is fine, that we got this.

"I warned you, Mila. I told you Zane was bad news. I see you didn't listen."

Zane's not saying anything, so I don't either.

Ryker continues. "Did you know Zane is under investigation for embezzlement? I told you that you shouldn't trust him and there's a reason why. He has stolen from his own father's business. Doesn't that disturb you? It should."

Zane stands there watching me, observing the

emotions that wander over my face.

Wait. Is he anxious about this revelation? Surely not.

Ryker already told me about Debra's false accusations against Zane. I never discussed it with Zane. I didn't feel the need. "I don't believe those accusations for even a hot second."

"Really? You don't care? You don't care that you're seeing a man who's a criminal? A man who steals for a living?"

"He's innocent until proven guilty as far as I'm concerned."

"He's a thief!" Ryker shouts, as if that'll convince me to shun Zane.

The only thing he's stolen is my heart. I debate over it, but decide it's best if I don't say that out loud.

"I came home for a few days—all the way from Japan—just to save you from him. You have no idea what a huge mistake you've made. You've fallen for his lies, hook, line, and sinker. He's manipulated you. Can't you see it? Are you really that blind? Everything in life is a competition to Zane. He wants to win, and you're the current prize."

Zane's face is now blank, giving me nothing to hang onto. It doesn't matter. My grip is tight and unyielding. "I don't believe you," I tell Ryker.

Ryker lets out a sinister laugh, like what I said is so ridiculous, there are no words to convey my stupidity.

"He's gotten to you, Mila. He's under your skin and you're so blind you can't see straight. He's a master manipulator. Did you really think he showed up on my doorstep by chance?" He shakes his head. "Oh, Mila. How could you be so naïve?"

That's sour grapes talking. I know it is.

"Did he feed you a sob story about his poor, neglected childhood? Did he toss the *dead mother* card your way? Girls love that stuff. They fall for it every time. They have his whole life."

"Never underestimate the power of the truth."

Ryker walks over to me and stands directly in front of me, blocking my view of Zane. It's a stance designed to intimidate, but I don't back down. "Did you really just say that? Are you serious right now?"

"Utterly," I tell him firmly.

"Then you're a fool. He's playing with you like you're his current favorite toy. He'll leave you. It's what he's good at. *Leaving.* If that doesn't scare you, I don't know what will."

"Listening to you makes me a fool." I'm fed up with Ryker and his twisted version of the truth. "Zane left for his Army commitments. Quit making it sound as though he ditched his responsibilities. I can see right through you. The game is over, Ryker. Give it up."

"You're wrong. He did ditch his duties. He left the family business, breaking my father's heart. Zane's only good side is his back, the side you see when he's walking away. And he will walk away. Mark my words, Mila. He won't stay. He'll leave you."

"You're such a jerk." I can't believe I never saw it.

"Proud of it."

"You can't come between us. Quit trying."

"Don't make me do this, Mila. It'll hurt, and that's what I'm trying to avoid."

"Don't make you do *what*?" I ask, confused.

"Don't make me hurt you."

"You can't hurt me, Ryker. You don't have that much power."

"Don't I?" he says, turning and pacing the room.

Zane hasn't moved. He's watching us with guarded eyes, watching the situation unfold, but refusing to indulge Ryker. I'm not sure if he heard our entire exchange, but he probably got the gist.

I remember Zane saying, when it comes to family drama, he takes himself out of the equation. He wasn't kidding. I've seen him do it in the past, once during our visit with Debra, and once when Ryker called and hollered at him for being at the penthouse. I hate that he doesn't fight back. At the same time, I respect his restraint, his refusal to sink to their level. I have a feeling it was a lesson he learned in early childhood, a survival instinct. He learned to play it cool and keep his thoughts to himself.

Regardless, I'm rattled by his silence, even though I'm fighting the feeling. I wish he'd defend himself, give Ryker an earful. His gaze is still glued to me, like he's trying to send me a message. But I can't hear what he's trying to convey. He's acting as though he's an observer, not a participant.

Ryker stops pacing, standing between us like a referee in a boxing match. He directs his next remark toward Zane. "Does she know, Zane? Does she?" He laughs as though he's disgusted.

That gets my attention. Do I know what? I can feel a subtle shift happening inside me. My confidence is slipping. All at once, I'm filled with trepidation.

"Does she know you're a stalker? Her stalker?" Ryker asks with an accusatory tone.

What? Zane said Ryker and Debra would mess with us, that it was a given. But this is verging on ridiculous.

Ryker laughs aloud, like the situation is terribly funny and he's the only one who knows the joke. "I have a cute little story for you, Mila. I'm sure you'll find it enlightening. Won't she, Zane?"

The only thing that moves on Zane's frozen form is the motion of his jaw joint, as though he's gritting his teeth. A denial is nowhere to be seen.

His demeanor scares me more than anything Ryker can reveal.

"You're gonna love this, Mila. I promise."

In spite of Ryker's odd laughter, his expression is the hardest I've ever seen it. I swear, his eyes are so cold, they're like looking in a dead man's eyes.

My fingernails dig into my palms as I steel myself for

his story. All the while, *he can't break us,* wanders through my mind. Over and Over.

I won't let him.

chapter twenty-six
♡

"ONCE UPON A time," Ryker starts, enjoying this way too much. "I had clients in town and I took them to see the Marin Symphony. It was last year's season. I attended three nights in a row, taking different people each time. Is this story good so far?"

"No, not at all," I tell him.

"It's about to get better."

Zane's shoulders are rigid, his posture tense. Is he nervous about Ryker's story? I swallow and say nothing more.

"All three nights were *lovely*, if you enjoy that sort of thing. Full disclosure here. I enjoy the symphony *somewhat*. I hated it as a kid. I thought it was the most boring thing life had to offer. It has since grown on me. Only just." He holds up two fingers very close together, to indicate a teeny amount.

"Get on with it, Ryker. Say what you want to say."

He's a mean man. I didn't know that about him. Duly noted. I will forever be careful in his presence.

"Some stories can't be rushed. Especially when the punch line should be savored."

He pauses and tendrils of fear wander up and down my spine. I was wrong when I thought Ryker didn't have any humor inside him. He does. Dark humor. Cruel humor. I never really knew this man. The thought bothers me more than I care to admit.

"Where was I? Oh yes. The symphony and how much I sort of, no, *barely* enjoyed it. My clients loved it, even though one of them snored through the whole darn thing. So rude and so unfair. I couldn't join him, I had to be the perfect host and pretend I was fascinated."

So, it was only for my sake that he pretended he loved

attending the symphony. Does he ever reveal his true self?

Maybe that's what he's doing right now.

Ryker goes on. "At any rate, a funny thing happened while at the symphony those three nights in a row. I saw someone there I knew each and every time. Can you guess who it was, Mila? I bet you can. But I'll give you three chances just in case."

My stomach clenches painfully. "I have no idea."

"You're such a bad liar. Not necessarily a bad thing, though. If you want to succeed in life, may I suggest getting good at it? But I digress. If you guessed my brother, you would be right on the money. Ding, ding, ding. All three nights in a row, there was Zane, enraptured by the symphony. Like I said, the symphony is okay, but let's face it, most of the time it's a real snoozefest. But not to Zane. Oh no, his eyes were glued to the stage, and I mean riveted. The man was freakin' mesmerized. Made me wonder if we were watching the same performance. Finally, I approached him and asked what he was doing there. Go ahead, ask me what he said, Mila. You'll love his answer."

Zane grants me another slight shake of his head in the negative. That's all—and I need more.

"It doesn't matter what he said." My hot cheeks and quivering lips betray me.

"Oh, I think it does. I think it matters big time. First, I'll tell you what he didn't say. He didn't say, *Our father just had a stroke and being here reminds me of time spent with him as a kid.* That would've been my first guess. I was wrong, I admit it. Gotta say, Zane surprised me when he didn't even glance my way. Instead, he said, *The pianist, she's amazing, isn't she?* So, if you don't know who that is, I'll tell you. That was you, my dear, sweet Mila. Yes, you. Our Zane here couldn't take his eyes off you. Y-O-U. He was captivated." Ryker scoffs. "News to you, isn't it? I can tell by that shocked expression on your face. Business 101. Learn how to hide your feelings. You missed that class,

Mila, didn't you?"

Ryker walks toward me acting casual, his hands in his pockets. He thinks he's won, that he's dealt the winning blow.

He might have.

"Didn't you?" he says, his lips snarling.

"Get away from me."

"Does that hurt enough or should I continue?" he taunts.

"Get out of my sight."

Ryker moves away, his hands in the air like he's surrendering. "The power of the truth, Mila. Never underestimate it."

He throws my own words back in my face. They hit me hard.

I wanted to present a united front, a barricade so tight, Ryker or Debra could never infiltrate it. But there are too many cracks. Zane and I aren't strong enough for this. He knows it and so do I. We were right to attempt to keep our relationship a secret from the enemy camp. We didn't have enough time to fortify ourselves from this attack. We need more. More time. More kisses. More hugs. More talks. Just more.

I think the wind could blow and knock me over. Shocked doesn't describe how I feel. Not even close.

Ryker continues, even though no one wants to hear another word he has to say. "Shortly thereafter, Zane had to leave the country, because that's what he does. Leaving is his talent, in case you haven't guessed."

I turn my heated gaze on Ryker. "Then you arranged for us to meet? You're such a hypocrite. Who stole from who?"

"Don't flatter yourself, my dear. We met by chance. I knew I'd have to be careful when Zane found out about us. I knew he'd try to steal you from me."

He's lying, twisting the truth. It's *his* talent.

My heart drops into my stomach and I feel physically

ill. Am I a pawn caught in the middle of sibling rivalry? Looking back, my first meeting with Ryker seems calculated. Ridiculous business card and all. He was at the symphony meet and greet to check out the woman he thought his brother was obsessed with. He was never in love with me, falling or otherwise. I was something his brother desired, so he went after me. It explains his lukewarm behavior coupled with his unwillingness to let me go. I was just something to win.

The thing is, I can handle Ryker. I don't care about him. He doesn't matter to me.

But, Zane. What about Zane? He has the power to crush my soul.

Am I just a prize to be won?

The memory of the usher speaking to Zane after opening night at the symphony wanders through my mind, the way he patted Zane on the back, the way he mentioned how he never missed a show.

I assumed the usher meant he was attending shows long before I ever played for the symphony.

I swallow hard and shift from foot to foot, feeling shaken to the core, stunned to the very depths of my soul.

I can't wrap my mind around this revelation. What does it mean? All this time, Zane knew who I was. He watched me play several times. He was mesmerized by me.

I don't understand. Why didn't he tell me? I thought we met for the first time that moment when I walked in on him in Ryker's penthouse.

Then I remember the way he froze, the way he stared at me as though he was in shock. *Frozen encounter.*

At the time, I thought it was because I had walked into the penthouse unexpectedly. Now, the scene plays out in my mind very differently.

Zane's face is a stony mask. He's still watching me with an unwavering gaze, saying nothing.

"Defend yourself," I say, pleading with him.

"Yes, Zane, defend yourself. Tell her you're not a thief, that you haven't taken a red cent from your father's company. While you're at it, explain why you haven't been arrested yet. Mom's in a tizzy over that one. But the doozy is your stalker-like behavior. Explain to us how you're not a stalker. I'd love to hear that one, wouldn't you, Mila? Go ahead, tell her how your behavior was completely normal and not weird at all. Tell her you weren't staring at her like some lovesick puppy while she performed. Declare your innocence, Zane, I dare you. We're waiting," Ryker prods. "This is gonna be good, I can feel it in my bones."

I hate the way he's gloating. If he thinks he can win me back, he is sadly mistaken. He's a poor excuse for a human being. Rotten to the core, every inch Debra's son. He's enjoying our pain, like it's his lifeforce. He feeds off of it. I've never seen him so animated.

"Shut up, Ryker," I say. Childish, maybe. But it feels darn good to say it.

He's not fazed at all. Ryker pretends like he's zipping up his mouth and throwing away the key. Like he's twelve years old. His dark humor disgusts me. I don't find this side of him amusing. I didn't know he needed to be cruel to find his funny bone, as sarcastic as it is.

I turn my attention back to Zane. "Please."

"I can't," is all Zane says.

He's like a statue, firm and immoveable, showing no emotion, and no reaction to Ryker's accusations. I feel like he's backing away, removing himself from the situation, removing himself from me. He's retreated within himself like he's pretending he's not here and this isn't happening. I have a feeling this is how he's handled Ryker and Debra his entire life.

My eyes fill with tears, but I don't let a single one fall. "Please, Zane. Say something."

He shakes his head in the negative again. "I'm sorry."

"Sorry? You're sorry?" Ryker roars. "That's not good

enough. Mila sees you for what you are now. A liar, playing with her emotions. Just so you can take what's mine."

Zane must know his silence makes him come across as guilty. This is killing me. I need him to say something, anything. Speak up. Put Ryker in his place. Tell me he loves me. Say this is all a mistake. That Ryker's not telling the truth. If he would only speak, I would listen. Doesn't he know that?

Ryker, in his element, goes on. "What's the matter, Zane? You don't have Dad to hide behind anymore, do you? No one will save you now."

Why does Zane simply stand there and take it? I remember him saying that arguing with Ryker or Debra is like spitting in the wind, useless and it never ends up where you intend. I understand that philosophy. I respect it. It's obvious Ryker wants to fight with him. He's hungry for it. By refusing, Zane puts out the fire before it has begun. I hate that he's lived with this all his life.

But this is different. Ryker is deliberately trying to tear us apart. Yet, Zane won't fight for me. He won't even speak to me.

I don't want to be here. I can't watch Zane behave like this. I turn to leave, to escape. To go cry my eyes out.

"Mila, wait."

It's Zane. He speaks.

I face him, hopeful. All I need is a few words of explanation and I'll believe him. Something. Anything. I'll forgive him and we'll move on.

But he just says, "I'm sorry," one more time.

What does that mean? He can't explain his actions? Is he admitting guilt? Has he been lying to me? Is he not who I think he is? Has our relationship been exactly what Ryker is insinuating?

"Let her leave. She needs time to process," Ryker hollers and continues slamming Zane, ignoring me, dismissing me.

"You came here to steal my girl, didn't you? That was your intention from the very beginning. Admit it. You're not in love with her. This is all just a game to you, some sort of sick competition."

Nothing changes. Zane maintains his silence.

My heart breaks in my chest. I turn again, ready to walk away. My hand has a mind of its own. It grips the doorjamb and holds it tight, hesitating, preventing myself from leaving. I don't want to leave Zane. No one ever stands by him, especially now that his father is unable to be there for him. He needs someone. And I want to be that someone.

I know Zane. There's a reason why he's not saying a word, a valid reason. I need to trust him, and not put any stock into Ryker's accusations. He knows how to twist the truth to make a situation sound dirty, how he wants it to sound. He wants to break us up. Why am I believing anything he says?

Actually, I don't. It's a light bulb moment, hitting me with enough strength to stun me. Nothing that comes out of Ryker's mouth is the truth. I will never believe anything he says.

I want to be the someone who tells Ryker to shut the heck up. Loudly and often. Not just now, all the time. I no longer care about the consequences or keeping peace in the family. Someone needs to put Ryker — and his horrible mother — in their place.

Ryker's shouting grows louder, closer, and I hang my head. This shouldn't be how brothers behave with one another. It breaks my heart for Zane. Calm and quiet Zane. The brother who refuses to engage, to fuel the flames of anger. I love him for it.

All at once, a blinding pain rips through my hand. At the same moment, I hear Zane yell, "NO!"

An inky blackness fills my mind, the pain in my hand so searing that I can barely react. Stunned, I turn, wondering what just happened. I fall to my knees, cradling my hand, horrified by the immediate swelling.

No. No. Please, no.

My chest heaves as I stare at my hand. I'm so shocked, I can barely react, barely comprehend what just occurred. It was so fast, so unexpected.

The door that Ryker slammed sways in front of me, still in motion from the force.

It's not just any door. It's a heavy twenty-minute fire door. It took strength to slam it as hard as he did. All that energy zeroed in on my hand, right at the knuckles, then bounced away, having no idea what kind of trauma it left in its path. My hand was the only thing stopping the door from clicking closed, a doorstop of the worst possible variety.

My hand, my hand.

When a response does come, it hits me hard and fast. Tears instantly pour from my eyes, blocking my vision from the horrific sight of my mangled hand.

My dreams, my life, everything is disappearing in one blinding moment. One small action that will change my world in huge ways.

Anguished cries are forced from my body, sounds I've never heard myself make. The pain is unbearable.

But the ramifications are excruciating.

A wave of dizziness makes me fall to the floor. I'm crying uncontrollably, writhing in pain. I can hardly catch my breath as waves of agony course through me.

The blackness is again at the edges of my vision and I feel myself going numb, slipping away. The pain is too much.

I open my eyes, tears blurring my view. Zane is above me, kneeling next to me. His lips are moving, but I can't hear a word he's saying above the ringing in my ears. He's holding my hand, gently cradling it in his own.

Ryker is standing there looking stunned, doing nothing.

Zane turns and yells at him. "Get ice! Now!"

I hear that loud and clear.

Ryker finally acts, leaving my line of sight.

The next thing I know Zane has gently placed a bag of ice on top of my hand. The cold makes me gasp as it invades me, conquers me.

Zane carefully wraps a towel around the ice and my hand, securing it in place. He positions my hand on my stomach and picks me up in his arms, cradling me like a baby. I bury my face in his chest, squishing my eyes closed and gritting my teeth against the waves of agony.

"Help me get her to your car!" he yells to Ryker.

He sounds frantic, yet determined.

There's several minutes of jostling while Zane gets me to Ryker's car at record speed. My hand remains cocooned on my belly, the cold ice causing sparks of pain to wander up my arm clear to my shoulder.

A sudden change of temperature tells me we've entered the parking garage in the basement. The strange echo of tires rolling against the pavement hits my ears.

More jostling, this time rougher as Zane begins to run to Ryker's car. I want to cry out, but I can barely remain conscious, much less utter a single word.

But I'm in Zane's arms. He's taking care of me. I'm leaving it up to him to get me the help I need.

When the manhandling stops, and the slamming of car doors stops bouncing through my head, I peek at the world around me. I'm still in Zane's arms, nestled against his chest, sitting on his lap. A seatbelt is awkwardly wrapped around us, cutting into my skin in various places. The tires are screeching as Ryker drives like a wild man to get me to the hospital.

Zane is holding me tightly, so tight I hardly sway with the motion of the car. He's looking down on me with fierce eyes.

"Everything will be all right," he says, his voice gritty. He presses his lips to my forehead.

I appreciate his words. I do. So much. But I know the

truth. It's staring me in the face.

My days as a professional pianist are over.

And there's nothing anyone can say or do to change that fact.

chapter twenty-seven
♥

WHEN I NEXT awaken, I'm lying in a hospital bed, my mind foggy. I'm dizzy and my mouth feels like cotton.

As I attempt to open my eyes and keep them open, I find Ryker and Zane sitting in my room. Zane looks ravaged with emotion and Ryker looks sheepish. A new look for him.

"Hey, sweetheart," Zane says softly.

Ryker winces, like Zane's words disturb him.

I bring my hands up to my face and that's when all my memories come rushing back.

I stare at my heavily bandaged hand for several tense moments, my heart sinking in my chest with each passing second. I can't stop the tears that roll down my cheeks. "My hand. My hand," I say, over and over, as though they're the only words I know.

"It'll be okay, Mila. It's going to be all right," Zane soothes.

"Don't say that. Nothing is good or okay or all right," I moan. I shouldn't talk that way to Zane. He's only trying to console me. "I'm sorry, I'm sorry."

He smirks. "Hey, you're right. This sucks."

There's the Zane I know and love. "Thank you," I say quietly, feeling validated. I don't want to hear a bunch of consoling words that have no meaning or truth in them.

"Give it to me straight." I'm still groggy, but I need to know. Right now. "I want to know everything. Don't sugarcoat it."

"You had surgery," Zane says, stroking my arm. "The brunt of the force hit your knuckles. It broke a few bones in your hand that are now held together with wires and pins. The bones should heal without a problem. But you also ruptured a tendon and that's what the doctor is most worried about. When a tendon is involved it takes longer to return to full hand function. Worst case scenario, full finger movement never returns. That's probably not the case here, but you should know it's a possibility. The doctor is hopeful that extensive physical therapy will result in a full recovery."

"A recovery that means I can function like a normal person or a recovery that means I can play the piano professionally again?"

I can see the sorrow in Zane's eyes, telling me what he can't put into words. "It's too soon to say, Mila. It's not a yes, and it's not a no. Time will tell."

I press my lips together. With sheer will power, I stop my tears and pull myself together. I'm not going to break down with an audience. Not again. The lingering anesthesia and the pain meds are messing with my ability to think clearly. Controlling my emotions is tough.

"Thank you for telling me the truth," I say, my voice trembling.

Zane reaches out, running his fingertips over my cheek. I love his quiet reassurance.

"I'm so sorry, Mila," Ryker says, subdued. "I had no idea you were still there. I thought you'd left. I didn't look before I slammed the door. I didn't know your hand was there. I didn't mean for this to happen and I can't apologize enough. I never wanted anything like this to happen, I swear. It was an accident, a terrible accident. I would never . . . I would never . . . do that to you."

Ryker sounds more like himself again, the spin-doctor politician who can smooth talk his way out of anything. I much prefer this side of him to the cruel-humored slayer of dreams.

Ryker might be a lot of things, but I know he wouldn't physically harm me on purpose. It's not how he operates.

I want to lash out and blame him—and I almost do. It's on the tip of my tongue. I'd like to tear into him and destroy him. But it won't change anything. What's done is done. My chest heaves with a long sigh. "I know it was an accident." I don't sound very forgiving, but the words have left my lips. They weren't easy to formulate.

"I'll cover all of your medical expenses and you'll have the best physical therapist money can buy," Ryker says. "You'll play again, Mila. I know you will. I know it's your dream, the only thing that truly matters to you."

The room is dead silent for several beats.

"No, it's not," Zane says quietly.

My eyes lock with Zane's. He knows me, even after the short time we've had together.

Ryker flinches like he's been hit. "You don't know her like I do." He can't help but sound churlish when he speaks to his brother.

"Not now, Ryker," Zane says firmly.

I close my eyes. I can't deal with this. *It's too much.*

Zane leans in close to me. His hand caresses my forehead, moving the hair out of my eyes. I love the comfort. There are so many things we need to talk about. His silence during Ryker's accusations spooked me. I know it's just his way, and I don't believe anything Ryker said, but I'm still consumed with uncertainty about our relationship and I don't like it one bit. *This is too much.*

"She wants more in life. So much more. The piano is not her only dream," Zane says almost inaudibly, and I wonder if Ryker heard.

"You don't know what you're talking about, Zane. You never do."

Oh, he heard. Even in this tender situation, he can't stop poking at Zane. Irritation stirs within me, a gathering storm. *Too much. I can't do this.*

On the other hand, Zane is reminding me that I have always wanted more in life, that the piano was not my only dream.

He understands me. He's right. I do have another dream. Love, marriage, children. Having that dream come true revolves around him. It's ours for the taking. And I want it.

But it doesn't take away the devastation of losing everything I've worked for, though. Not even close.

Zane runs his fingers through my hair, smoothing it out. I'm grateful he's at my side. I love his touch, the way he expresses his love through his ministrations.

"Leave her alone, Zane. Let the poor girl get some rest."

But I can't deal with Ryker's constant barrage. Can't he let it go for the moment? My life is a disaster and he doesn't have the decency to cool it.

This is too much.

Zane and I need time alone. I need him to explain his silence earlier today. Or was that yesterday? I don't even know what time it is, much less what day it is. I need to think things through. I can't do it with a fuzzy head.

"I called your parents," Zane says, his voice soft. "They'll arrive this evening, only two days earlier than planned. Your brother's coming too."

Thank goodness. I need them. "Thank you."

The pity in Zane's eyes overwhelms me. He knows, like I do, that this is probably a career-ending injury, the closing of a chapter in my life.

I can't do this. My hand is throbbing, but not as much as my heart. It's aching in a way I've never felt before.

I turn onto my side, my back to Ryker and Zane, and burst into bone-wrenching sobs, the kind that physically hurt, the kind that involve every muscle in my body. I don't want to break down, but I don't seem to be able to control myself. I blame the drugs, even though I know the current circumstances are really at fault. My entire body shakes with the force of my sobs. I cry so hard I can barely catch my breath.

Zane rubs my back, a show of comfort that I desperately need. Even though I feel and appreciate his comfort, I can't stop weeping.

I. Can't. Stop.

When my convulsing cries don't end, when it's clear I can't control my emotions, I hear Zane say to Ryker, "Call the nurse."

The nurse rushes in, slightly alarmed by my mental state.

I am too. I'm overwhelmed with waves of anguish that are washing over me as regularly as the waves hit the shore.

She puts something in my IV. I feel it hit my veins as it trails up my arm in an icy path. It brings me the relief I need. The world around me disappears and fades away, giving me a blessed respite.

I'm awakened by my mother's sweet voice.

"Hello, you must be Zane. I can't tell you how happy I am to meet you. I wish it was under different circumstances, though."

I open my eyes to see Zane engulfed in a motherly bear hug. I'm presented with my mother's sweatsuit-covered backside. Zane is facing me, looking like a man who won a gold medal, but can't believe it's true.

It hits me that he's never experienced motherly love. Not that he can remember, anyway.

Awkwardly, he lifts his hands from his sides and wraps his arms around my mother, returning her overexuberant hug. Perhaps I should've warned him. If he's with me, my family will accept him wholeheartedly and love him as though he's one of us. I don't know if he's ready for so much love and acceptance.

No need for him to remain silent here. This is a safe zone.

Ryker's nowhere to be seen. I'm relieved he finally left.

My eyes are so swollen, they hurt, and my throat is scratchy. The muscles in my neck are strained from crying so hard and my head is pounding. I think the loss of a dream deserves a little pout. I'm allowed.

I'm the next one to be embraced by my mother, followed by my father, and Martin, my brother. They surround my bed and cry with me.

Mom runs her hand over my forehead. "You'll play again, Mila. I know you will. Nothing can stop my baby girl when she's determined to do something."

"Are you kidding? Remember that summer she wanted a treehouse? Our Mila hounded me until we built it together. It took us days, but she never gave up or said she was too tired. When she wants something, she works until she gets it. If she's told it's impossible, my girl will find a way." Dad holds my good hand, patting it softly.

"Seriously. A whole lotta babysitting hours went into that baby grand of hers. I still can't believe she saved up enough to purchase it." Martin rubs my arm. "You got this, Mila."

I smile through my tears that I still can't seem to control. I didn't let Zane encourage me earlier. But I let my family lay it on thick. I soak it all in, knowing it could all be false hope. But I don't care. Somehow, I'll tap into that determination inside me. Right now, it feels elusive.

I glance at Zane. He's standing back, watching the scene before him with serious eyes.

"Zane, get over here. You're practically part of the family now," Mom says. "Our Mila can hardly stop talking about you. You've made our girl so happy. If Mila loves you, then so do we. That's how it works."

He moves forward with reluctance, taking the seat next to Mom. She puts her arm around him, holding him close.

Zane had his father while growing up, but a family circle is foreign to him, and it shows in his subdued expression.

"You picked a handsome one, Mila." Mom sends me a thumbs up. "This guy's a stud. You two will have beautiful children."

My cheeks grow hot.

"Mom, don't embarrass Mila," Martin warns.

Dad pats Zane on the back. "She's just trying to make me jealous. Keeps our marriage alive." He laughs heartily at his own joke.

While my family volleys lighthearted jokes back and forth, I find myself observing Zane unnoticed.

He doesn't laugh or even crack a smile. The look in his eyes can only be described as haunted.

Finally, our eyes meet. We stare at each other, our faces somber. His eyes burn into mine. I'm surprised I don't catch on fire from the heat of his stare.

The simple truth hits me hard. Something is terribly wrong.

Has Ryker caused a rift between us? Exactly what I swore he couldn't do.

No, I don't believe any of Ryker's accusations against Zane. Of course, Zane doesn't know that. Does he realize I know Ryker is a master at twisting the truth?

Zane has not confirmed or denied a single thing. But we haven't had a moment to ourselves to talk, either.

For the first time, I begin to wonder if I could be wrong about Zane Martel.

Maybe he's not who I think he is.

The thought enters my heart like a painful sliver.

chapter twenty-eight
♥
Two weeks later

I STARE AT the vases of flowers crowding my dining room table, almost all sent to me by my symphony cohorts. Most were accompanied by a card, filled with get well wishes. Many reminded me I'll be back in no time at all.

Hope can be so deceiving. Especially when faced with reality.

I constantly remind myself I'm not alone. I have a huge support system. Yet, here I am feeling lonely, trying to convince myself I'm fine.

I'm not.

Mom, Dad, and Martin were here with me for about a week and a half. Mom and Dad had planned to stay longer, several weeks to a month, if needed. But Mom became ill with the flu. Dad thought it was best to take her home to let her rest. Now he's coming down with it too.

So, here I sit. Alone. I never realized how excruciatingly slow time passes. Sixty seconds make up a minute. Sixty minutes make up an hour. The cast has to stay on my hand for six weeks. Four more weeks to go. Twenty-eight more days. Six-hundred and seventy-two more hours.

Might as well be forever.

My phone rings, startling me out of my stupor.

"Mom? Hi, how are you feeling?"

"Not so good, sweetheart." She breaks into a coughing fit, hardly able to speak.

"How are you, Mila?" Mom croaks. "Are you okay?"

"I'm fine, Mom, really. Don't worry about me. Just get better." Such a lie.

"No sign of coming down with the flu?"

"None at all. All the antibiotics they pumped into me must've strengthened my immune system and helped me fight it off."

"I'm so glad. You don't need any more on your plate." Mom holds the phone away as another coughing fit overcomes her. "I wish you would've come home with us, but I'm glad you have Zane. It's a relief to know you won't be alone, sweetie. Is he back yet?"

"Not yet. Any day now, I'm sure."

Do I have Zane? I don't know for sure. I hate my doubt, but it's there, creeping around my soul. I don't express my feelings to my mom. She'd just worry.

"Get some rest, Mom. No more talking, it's making you cough. Take it easy. I hope you'll be feeling better very soon."

We hang up, and I let out a heavy sigh. The last two weeks have felt like two years. That's how it goes when I have nothing to do but heal.

I've been taking lots of walks through the streets of San Francisco to help stave off depression. I take a new route every day to keep things interesting.

If I don't get outside right now, I'm going to plummet. I grab a hat, sweater, and sunglasses and head out the door.

I manage at least five miles, pushing myself hard. My blood is pumping through my body and my heart is beating steadily. The sun on my skin somehow grants me peace. I'm trying to maintain a positive frame of mind, but it isn't easy.

It's a daily struggle. The Great Big Dark, as I've nicknamed depression, takes over from time to time. But I'm giving him a fight. I won't let him have me. It's like we're standing in a boxing ring, each in our respective corners. I'm determined to deliver the knock-out blow. So is he.

When I was released from the hospital, I didn't return to Ryker's penthouse. Instead, I went with my parents and brother to their hotel to convalesce until I was able to care for myself.

Living with only one working hand is harder than I imagined it would be. Simply getting dressed, feeding myself, and managing my personal hygiene presents a daunting challenge.

Mom left me with a freezer full of easy-to-make food. Thanks to her, I won't starve or subsist on take-out. Since she left three days ago, she has called every morning to help keep the Great Big Dark away, but now that she's getting worse, I can tell talking on the phone is tough. I hate that she's so sick. I feel like she worked so hard taking care of me that she wore herself out, making her resistance low. It makes me feel guilty.

I try not to think about the piano. My fingers itch to play again, to fly over the keys, to produce the music of my soul.

The doctors are doubtful. I plan to prove them wrong. No, I *will* prove them wrong. I have to hang onto hope or I have nothing.

I round the corner and see a man standing on the doorstep of my apartment. My heart rate quickens, when I think it's Zane.

It plummets when I realize it's Ryker. I didn't know he was still in town. I'm still angry with him for deliberately causing issues for Zane and me.

Amongst other things. Like the cast on my hand. Trying to let that one go, though. It's not easy.

"Hello, Mila."

He's holding a shaking Arthur in his arms. Artie is the only reason I approach to talk to him. Otherwise, I'd turn and walk away. Artie's dog bed sits on my doorstep, along with his food, water bowls, and a bag of dog food.

Artie starts to wiggle out of Ryker's arms when he sees me, emitting a high-pitched cry. I rush forward and hold him, keeping my injured hand away from his excited movements. He licks my face, my hand, my arm, greeting me and letting me know he missed me. I'm just as happy to see him. It takes him several minutes to calm down and relax in my arms. He sniffs at my encased hand, curious about the cumbersome monstrosity.

"I know. I hate it too, Artie." I hug him to my chest. There's something about this sweet dog that calms my soul. I needed this. He makes me happy, and I need to do things that make me happy right now. Desperately. I'm hanging on by my fingernails. The Great Big Dark wants to be my roommate.

I keep insisting I live alone.

I turn my attention to the person—who can barely be called a human being—watching our reunion. "What are you doing here, Ryker? Have you come to destroy more of my life under the guise of saving me?"

He mulls that over. "No, of course not. I'm here because Arthur misses you. He stands by the door all day and all night, waiting for you to return. He's hardly eaten. I guess you could say he's miserable without you."

"I get it. So, you want me to take care of your dog while you finish your business trip in Japan?" The gall.

"No, I won't be returning to Japan. I'm sending another employee in my place. As for Artie, I'd like to give him to you, that is, if you want him. To be honest, we've never really bonded. You seem to love him, and he adores you. I know you'd be a good home for him."

Tears prick at my eyes. "Yes," I say right away. "Yes, I would love to have him." He'll be my very own little ray of sunshine. I understand why hospitals allow visits from therapy pets. They make a difference to a patient's mental health. I need that right now, more than anyone realizes.

I nuzzle Artie's head with my chin, love burgeoning inside me. Me, Artie, and Zane, we're a trio. But the third leg of our stool is missing. And I'm falling over without him. I miss him desperately.

I study Ryker. There's something different about him and I can't quite figure out what it is. One thing I know for sure, his demeanor is strangely downcast.

"Can I speak with you?" he asks.

My mind races as I try to make sense of this visit. I can't handle any more drama. I'm struggling to keep my head above water.

"Why? So you can destroy more of my dreams?" Am I talking about Zane or the piano? I don't think he knows. Neither do I.

He shifts uncomfortably. Do I detect a bit of guilt? I'm sure it's a new emotion for him. "No, it's something else. It's important."

He brought Artie to me, so I guess I can at least speak to him for a few. "Yeah, okay. For a minute. I'm *super* busy."

If he detects my blatant sarcasm, he doesn't let on.

I unlock the door to the new place I call home. I call it my palace. It's a standard one-bedroom apartment. Nothing special. But I'm on my own again and free of any obligations to Ryker. That alone makes it the most wonderful palace in the world.

Shortly after I was released from the hospital, I enlisted my brother to go to Ryker's penthouse to gather my belongings. My father found me this apartment and rented it on a month-to-month basis. They moved all my stuff in, organized it for me, and here I am. My baby grand is still at Ryker's penthouse. I don't want it here. I couldn't bear to see it every day.

My family wanted me to return home with them to Twin Falls to take some time to regroup and figure out what to do next.

But I have unfinished business here in San Francisco.

The unfinished business is Zane.

They understood. I knew they were disappointed, but they supported me anyway.

The thing is, I didn't tell them what had happened. I couldn't bring myself to talk about it. I didn't want to shed a bad light on Zane or give my family a reason to dislike him. Hence, Mom thinks I have Zane, the man I'm crazy about, to look after me.

I'm not positive that's true anymore. His silence says so much. It makes me wonder if everything is still okay between us.

I regret not spilling my guts to her and asking for her advice. I usually tell her everything. But I'm dealing with too much right now. It's overwhelming.

I know staying here is a risk. But I must know if there's anything real between me and Zane. I can't leave until I get my answer. Believe me, I'm already questioning the wisdom of my decision. After all, he's the only thing keeping me here now.

"This is quaint," Ryker says.

Translation: This sucks.

"It's horrible. Just say it." Especially compared to his luxurious penthouse.

"No, that's not what I meant. It's . . ." He pauses. "Okay, yeah, it's horrible."

"Did that hurt terribly?'

"Did what hurt?"

"Telling the truth."

"Mmm, it's not so bad. Not my usual style, though."

I think we finally understand each other, Ryker and I.

"You're hopeless and I pretty much hate you. Tell me what you want to say that's so important and get out."

A flash of anger doesn't cross his features at my words. He's still a touch sheepish around me. Good. He should be.

He's also done with me and has probably already moved on to other nefarious schemes. I wish it were easy for me to move on from the mass devastation he created in my life.

"Have you heard from Zane?"

Sore subject. "Not recently." I haven't seen him since that tense moment in the hospital when he looked at me with fire in his eyes, the moment doubt invaded my soul.

I was discharged from the hospital the next day. I received a text from Zane shortly thereafter. He tried to call, but I was taking my first challenging shower with a plastic-covered cast. So, I missed it. Something I deeply regret.

Zane: I'm being sent overseas. Emergency mission. Have to leave within the hour. Not sure how long I'll be gone. Really bad timing. Can't get out of it. We need to talk when I get back. I can explain, Mila, I promise. Please let me. Take care, heal, and enjoy your time with your family. Everything will be okay. I love you.

I responded with a simple *Be safe. I love you and I'll miss you.*

There's an ache in the pit of my stomach with Zane gone. I long to hear his explanation. I want to get it out of the way so we can return to the way we were.

At least, that's what I'm hoping for. Maybe I'm a fool.

Other than a beautiful vase of roses and a get-well card, I haven't heard another word from Zane.

Nothing. Like he disappeared off the face of the earth. It's killing me. A long, slow, torturous death.

Was Ryker right when he said leaving was Zane's talent? Has he left me?

I hope I haven't made a huge mistake. Without him, I wonder what the heck I'm doing here in San Francisco.

"We tracked Zane down."

"No surprise there. That's your specialty." This time, my sarcasm is not lost on him.

"He's been out on assignment, some overseas mission where he doesn't have cell service."

I hide my stunned reaction. I'm relieved to hear he doesn't have cell service. Maybe that explains everything.

I hope.

"We had to go through official military channels to reach him. He's on his way home now."

"How did you manage that?"

"If there's a bereavement in the family, the military is

very cooperative."

Wait. What? Heat rushes to my cheeks. "Bereavement?"

"Yes. That's why I've been trying to reach Zane. My father passed away two days ago. The funeral is tomorrow. Zane ought to be there. I was hoping you'd heard from him."

Stunned again, my lips form a silent O. Zane is going to be overcome with grief. His beloved father meant the world to him.

Now I understand Ryker's current expression as well. Grief has a way of making an appearance on people's facial features.

"You mean *our* father, not *my* father. Right?" I'm always inclined to defend Zane. He needs someone on his side.

"*Our* father," Ryker snaps, sounding irritated.

Oops. There's the real Ryker, shining through.

"Will you let him know the funeral service is at two PM tomorrow? I wanted to make sure I've made every effort to inform him. Otherwise, he'll accuse me of cheating him out of *our* father's funeral."

He assumes I'm still in contact with Zane, that even without cell service he's somehow keeping in touch.

Nope.

"But the military did give him the message, right?" I ask.

"They said they did. They said he was on his way home. But I haven't heard a word from him."

"I'll send him a text. But I can't guarantee he'll receive it."

"Thank you. You're more than welcome to attend the service tomorrow. My father liked you."

Zane will need support—and I want to see him. "I'll be there."

"I appreciate that. It's been a tough couple of days."

I'm only thinking of Zane when Ryker lost his father as

well. It's not a time to hold grudges. "I'm so sorry for your loss." So trite, but I don't know what else to say.

He takes out a business card and jots down the address of the cemetery. Huh. Another business card from Ryker. I'm so lucky.

"Graveside services only." Ryker pinches his nose to control his emotions. "I'd better go. Lots to do."

He leaves in a hurry, not even giving Artie a last glance.

Or me.

I know he's mourning and distracted.

But I can't help myself. I say to the thin air, "My hand, you ask? It's healing, but I might never play the piano again. No worries, it was only my lifelong dream, no big deal." I let out a fake, fluttery laugh.

"Pain? Hey, on a scale of one to ten, it's only an eight. Hardly hurts at all." I wave my good hand in the air.

"Oh please, stop apologizing, I forgive you for slamming that heavy door on my hand. I know it was an accident, don't give it a second thought." I manage a fake smile.

"By the way, thanks for exposing Zane's true colors. He was only the love of my life. It didn't really hurt all that much."

Artie looks at me with his huge dark eyes. He whines as though he's expressing sympathy.

"It doesn't matter, does it, Articus? We don't believe that brute. We still love Zane. Even if we do require an explanation."

I collapse onto the couch, holding Artie close. The Great Big Dark tries to take over, but I keep him at bay.

Only just.

chapter twenty-nine
♡

I ARRIVE AT the cemetery early. It's a beautiful resting place. The perfectly manicured grass is a vibrant green and the entire area is dotted with mature trees.

My eyes search the area for Zane. I don't see him.

I texted him last night. I debated over what to say, how many details to include. In the end, I kept it simple.

Me: So, so sorry about your father. Funeral service is at two PM.

I don't know if he received it. I haven't heard back. I hope he'll be able to make it home in time. He would be devastated if they held the service without him.

A crowd has already gathered at the graveside, quietly visiting and taking turns to sign an elegant guestbook. Soft organ music plays from a hidden device.

Ryker approaches when he sees me. He hugs me tightly. "Thank you for coming, Mila. Come sit with me."

I hug him only because of the circumstances. After the funeral, the truce is over.

There are six chairs in the front row, designated for family. I agree only because I'd like to sit with Zane.

Debra is already seated. She's wearing a sequined black number with thigh-high slits up the sides. The only thing that makes it appropriate for her husband's funeral is the color. In every other way it's entirely inappropriate for her age and the occasion.

She looks me up and down. "Too bad about your hand, Mila. But there are so many other things you can do with your life. Things that really matter."

I lean down to her level. Which is low, very low. "Or I could marry a well-to-do man and live off of him."

A Kleenex is tightly gripped in her fist. She wipes at her eyes, even though there are no visible tears to mop up.

Her mascara is perfect with not a smudge.

"Aren't you clever?"

"I'm learning," I tell her, and take my seat.

Ryker turns toward me, casually placing his arm around the back of my chair. He quietly whispers in my ear, "Did you hear from Zane?"

"No, I didn't. I hope he makes it in time. Did you hear from him?"

"No, nothing."

And yet, he went ahead with the funeral service. As though it didn't really matter if Zane was here or not. The thought makes my blood boil. At least he put forth effort to notify him. But he should've waited until he knew Zane could be here for sure.

As we begin the opening hymn, a Jeep screeches to a halt on the street.

And there he is.

My stomach flutters at the sight of him. I take a deep breath to calm my racing heart.

Zane exits the car wearing sunglasses, black suit pants, and a white dress shirt. He walks around to the passenger side of his jeep and grabs his suit coat. He puts it on as he walks toward the service. He pulls a black tie out of his pocket and wraps it around his neck, tying it as he approaches.

That's Zane for you.

He straightens his tie and buttons his suit coat as he arrives under the canopy where everyone is seated, looking refined and polished, and like he didn't just finish getting dressed as he approached. The man can wear a suit, the suit doesn't wear him. Despite the somber occasion, he looks amazing. A little thinner, his skin more bronzed, but amazing all the same.

Due to his sunglasses, I can't see his eyes. The firm set of his lips and the knit of his eyebrows expresses his mood, though. He's upset, naturally. I know his grief runs deep, much more so than he's letting on.

When he looks in my direction, he does a double-take and goes completely still. Promptly, he turns away. He doesn't approach or take a seat. He remains standing.

It's then I realize how it must look to him. I'm sitting with Ryker in the family section. And he has his arm around my chair, not around me, just around my chair.

From Zane's point of view, it's a minor technicality.

Ryker did this on purpose. I know he did. He's still in the game. And I fell right into the trap.

When I stand, Zane looks my way. I motion with my good hand toward my chair, inviting him to sit.

He shakes his head in the negative ever so slightly, his jaw joint flexing like he's gritting his teeth. It's a response I've only seen twice. Now, and that horrible moment in Ryker's penthouse. It's so unlike the Zane I know.

I stand for a few more minutes, unsure what to do. I want to go stand by Zane, but I'm not certain he'd welcome my presence. He looks unapproachable, his expression hard. I'm not going to make a scene at his father's funeral.

There's nothing left to do but sit back down.

This isn't how I saw this going. I wanted to be here for Zane, but I'm completely thrown by his demeanor. I knew he'd be grief-stricken, but I didn't know he'd be standoffish.

The funeral is a blur. I hear nothing as I sit there with my heart in my throat. All of my doubts have been confirmed.

Memories wander through my mind. Zane's hands running through my hair as he gently brushed my long locks. Riding a cable car with Zane while hanging off the sideboards. Walking through Chinatown hand in hand. Dancing with Zane while cooking chili. Watching Jeopardy. Shopping for colorful trinkets for Ryker's penthouse. Riding pedal boats at Stow Lake. Jumping on Ryker's bed and sharing our first kiss. Sharing that crazy kiss when he responded to the bomb-threat at the Golden

Gate Bridge. Eating Lucky Charms for breakfast. Kissing wildly in a dark storefront while dressed to the nines in our symphony attire.

I want that life back. I want Zane.

I want his laugh, I want his kiss, I want his smile. I want his bare abs and chest to stare at me as he walks around in jeans and jeans alone.

Am I wrong to want him? Is there a valid explanation he can offer me? Is he a thief? A stalker?

Do I believe Ryker or Zane? The thing is, Zane hasn't given me a story to believe or not to believe.

Just radio silence.

The accident took everything that'd happened beforehand and placed it on the back burner.

Now I'm back to that horrible moment. That moment when Zane looked me in the eyes and said, "I can't," meaning he couldn't explain. He had nothing to offer me.

What am I doing here? I'm here for Zane and if I don't have him, there's no reason for me to be here.

When the service is over, I remain seated as Zane stands next to his father's coffin. He stands there a long time, saying his final goodbyes. I watch his lips move silently as he speaks to his father. I watch as he reaches out and pats the coffin a few times.

Then he turns to leave.

Without acknowledging me.

I follow him to his Jeep. "Zane, wait."

He does everything he did when he arrived, only in reverse. He removes his suit jacket, takes off his tie, and unbuttons the top few buttons of his dress shirt.

His face could be made of stone. I've never seen him like this. Of course, I've never seen him devastated by loss, either. He shared a strong bond with his father, his only real family. I can't imagine how he must be feeling.

His eyes look down at my heavily-casted hand. "How's your hand?"

With everything that's going on, that's his first

question. He's concerned about me.

In that moment, I'm sure I'm not wrong about him.

"It's healing. Thank you."

"Good. I've been overseas on assignment. No cell service. Sorry I couldn't call. I've been worried about you."

"I'm glad you made it home in time to be here."

He nods. "Me too." He scrubs his face with one hand. "All night flight. I've hardly slept in two days. Barely made it here in time."

"You must be exhausted."

"Yep." He looks down for a moment. "So . . . you're here with Ryker?"

Doesn't he know me well enough to know I would never go back to Ryker? "No. Just being polite after his father died. Temporary truce."

I swear, he could be a statue. Or turn me to ice with his glare. "My father just died too, Mila."

Slip of the tongue, I want to scream. *That's not what I meant.* But there's no time to speak.

He turns abruptly, gets in his Jeep, and drives away, his tires screeching.

Stunned, I stand there in his dust, wondering what just happened. I threw out an olive branch and he rejected it.

He's upset, he's consumed with grief, he's exhausted. This isn't normal behavior for Zane. In my heart, I know this.

Regardless, everything inside me plummets, like I crash landed and hit the earth hard and fast. I feel blackness descend on me, invade me.

I'm a throbbing mess. My hand is throbbing and my heart is throbbing.

Worst of all, the Great Big Dark just signed a lease to join me in my apartment.

I can't fight it anymore. I now have a roommate.

TAYLOR DEAN

chapter thirty

♡

FIVE DAYS PASS. Five days of sitting in my apartment, mindlessly watching TV, never wearing anything besides pajamas. The same pair.

And ice cream. Lots and lots of ice cream. Straight out of the tub. Who needs a bowl? They come in serving-sized tubs for a reason. I have to prop the tubs in between my feet to open them one handed. Where there's a will, there's a way.

No more walks. No more sunshine. I keep my blinds firmly shut, the drapes closed, my butt on the couch, my eyes on the TV, and the lights off.

I had Lucky Charms for dinner last night. They remind me of Zane. They were even better than the popcorn I had for dinner the night before.

Artie's always on my lap, my partner in crime, my only friend. He's my lifeline, my thread of sanity. Without him, I'd be lost.

I tell myself I'm recovering, that I need to rest. Who am I kidding? I'm wallowing in the depths of despair, the valley of the shadow of death. I'm not on vacation, I've built my summer home there.

I heard from Zane once. Once! He sent a text shortly after the funeral.

Zane: I'm so sorry, Mila. Forgive me. Really tough day. Crazy busy with legalities. Will see you soon. As soon as I can. We need to talk. I love you. So much.

Not a peep since. Nothing. Nada. Zip. Zilch.

I know he's busy. With his father gone, I imagine dealing with his estate and working through the changes to his father's company are extremely complicated. There's so much to do when someone passes. It's a time when all you want to do is grieve. Instead, there's mounds of small details to take care of.

But is he really so busy that he can't make an effort to see me? To check up on me? Another text. A quick phone call.

Anything. I only want a crumb.

I stayed here to give us a chance. He says he loves me, but his silence speaks louder than his words. Maybe I've already received my answer and it's a big fat NO. Maybe that's what his silence means.

Did Ryker reveal things Zane didn't want me to know? And now that I do know, does he figure the game is up and it's useless to even try? Was everything a lie? Was he simply trying to one-up his brother?

I don't know. I'm speculating constantly, trying to reason it all out. I have too much time to dwell on it. My imagination is my worst enemy.

There's only one thing I know for sure. Zane is not here, and I'm all alone. I've lost everything.

So, I'm having a pity party. And no one is invited.

Without Zane, the injury to my hand feels like a death sentence, like I no longer have a life. I'm useless and washed up. I peaked early. It's all downhill from here.

I probably shouldn't have portrayed such a brave face to my family during the time they were here. I gave everyone the impression I could handle this major setback.

I can't.

I should have told them about my worries over Zane. I assured them he'd be here taking care of me once he returned from his overseas mission. Of course, I didn't expect the way events have played out.

Mom and Dad are both very ill now. Mom's cough turned into pneumonia and Dad has bronchitis. Neither one of them feels like talking on the phone, understandably. They're on antibiotics and are telling me they'll be fine soon, not to worry. Martin's on a business trip. I don't want to bother them with my *poor me* sniveling. So, I've kept to myself.

The Marin Symphony found a replacement pianist. A little too quickly. They flew her in from Russia, so I wasn't exactly easy to replace. Just quick.

Life goes on. For everyone except me. I've come to a screeching halt.

I've never felt so alone and forgotten. Abandoned and overlooked. Yep, I've succumbed to the Great Big Dark. He loves me and keeps me warm at night.

No one cares that my hand is injured and my dreams are ruined. The Martel men have their own lives to worry about. I'm history. Someone they ruined and forgot about.

They've probably already moved on to another sick and twisted competition.

I grab the remote and flip through the channels. When I come across Jeopardy, I flick the TV off and stare at the blank screen. For a long time.

What is duped by a stalker?

I rub my forehead in a circular motion. This is what an all-time-low feels like. I know I need to do something to save myself. But I don't have the energy. All I want to do is watch TV and fade in and out of sleep.

I need help. I should reach out, call some of my symphony friends. Plan a lunch date. Some retail therapy.

But I don't want to. That's the catch-22 of the Great Big Dark. It's like I'm drowning and no one's there to save me. Yet, if I scream for help, I know someone will come. They'll pull me out and I will be fine. The thing is, I don't want to call out for help. I want someone to notice and come to my rescue of their own accord.

Notice me. Save me.

It's not a healthy viewpoint. I know it's self-indulgent. But knowing that changes nothing. It is what it is.

The longer no one comes, the further I sink into the water. My head is covered. I've been underwater for days and I'm powerless to save myself. It's like my hands are tied behind my back.

I hate the Great Big Dark, and yet I embrace him and

hold him tight. Because I don't have anything else.

I grab another tub of ice cream from the freezer and indulge in the only happiness I can find.

When my phone rings, I nearly jump out of my skin. It's been eerily silent for so long, I hardly recognize the ringtone. I have no voicemails and no texts. Nothing. It's enough to make a girl feel invisible.

Ryker's name flashes across my screen. The devil incarnate is calling.

"What do you want?" I ask, my voice sounding like a croak at three in the afternoon.

"Mila?"

"Why does that surprise you? That's who you called. Or did you butt dial me?"

"Are . . . are you okay?"

"I'm fantastic. Never been better. Why wouldn't I be? If you can't answer that, you don't deserve to be speaking with me." My voice shakes with emotion, betraying me. Tears are never far from the surface these days. Okay, constant. Same difference.

"I, uh . . ."

"Never mind. Why are you calling me, Ryker?"

"You sound weird. What's wrong?"

"Really?" I ask, heavy on the sarcasm. What could possibly be wrong?

"Really. You don't sound like yourself."

"I'm not myself. Things have changed in my world."

"I know they have. I'm sorry about that."

"So you've said."

"I mean it."

"Why the phone call, Ryker? Please get to the point." I'm positive he didn't call to check up on me. He never does. No one does.

Oh man, I'm sinking fast. In the self-pity pond.

Ryker is silent for far too long.

"Hello?" I say.

He clears his throat. "Listen, the reading of my father's

will is tomorrow morning. Will you go with me?"

Is he serious? "Why would I do that?"

"I would love to have you by my side. I need a friend. That's all."

No, he doesn't. He wants Zane to see us together. He's so transparent. The twisted competition hasn't ended.

"And you think I fall into the category of friend?" I curse my trembling voice. It announces I'm on the edge.

No, I'm not on the edge. I'm freefalling toward the ground.

He's quiet again, this time for several moments. "What's wrong with you?"

Does Ryker actually have a perceptive bone in his body? Who'd a thought? "Do you really want me to answer that? You would probably regret it."

"Mila . . ."

"What?" My tone is challenging.

"Will you go with me or not?"

I bow my head, my thoughts whirling. If I go, I will have a chance to see Zane. Maybe afterward I'll have the chance to corner him and demand to hear an explanation. I'm torturing myself, but I need to hear Zane's side of the story from Zane's lips. I can't give up on us until that happens. Is Zane the bad guy Debra and Ryker purport him to be? I don't think he is. I can't turn tail and run back home to Idaho until I know without a doubt.

The only way to know is to face Zane.

That means I have to take a shower and get dressed, which seems like a lot of effort. I don't know if I have the energy. It's something I need to do, though. If I don't pull myself out of this rut, I might never get out. No one's going to do it for me. Prince Charming doesn't exist.

Well, he does, but he's dealing with settling his father's estate—and grief. He's busy. He can't hop on his white horse and save me.

And maybe, just maybe, he's filled with regret because he let himself get entwined in sibling rivalry. Maybe he's filled with guilt and can't face me.

There goes my imagination again.

"Sure. I'll go with you."

"Thanks, Mila. I'll pick you up at ten-thirty."

"No, I'll meet you there. Give me the address." I jot it down on a soiled napkin and toss it onto the cluttered coffee table. Then we hang up.

I contemplate taking a shower, but a new episode of Judge Judy is on. And the couch is really comfortable. And getting up is so hard. My body feels like it weighs a ton.

I might not ever get up again. I have no reason to, anyway. Other than tomorrow morning, that is. If I decide to show. Why should I go after Zane? Shouldn't he come after me?

Yes. Yes, he should.

chapter thirty-one

♡

THIRTY MINUTES LATER, there's banging on my front door. I curl up tighter, pull my blanket over my head, and ignore it. I don't feel like getting up or seeing anyone or talking to anyone. I only want to wallow in the dark world of nothing.

"Mila, I know you're in there. Open the door."

I breathe in and out deeply. It's Ryker, the dream slayer. Fantastic.

I let him bang on my door for another five minutes, to see if he'll give up.

He doesn't.

"If you don't answer, I will break down the door. I'm not joking. Remember? I don't joke. So, let me in right now."

I shuffle to the door and throw it open. "Or what? You'll huff and you'll puff?"

"Does that make me the big bad wolf?"

"If the shoe fits."

I navigate the minefield of my palace, return to my comfy couch, and pull my blanket up to my chin. Artie resumes his position cuddled up at my side. We're a pity party team.

Ryker slowly enters the apartment, stepping over the bags of garbage that are stacked up in the foyer. I have the feeling he wouldn't call my home a palace. He looks in my kitchen, distaste marring his features. I didn't expect him to love my new decorating style. It's where you let all of your takeout and pizza boxes clutter the countertop. It's a great look.

I gave up on the healthy freezer meals my mom left me. Instead, I've been indulging in all sorts of fast food. Anything that's batter-coated and fried in oil is my new best friend.

Ryker deliberately stands in front of the TV, his eyes perusing the stack of garbage on the coffee table, his lips turned into a frown. When his gaze lands on me, there's little change to his disgusted expression.

Artie climbs closer to me, shaking in my arms, his whine piercing the air.

"He never did like me," Ryker says.

"Can't think why." I wipe a few tears from my cheeks. They fall unbidden. All the time. It's the norm, rather than the exception.

I sit up. "You're blocking my view. I haven't seen this episode."

"Where's Mila and what have you done with her?"

"Ryker, was that a joke? If so, it wasn't very funny. Try again."

"What are you doing?"

"I'm recovering. You slammed a door on my hand after you ripped my heart out of my chest. Remember? Think hard. I'm sure it'll come back to you."

He walks forward and tries to grab the remote out of my hand. We struggle for a bit, but he wins. He flicks the TV off.

"I was watching that."

"How long have you been watching that?"

I do a quick mental calculation. "Oh, about five days and four hours."

"Maybe it's time to give it a rest." He approaches a window and yanks open the drapes.

My eyes squint from the sudden bright light. "Now I'll turn into a gremlin."

"My dear, you already have."

He removes his suit coat and starts to roll up his sleeves.

"I think you should leave. I don't even know why you're here," I tell him. Perhaps guilt, the great motivator.

"I don't know why I am, either. Don't question it and

everything will be fine."

He opens a window, letting a fresh breeze into the apartment. He grabs the garbage can and starts picking up all the trash piled on the coffee table. The only survivor is the napkin with the address on it for tomorrow. He hangs that on my fridge with a magnet.

"Ryker, please stop."

He casts me a raised brow. "Make me."

I sink further into the couch. "I'll pass."

"That's what I thought."

When he's done with the coffee table, he moves to the kitchen, doing the same thing in there.

I remain firmly planted on my couch, with no intention of getting up. There's a permanent scowl etched into my features. Not sure it'll ever fade. Turns out, my mom was right. If I distort my face long enough, it'll stay that way. I thought it was just something mothers say to make their children behave.

Ryker's gone for a while as he disposes of all the trash in the parking lot dumpsters. I consider getting up and locking the door, shutting him out, but I can't make my legs move.

When he returns, he searches a few closets until he finds the vacuum. He proceeds to not only vacuum my apartment, but to dust it. Then he cleans the bathroom and the kitchen. He even mops the floors. There's a reason why his penthouse was always sparkling clean. He must scour it all the time. Probably on a daily basis.

No wonder he's so good at it. Surprise, surprise.

When he's done, I hear the shower turn on. At first, I think he's still cleaning in there. Then I hear him say, "Right now."

I look up to find him standing in the hall with his finger pointed to the bathroom. "Get in of your own free will and choice while you have the chance."

"You wouldn't dare."

"Try me."

Uh, no. I get up and walk toward him. "I was going to take a shower today anyway."

"Were you?"

"We'll never know for sure now, will we?"

"Just get in."

I decide to ask him the same question I asked Zane. "Tell me something, Ryker. Are you the good guy or the bad guy?"

"Bad guy," he says with no hesitation whatsoever. "That won't change. Don't expect it to. Now get in the shower and don't come out until the grease from your hair has melted down the drain. It might take a while."

"You're a mean man."

"Proud of it. Now quit stalling."

"Will you wrap my hand for me?"

"You can't do it yourself?"

"I don't know. I haven't tried. But I can't get it wet. How am I supposed to wrap it one-handed and make it waterproof?"

"Oh my gosh. You're such a baby."

But he wraps my hand for me anyway. He does a really good job too. And he's gentle. He ignores the tears falling down my cheeks as if they aren't there, which suits me fine.

I take a long, hot shower while contemplating Ryker's actions. I once loved him, but those feelings have long since been replaced with . . . let's just say, very unkind feelings. I don't know what's happening right now on the roller coaster of my life. I only know it's an odd turn of events.

It makes me realize that most people are not all bad or all good. We all have our strengths and weaknesses, our own set of life experiences that shape us.

Ryker's done some bad things, but here he is, helping me when he sensed I needed it. So unexpected. Like a wardrobe malfunction, his good side is showing.

I exit the bathroom with wet hair, dressed in fresh

pajamas. It doesn't make the Great Big Dark go away. But it sure does give him a run for his money.

My apartment is fresh, clean, and happy. Not at all how I want it. It no longer matches my mood.

Ryker's sitting on the couch, and there are two plates of take-out on the coffee table in front of him. Artie's in his dog bed, as far away from Ryker as he can possibly get. Maybe I need to pay attention to the message Artie is sending me.

Unfortunately, I already know the content of the message from firsthand experience. Ryker's an ogre dressed in a really nice suit. He might have a soft side, but he also has a mean streak inside of him that I'd rather not tangle with.

I join Ryker on the couch, pulling my blanket around me as though it will protect me from him. He flips on the TV and we eat our dinner in silence that's only marred by the muffled sounds of my tears. I can't help myself. The tears fall easily and often lately.

Ryker again pretends like he doesn't notice. That's okay, if he tried to comfort me, I think I'd slap him.

He cleans up our plates, rolls his sleeves back down, and dons his suit coat.

"Are you okay?" he asks.

"Do I look okay?"

"No, but I know you. You're stronger than you think. Give it some time and you'll eventually be okay."

Will I? Why does everyone have so much faith in me? Why don't I have faith in myself?

He folds his arms, his stance wide. "I've been wondering about something and I can't let it go. If you don't mind my asking, what happened to us, Mila? Where'd we go wrong? I'd really like to know."

That's a loaded question. "We're different, Ryker. We're just very different people."

"How so?"

"I like butterflies, you like scorpions."

He looks down at the floor while he thinks about what I said. "Was that sort of a metaphor-slash-joke?"

"Yep."

"Clever. I'll have to remember that one."

"Want me to write it down on one of your business cards for you?"

"Nah. Thanks, though."

That one went right over his head.

Ryker approaches, sitting on the coffee table in front of me. He reaches for my good hand and holds it in both of his. Oh no, here it comes. The last-ditch effort to win the competition, I mean, the girl. I will never know if he is really sincere.

"One more thing, Mila. I have to ask. And I'll only ask once. Is there still a chance for us? Any at all?"

I study his face and realize he's utterly serious. Huh. That surprises me. I gently slip my hand away from his. "Nope. Not in this lifetime. No reason to ask a second time."

He stands, adjusts his suitcoat, and puts distance between us. "That's what I thought. Can't hurt to check, though."

Business 101. Learn how to hide your feelings. He has that one mastered. It's like I told him the time of day. "Can I ask you something?"

His eyes narrow. I wonder how many secrets are hidden inside that brain of his. "Sure."

"Did we really meet by chance?"

"No."

His answer is immediate. The truth at last. So refreshing.

"You pursued me just because your brother was obsessed with me?"

He shrugs. "It started out that way, but once I got to know you . . . the rest was easy and I found myself really liking you."

Okay. At least, part of it was real. "Then why accuse

Zane of trying to steal me from you when it was the other way around?"

"Why not?"

Why not, indeed. "Your mother taught you well, Ryker."

"Yeah, she's great."

"Is she?" He can't possibly miss my sarcasm.

"The best." Yep, he does.

"She's certainly loyal to her son." That's the only nice thing I can say about Freddy.

"Yes, she is. By the way, this, today, never happened. If you tell anyone, I'll deny it."

"I wouldn't want anyone to know you did something good."

"Exactly."

Wow. Humor and Ryker—it's worse than I thought.

I can tell he's ready to make his exit. "Ryker, wait. One more question. I really need to know. Is Zane the bad guy?"

He places his hands in his pockets and cocks his head to one side. "Do you really like him?"

"Yes, I do."

"Why?"

I splay my good hand. "Lots of reasons you wouldn't understand."

He breathes in and out deeply. "Okay, whatever."

"Is he the bad guy?" I ask again.

"Of course he is. Always has been. He's the bane of my existence."

"But is he really the bad guy? Tell me the truth."

His lips smirk as he mulls it over. "Yes," he says with raised shoulders. "See you tomorrow morning."

Without further explanation, he grants me a nod, turns and leaves.

chapter thirty-two
♡

IT FEELS GOOD to be dressed. I guess I'm still human after all. I'm wearing a black pencil skirt, a white silky top, and a light sweater. I normally wear a button-up blouse with my skirt, but I couldn't button the buttons. I tried to accessorize with a necklace, earrings, and bracelets, but I couldn't manage the clasps. At least I tried. Yay, me. This is my attempt to join the world of the living. I have one foot in the Great Big Dark and one foot in the world. I don't know which way I will step next. I'm teetering.

I meet up with Ryker in the law office foyer.

"Well, look at you. I knew the real Mila was buried under there somewhere," Ryker says when he sees me. "Huge improvement."

"Yesterday didn't happen, remember? Therefore, I don't know what you're talking about."

Ryker gives me a quick hug and pats my back. "Oh yeah. Forget I said anything."

We have an odd sort of truce between us. I'm still angry with him, and yet he came to my rescue yesterday. It was sweet and weird all at the same time. I don't know what to think of it, or of him.

"Thanks for coming today, Mila. I'm glad you're here."

I'm not here for Ryker, but I don't need to say it. He knows.

"Zane hasn't made an appearance yet. He should be here soon. Shall we go inside?"

"Okay."

It also feels good to be out of my palace for a change. Still, my heart is heavy. Zane's silence is weighing on me. I know he must be swamped, but doesn't he realize what total silence is doing to me?

Zane must know how much I need him right now.

Doesn't he? I know he must need someone as he deals with grief. Plus, he needs someone who will be on his side and I'm the first person in line. With my arm raised high in the sky. We can be there for each other. We can heal each other.

And yet we're not. We're both alone as we deal with the cards life has dealt us.

We enter a small conference room that's downright luxurious. My feet are sinking into deeply padded carpet. The air conditioning is locked on the keep-ice-frozen setting. Light is streaming in through the large windows, accentuating the polished cherrywood furniture. Expensive paintings dot the walls. The décor gives the impression of money, or maybe it represents someone who would love to take your money.

We're directed to sit at a large table with cushy chairs. I sit next to Ryker, but it's more than obvious we're not together as a couple. He's at least a foot away and doesn't have his arm around me. Nor will I let him pull that stunt again.

Zane knows me. Surely, he'll know I'm here for him. Won't he?

He didn't seem to know at the funeral. Maybe this is a mistake.

Debra flanks the other side of Ryker. She's consulting with one member of the team of lawyers they have with them. Whispering constantly. Planning to do evil things with her riches, no doubt.

"Are you ready for this, Mila?" Ryker asks, a gloating tone to his voice.

"What do you mean?"

"You do realize this meeting will not go well for Zane, right?"

What?

"It's the reading of his father's will. Of course it will go good for him." I assume today won't go as well for Ryker and Debra as they think it will.

"Remember the ugly little word called embezzlement? Dad knew about it. It's all hitting the fan today."

Oh. That's the real reason Ryker brought me here. He wants me to see Zane get cheated out of his inheritance. He wants me to have a front row seat to Zane's humiliation.

I'm an idiot. I should've known better.

Even when I think I'm going in with my eyes wide open, Ryker has an ace up his sleeve. Today it's not about making Zane think I'm with Ryker. It's about me seeing Zane's life crumble around him.

"Is that why you wanted me here?" I hiss.

"You need to see and hear this. It'll make you see things as they really are. Your eyes need to be opened. I'm doing you a favor."

"Don't pretend this is about me."

I don't want to be here. I shouldn't be here. I don't belong. This was a huge mistake. I need to leave. Now.

I scoot my chair back with the intention of making a hasty exit, when a side door into the room opens.

Zane walks in, looking every inch the high-class executive. I've seen him in a suit twice. Once at the symphony and once at his father's funeral.

Today is different. He's somehow more elegant, more commanding. He's wearing a crisp tie with a matching hanky in the pocket and silver cuff links catch the light at his wrists. He looks nothing like my man with the easy smile who loves to wear ripped-at-the-knees jeans. Today he exudes authority and confidence, like he's a force to be reckoned with.

Of note, he's utterly serious, but he doesn't look nervous or scared, or like he has a reason to be.

I doubt Ryker knows what will really happen during this meeting.

Zane's eyes zone in on me immediately, like I am the thief of his gaze. It's as if nothing else matters to him, as if no one else exists. His expression softens and turns tender.

He always looks at me like that and I love it.

He gives me a brief nod, and the fleeting look of tenderness is gone in an instant as his poker face returns.

I know he wasn't expecting me to be here. I wanted to be here for him, but he certainly doesn't look like he needs me—or anyone. He's his own man and can handle himself.

Do I know the real Zane? I'm not so sure. I'd like to think I know the real man, and the executive in the fancy suit is his façade, his work persona. I wish I knew for certain.

Then, from the same side door he came through, two armed security guards enter the room and stand on either side of Zane.

His expression doesn't change or show any emotion whatsoever.

Something inside of me dies at the sight. Why are they here? Will Zane soon be under arrest? What's going on?

An older man enters the room from the same door we entered. "Edward Hanover, Mr. James Martel's attorney," he says, introducing himself. "Shall we begin?" He motions with his hand toward Zane. "Please, Mr. Martel, have a seat."

Zane sits at the head of the table. The security guards step forward and stand on either side of him.

I glance at Ryker. His lips curve into a half smile and he laughs quietly. Debra has a small evil smile on her face too. They're enjoying this.

I scoot my chair toward the table. I can't sneak out now. Whatever happens, I'm here for the duration.

Mr. Hanover says, "Mr. James Martel asked that the following video be shown upon his death, at the reading of his last will and testament. Without further ado, we shall begin."

He picks up a remote and blinds slowly cover the windows. He presses another button on the remote and a screen lowers at the front of the room.

I peek at Zane and find him staring at my broken hand that's resting on the table, a deep frown on his face. Yeah, I want to say, I feel exactly the same. It sucks. Big time.

And I'm drowning without you.

I can't think about it now. I'll fall to my knees and break down, sobbing like a baby.

The lights in the room lower. The lawyer presses another button on his remote and James Martel appears on the screen, stealing our attention. It's a James I never knew, since I met him after his stroke. He's sitting at a desk, a suit covering his slim frame.

"Hello, my beloved family. If you're watching this, it means I'm gone. Believe me, I'm as sorry to hear that as you are." He smiles into the camera.

Light laughter trickles around the room. When I glance at Zane, I notice he doesn't find his father's words amusing.

James is handsome, vibrant, and authoritative in all his mannerisms. He looks and acts like a man who is used to being in charge of his domain. I wish I had known him like this, when he was lucid and coherent.

He loved Zane, and I do too. We would've had a lot in common because of our feelings.

"The doctors tell me it's time to slow down and that's not something I've ever done. Not sure I know how to slow down, but I suppose I'll learn. I thought I'd start with putting my affairs in order. My blood pressure seems to enjoy going as high as it possibly can, and my cholesterol must be best friends with my blood pressure, because they like to join each other."

Again, a few people chuckle. Now I know where Zane gets his sense of humor.

"Regardless, I'm still here and I'm taking the proper precautions to get my health under control." He pauses as he looks down at a few pieces of paper on his desk. "My lawyer can read you my will, which is in perfect order, I assure you. But it's a whole lotta mumbo jumbo no one can understand, but him. So, I'm here to explain in layman's terms exactly what will happen to my estate upon my death."

James shifts in his chair, resting his forearms on the desktop. "Before I begin, there's a few things I'd like to say to my family. Zane, I'll start with you. The first year of your life was a rocky one for me. Even if I could do it over, I wouldn't change my reaction to losing your mother. It devastated me and I was a lost soul if ever there was one. I loved her like I've never loved anyone in my life and that's just the way it was. No regrets. Zane, as our son, you were my only comfort. I'm guilty of loving you too much, if that's possible. To this day, every time I look at you, I remember her, and it comforts me. You've been the joy in my life. Zane, I love you, son. Know that I'm with your mother and we're watching over you. Every second, we're cheering you on. Never doubt it. Don't spend all your time mourning me. Move forward with your life and be happy. That's all I ask."

If Zane's not going to burst into tears after that, I am. But when I glance at him, he's still stone-faced.

James continues. "At any rate, lucky for me I met someone new. A beautiful young lady named Debra. She charmed me from the get-go and saved me from the depths of despair. I'll always be thankful to her for that. She's stood by my side all these years and supported me every step of the way. We've had some strife here and there, but she's always been my biggest champion. I love you, sweetheart."

Debra flutters and wipes at her non-existent tears.

Strife? Yikes. I'll never understand why James stayed with Debra. He was certainly loyal.

"Debra also blessed me with another son, making me feel like the luckiest man in the world. Two boys to carry on my name and follow in my footsteps. I couldn't have been happier. Ryker, I love you, son."

Wait, that's all Ryker gets. I see where the problems

arise. I don't think James even realizes what he just did. He said so much more to Zane than he did to Ryker. Unwittingly, perhaps, but I don't doubt that Ryker noticed. Of course he did. I'm sure he's noticed all of his life. It smacks of rejection, because everything James said told him that his father loves Zane more.

However, if Debra clearly doted on Ryker and wanted nothing to do with Zane, it makes sense that James felt he had to make up for Zane's lack of love from his mother figure.

It's like the age-old riddle. Which came first? The chicken or the egg?

Which came first? James' preference for Zane or Debra's obvious dislike of Zane? I don't know.

Regardless, what a mess. Everything wrong in this family could've been resolved with love.

Love is the answer. It almost always is. It solves so many problems.

TAYLOR DEAN

chapter thirty-three
♡

JAMES GOES ON. "That being said, the love I have for my family is what makes the reading of my will so incredibly difficult."

"Yes, it does," Debra says aloud.

All my talk about love comes back to bite me, because I'd like to smack her in the face.

"It came to my attention not too long ago that Martel Investments was coming up short financially. The numbers weren't adding up. After an in-depth investigation, we realized someone was skimming money from the business. We knew it had to be someone on the inside, someone who I trusted, who had access to my personal accounts."

James pauses for effect.

"Imagine my shock when I realized who it was, and that it was someone close to me. It was enough to destroy my faith in the human race."

"That's right," Debra says as though her husband is really here and she's having a conversation with him.

"Let me say right now and let me be very clear, my will reflects the aforementioned situation. The person responsible will not be happy with their inheritance. It grieves me to do this, but it must be done. I will not, nor will I ever, tolerate dishonesty."

I close my eyes. I can't stand seeing Debra and Ryker gloating in my peripheral vision.

So, Zane is guilty. That's why he's not speaking to me. He doesn't want to fess up. It doesn't seem possible. The man I knew would never do such a thing. I hang my head.

"All right, let's get on with it," James says next. "Ryker, I'm going to start with you. You've been vice-president of Martel Investments for quite some time and you've done an excellent job. I'm very pleased with your efforts. It is my wish that you remain in that position. The new president will have a say in this decision, but that's my wish. I hope it will be honored. Forty percent of my estate belongs to you. Use it wisely, son."

Debra inhales loudly. "Vice president?"

And I think *really*? Vice president and forty percent of the estate is not enough for her son? If the estate is going to be divided three ways, does this mean it's not going to be divided equally?

Thankfully, James can't hear her objection. "As you know, due to my health, I stepped down from being president of Martel Investments not too long ago. I publicly named the board of investors as the acting president until a new president could be named. Prepare yourselves, this will come as a surprise, but they have been my front men, so to speak, my smokescreen. My son, Zane Martel, has been the acting president and will remain as the president of Martel Investments upon my death, which, unfortunately, has happened since all of you are watching this video."

This time, no one chuckles at his gallows humor.

"Zane has been a silent president up until now, but that changes immediately upon my death. Due to family strife, Zane was unable to operate in the company without interference. We both thought it best for his position in the company to remain silent, but ever-present. He will need to complete his commitments to the Army, but I assure you he can handle both. Zane, my son, my company is yours, along with sixty-percent of my estate. This keeps you as the majority stockholder, and therefore, in control. I know you can do it. I have faith in you."

Debra rises to her feet, her chair hitting the wall behind her. "What? That's not possible. He's a thief. He's the one who was taking the money. It was him!"

The two security guards standing next to Zane stand at attention, alert and ready to act, if necessary.

The lawyer pauses the video. "I suggest you take a seat, Mrs. Martel."

"This is ridiculous. I won't stand for it."

Her lawyers whisper to her. I can't hear what they're saying, but she's listening to them.

"Mom," Ryker says. "Sit down. Let's hear the rest before you object."

"That would be a good decision. Shall we?" Mr. Hanover says.

Debra takes her seat. I swear, smoke is coming out of her ears, she's so mad.

James unfreezes and comes to life again as the video continues.

"This brings me to my dear, sweet wife, Debra. I suppose you're wondering at this point where your inheritance lies. I will tell you what you already know. It's in a bank account in Switzerland, exactly where you placed it when you took money from Martel Investments and opened up a personal account for yourself."

"What?" Ryker says loudly, his hands clenched into fists.

"I have no idea what you were planning to do with it or if you had decided to leave me, but you have more than enough to live quite comfortably for the rest of your life. Consider it your inheritance, my dear. By the way, if you hadn't taken the money behind my back, you would've inherited a lot more. Ponder over that one for a while."

Debra lets out an odd sort of wail, half shock, half outrage. Ryker bows his head, shaking it with disbelief.

"As for the house, it's in Zane's name. I'm sure he will allow you to continue living there. As a matter of fact, I'm sure he will show you the same kindness that you have always shown him throughout his life."

Debra places her head in her hands.

"Mother?" Ryker says.

She doesn't answer.

"Ryker, I call upon you to take care of your mother and

see that she has all she needs. Debra, you have two options. You can accept your fate, or you can fight me on this and be escorted out of the room and arrested immediately for embezzlement. Your choice, my dear. I strongly suggest the first choice. Under the circumstances, it seems extraordinarily fair."

Zane nods at the two security guards and they move to stand behind Debra.

The game just changed.

I study Zane for a moment. The prince has taken back his kingdom. He doesn't look happy, even though he's won. It isn't a glorious victory for him. It's taken a lot out of him. It's the first time I notice how haggard he looks. His face looks ashen, even in this low lighting, and he has dark circles under his eyes.

"All right, that's it in a nutshell. Zane and Ryker, I implore you to work together and take Martel Investments to new heights."

The camera slowly pans out away from James' face, and we see a small purple gun being held to the temple of his forehead.

The entire room gasps. What? Was he coerced into saying what he just said? Is this some kind of joke?

The camera continues to pan out, and we see Zane holding the gun. He presses the plastic trigger and water shoots out all over James.

They both break out into laughter. James leans toward Zane, wrapping his arm around his waist and hugging him tightly.

The camera pans over to Mr. Hanover. He shakes his head and laughs. "Their idea, not mine. I advised against it. But this is legal, I assure you."

The camera pans back to James and Zane. They're still laughing, James still has his arm around his son.

And that's where the camera freezes as the video comes to an end. We're left in stunned silence as we stare at the father and son on the screen, caught in an embrace, their laughter evident, frozen forever.

Debra turns and huddles in the corner, whispering with her lawyers. It sounds heated. I don't doubt she'll fight with everything she has to overturn James' will.

"All right," Mr. Hanover says. "Those were Mr. Martel's wishes in layman's terms, as he put it." He addresses Debra's lawyers. "Copies of the legal documentation are available for your perusal." To Zane and Ryker, he says, "Gentleman, I have some documents that need your John Hancock, if you will."

Zane and a dazed Ryker head to the front of the room. I imagine they're going to be busy for a while. I head for the exit, my mind whirling. I look upon Zane so differently now.

He's been the puppet master all along, the one pulling the strings. He was always several steps ahead of everyone else.

And he never told me one single thing.

No, he remained silent about it all and I feel betrayed. So many secrets. So many things he never told me. Honesty is so important in a relationship. He never lied to me, but he omitted a lot. It's so much to process and I'm not thinking clearly. I only know one thing. I want to escape, to get away and never look back. I don't know what I was to Zane, but it wasn't what I thought. It makes me want to cry my eyes out.

Debra gets to her feet and turns her evil gaze on Zane. "The joke's on you, Zane."

I pause in the doorway.

"Is it?" Zane says coolly.

"Yes. I was only taking what was rightfully mine. I knew he'd give everything to you and leave me out in the cold. I'm not stupid. Did you think I wouldn't cover my tracks?"

Her lawyers quickly whisper in her ear, and she seals her mouth shut. She just incriminated herself before she could catch her slip of the tongue. Oops. Until this moment, she could've claimed James was wrong, that it wasn't her taking the money.

She lifts her chin and starts again. "You set me up, framed me, made your father believe it was me who took the money. I have all the proof I need to show that you're the one who stole money from your father's company," she spits.

Her lips pull away from her teeth and she resembles Freddy Fazbear in ways that make me shiver.

"I took my proof to the board of investors and smeared your name. I'm here to tell you, they'll demand your resignation. You won't be president for long."

I fully expect her to say, *I'll get you my pretty. And your little dog too.*

Zane says nothing.

"By the way, I took the proof to your father as well."

Zane can't hide the surprise that washes over his face.

"Oh yes," she continues. "I presented all of my evidence and I swore that if he didn't do something to set prosecution in motion, I would. I told him I would see to it that you spent your sorry life behind bars. It's irrefutable evidence, Zane. You don't stand a chance. I will see to it that you go down. Hard and fast."

Her eyes bulge as she speaks, like she's about to burst if she doesn't say what she wants to say.

"Would you like to know how your father responded to the news that I had the power to ruin his precious son's life?"

"How?" Zane says. "Please share."

"He responded with a stroke," she hisses with vehemence.

Zane turns and faces her fully, his face white as a sheet. "Excuse me?" His voice is low and threatening. I wouldn't want to be Debra right now.

"You heard me. A stroke, Zane. A massive stroke that led to his demise. I guess you could say the knowledge of your embezzlement scheme killed him. Sleep on that tonight," she snarls.

"What?" Ryker says. "Mom, what are you saying? Why would you do that to Dad?"

Zane stands very still, like a predator about to pounce on his prey. I wouldn't be surprised if he leapt through the air and attacked.

Instead, he nods to the security guards. "Escort the lady out immediately, please. To the door of her car and watch her drive away."

"You can't make me leave. I promise, I will fight this with every ounce of strength I have," Debra screams, losing all self-control. "I have proof it was you! Your father knew I could destroy you!"

The manner in which she'd framed Zane must've been highly alarming to James—enough to bring on a massive stroke. Or maybe it was the shock that she'd go to such lengths to hurt Zane that upset James so much. We'll never know.

Ryker's expression says it all. He's looking at his mother with new eyes, shocked eyes. "Mother? I don't understand. What are you doing?"

I think Ryker is experiencing that devastating moment when he realizes his mother isn't perfect. We all knew it would happen one day. That day is today.

It's about time.

Debra continues with her rant, and I can't listen anymore.

I feel so . . . betrayed. I know Zane's been overwhelmed these past several days and I understand. I really do. But my life is in shambles too. I tried to reach out to him. I got nothing in return. I didn't need much. Just a tiny crumb. A few words of reassurance.

I'm done.

I turn and slip out the door. No one notices. I didn't expect them to.

The tears start before I even reach the elevator. The wait seems interminable, so I take the open staircase in the center of the building. Architecturally, they are amazing, but it's not something I appreciate right now. I run down the stairs as fast as I can, my tears blurring my vision. I'm almost to the bottom when I hear my name.

"Mila, wait."

It's Zane. He's actually coming after me. I'm surprised he noticed I left.

I keep walking as fast as I can. I just want to get away. I'm not in a good frame of mind and facing him won't turn out well. My mind is a dangerous place right now.

I feel his hand on my shoulder, so I stop without turning around. "Mila, please."

He walks around me until we're face to face. "Mila, I'm so sorry. I've been facing twenty-hour days with everything that needed to be done and I didn't want to disturb you in the middle of the night and . . . Mila?"

He cups my chin and gently pushes my face up. He seems surprised by my tears. "Tears?" He caresses my cheek. "Tears?" he says again. "Hey, everything's okay. Please don't cry."

I'm finally with Zane, where I've yearned to be. I want to fall into his arms and let him comfort me like only he can. But I feel such a strange disconnect between us.

"Everything is not okay," I say quietly.

He seems taken aback as he studies my face. "Are you all right?" he whispers.

I blink my eyes heavily, tasting my salty tears as they dribble onto my lips. I don't answer his question.

"It'll all work out. I promise." He cradles my broken hand in his, running his fingertips over my cast.

"That's not a promise you can keep."

"Yes, I can. I can promise you happiness."

Can he? I don't know anymore. "Let me leave, please."

"Mila . . . I know we need to talk. I'm sorry this week has been so crazy. I haven't had a moment to myself, so much has happened, I . . ."

"I know. And I understand. I really do. It's a lot to

process, though. Please, I need to go."

He remains quiet and doesn't move. I look up at him and we share eye contact for a few moments. So much has happened over the past couple weeks, it's like we're strangers. We shouldn't be. We should've been clinging to each other amidst the trials in our lives.

His expression changes as he studies me. "Hey, are you sure you're all right?"

I'm still baffled that anyone can ask me that question and expect a positive answer. I shrug.

His posture rigid, he frowns. "Mila?"

Zane's eyes wander to the right of me as a deep voice interrupts us. "Mr. Martel, you're needed upstairs."

"I'll be right there." He runs one hand over his face.

He searches my eyes, his expression clouding. "I'm sorry, I . . ." He lets out his breath, frustrated at being pulled in so many directions.

I need to let him go. Free him. "Please, I really need to leave. Right now. I have to be somewhere."

I have an appointment with my apartment. It's waiting for me to go home and cry, stare at the walls, and sulk. Because that's my life now and I'm very, very busy doing it. Feeling sorry for myself is time consuming. His life is eventful. So is mine. In very different ways.

He doesn't step to one side, so I walk around him and practically run out of the building.

I doubt I'll hear from Zane Martel again.

chapter thirty-four

♡

I FOREGO A taxi, and walk the streets of San Francisco, my head down, my sunglasses firmly in place.

The tears won't stop. They. Won't. Stop.

I don't want to go home to my apartment. If I do, I'll spiral even further into darkness and I'm not sure I'll have the will power to escape.

I need to stay outside, keep walking.

I've never felt this way before and I don't know what to do. I need help. I've known it for a while, but I'm finally admitting it to myself, head on. Not even the fresh air or sunshine can shake my mood. The Great Big Dark has taken me over.

After walking for over an hour, I pull out my phone and search my contacts. I know what I need to do.

Seek help.

My finger hovers over my general practitioner's name. I've only seen her once when I had a sinus infection and needed antibiotics. But I'm still registered as a patient. Perhaps I can get in to see her today.

I make the phone call and I'm told she can see me today at three in the afternoon. I have a couple hours to kill. I find a restaurant and tuck myself into a booth, hidden from prying eyes. I force myself to eat and give my body the strength it needs.

I also force myself to think about everything that's happened in my life recently. I have to face my future, figure out what I'm going to do next.

Zane has his own life to deal with and he has a lot on his plate. That's the cold, hard truth. Time to face it.

I tried to stay here for him. I think that was a mistake.

Having Zane in my life is not the end-all solution to my happiness. I need to stop putting him in that category and take responsibility for myself.

I know what I need to do. I need to pack up and head for Idaho. It's what I should've done in the first place. I need my family. I need their love, their comfort, and their support to pull me through this difficult time. It's the only way out of the rut I'm in.

It feels good to think clearly.

I stopped taking my pain pills last night. I read that they can contribute to the Great Big Dark. It'll take time for the medication to leave my system. Then I'll see how I feel. It makes me wonder if I'll pull out of this easily without them. Except I know I can't put the total blame on the pills. Loss of a dream is a real downer.

Tylenol is doing the trick for my pain today, thank goodness. But I'm still groggy and out of whack. Emotional and weepy. I feel useless and invisible, like everything is wrong in my life and I have absolutely nothing to look forward to. I can't shake the feeling. Which is why I'm seeking help today, admitting my weakness. I shouldn't feel ashamed, but I do. Mental health issues have a stigma attached to them, but they shouldn't. It isn't fair to expect people to take care of their bodies, but keep quiet about their mental state, as if it's taboo.

At the appointed time, I grab a taxi and head for the doctor's office.

I don't have to wait long before the doctor enters the examination room.

"Miss Westerman, what can I do for you today?" She pauses when she notices the cast on my hand. "Oh, what did you do to your hand?"

I look down at the cast like it's an intruder. "I w-was involved in an accident and I b-broke it," I manage to say through a few sobs.

I told myself I would control my tears during the appointment, that I would speak to the doctor calmly and logically and explain how I'm feeling.

But I can't control anything. The tears flow down my face while my emotions make it difficult to speak.

"I see." She glances at my chart. "I saw you perform with the Marin Symphony once. You were amazing . . ." She inhales sharply. "Oh." She takes a seat, looking at me with new eyes. "So, how are you feeling?"

It's the moment of truth and I can hardly spit the words out. "I'm still in a lot of pain." Not what I meant to say at all.

"Physical pain?" she probes.

"Yes. But . . ."

"It's more than that?"

She's perceptive. But then, I suppose my tears make it obvious. I nod in the affirmative, still finding it hard to explain how I feel.

"Can you describe your pain?" When I don't answer right away, she adds, "Take your time."

I've come all this way. I'm here in the doctor's office. Now is the time to spill my guts. I have to do it. *I have to.*

"I feel . . . horrible and . . . I can't stop crying and . . . I don't know what to do." There. I said it out loud. It was harder than I thought it would be.

Her lips compress in a straight line. "Understandable. Tell me something, do you have a history with depression?"

"No, I've never felt this way before. It's hard to describe. I feel blank, as though part of me has been erased. I'm stuck in a big black hole and there's no way out and I'm surrounded by . . . despair. There's a weight on my chest and it's hard to breathe. Happiness feels foreign, like it's a lie, and everyone around me is just pretending."

"That's a pretty good description right there. I'm glad you came in today. The first step is always the hardest, but I want you to know you did the right thing. I can help. There are so many things we can do to get you feeling better. I need to ask you a few more questions first, okay?"

"Okay."

"Are you feeling suicidal?"

"I want to escape this feeling. But, no. I want to live."

"Are you still on pain medication for your injury?"

"I stopped taking them last night. Is it true they can contribute to this feeling?"

"It is. How's your pain? The pain in your hand," the doctor clarifies.

"Tylenol seems to be working today."

"Excellent. If you can, stay off the pain pills."

I nod.

"Besides your injury, have there been any other major changes in your life?"

I mull that over for a few moments, still embarrassed by my constant tears. "Yes. I think I've lost someone who was very important to me."

"A love interest?"

"Yes."

"Okay. That's a lot all at once. I believe what you are experiencing is situational depression. It can hit any of us at any time. Major changes in our lives can sometimes be very difficult to handle. So often we're convinced that life should always be happy, when that's simply not the case. Hard times come and go. The good news is that it will lift with time. It doesn't happen overnight and there's no magical cure. For now, I can give you something to help you cope."

"I don't want medication."

"It will help, and I think it's necessary right now. Just for thirty days, then we'll reevaluate. There's no need for you to be on medication for a long period of time."

I nod through the blubbery mess I am. She's right. It will help, and I do need it.

"I also think it would be helpful if you see a therapist." She glances at my hand. "This is a major change in your life. I think you need to talk it out."

"Okay. I think that will help."

"Will you be able to play again?"

"I don't know yet."

"I'm very sorry. You were wise to come in and seek help. You did the right thing. There's no shame in feeling down. We all feel it at one time or another, but it can get out of control. If things don't improve, I want you to call me right away, all right? Don't suffer alone. Reach out to loved ones or friends. Tell them you need help. Surround yourself with the people who love you. The worst thing you can do is keep this to yourself or isolate. Call upon family for help. This is a time in your life when people need to be there for you. There will be other times when they need you, but right now it's your turn."

"All right. Thank you."

I thank her ten more times before I escape her office, feeling validated and thankful for an astute doctor who took the time to listen to me.

I walk for another long while in the bright sunshine. I'm glad it's not a foggy day. The sunshine doesn't cure the Great Big Dark, but it makes me feel alive, like life isn't over.

Finally, I turn for home. It'll be getting dark soon, and I need to let Artie out. I'll take him for a walk while I fill my prescription. The doctor arranged for an appointment with a therapist for the day after tomorrow. I told her I would be making plans to go home to Idaho soon. She still felt I should see the therapist right away. The idea of unburdening myself of my toxic thoughts definitely appeals.

So, there it is. This is my life now. Instead of waiting for the handsome prince to save me, I saved myself.

The thing is, I still want the handsome prince.

Slowly, I approach my apartment, feeling worn out after all of my walking and crying. It's a good tired, though. I'll sleep well this evening.

As I get closer, I realize someone is sitting on my doorstep.

And it's not Ryker.

chapter thirty-five
♡

IT'S THE MAN who has stolen my heart. Maybe he's here to give it back. Maybe that's why I'm so down. I can't function without it.

When Zane sees me, he gets to his feet. He walks a few steps towards me, holding a bouquet of roses in his hands.

Zane. He's here. The prince with no princess.

Is he here to see if the shoe fits? There's not a glass slipper in sight. Maybe he doesn't need one. Maybe he's here to fight for me because he already knows I am the one for him.

If only.

My eyes are drawn to my small, fenced-in patio behind him. I can only see a slice of the scene through the open gate, but what I can see is magical.

A small round table boasts a pristine white tablecloth. Several candles are aglow on top of the table. Two dinner plates are covered by steel domes. I can also see a glimpse of more candles dotting my tiny patio. A string of twinkling lights crisscross overhead, forming a canopy of stars. Achingly beautiful violin music wafts through the air from a hidden speaker.

It's beautiful. As the sun goes down, it will be even more so. I'm stunned by his efforts.

The man, the music, the setting. It's everything I want, the touch of romance I need.

My eyes return to Zane. His expression is a mixture of sympathy, vulnerability, and tenderness. He also appears hesitant, perhaps wondering if I'll accept his grand romantic gesture.

I don't.

A flash of anger takes me by surprise. I didn't think I had enough oomph in me to conjure up anything other than my blah feelings. Perplexed, I turn around and walk away.

Something makes me stop after only a few steps.

I change my mind, walk a little further, and stop again.

What am I doing? I bring my good hand to my forehead and rub one temple with circular motions.

Zane is making an effort. I wanted him to come for me, and he has. Yet I'm a bundle of angry and confused and sad feelings. They're all inside me, jumbling around, each one vying for the opportunity to surface.

Slowly, I turn around again. Zane's still in the same spot, watching me battle with my emotions. There's a pleading expression on his face now, along with deeply furrowed eyebrows and slightly wild eyes.

I study him and see that the events of the past few weeks are written in his handsome features.

I haven't had it easy, but neither has he.

He's still in his suit, tie undone and hanging loosely around his neck, his top buttons unbuttoned, making me wonder how long he's been waiting for me. His state of undress only adds to his appeal, and makes me swallow. Hard. Man, he looks good.

My indecision over, I approach him. I stop walking when we're about two feet apart.

"Hey," he says.

I want to scream *Where. Have. You. Been?* But I don't. Instead, I return with, "Hey."

We stare at each other for what feels like forever. I absorb his lifeforce like a starving parasite. I want to latch onto him and never let go. At the same time, I'm angry, an emotion I wasn't expecting when and if Zane returned to my life. I don't want to feel angry. But I do. It isn't fair to him and what he's been through recently, though.

Zane breaks the silence. "I was worried about you. I've been trying to call."

I pull my phone out of my purse. I have twelve missed calls, all from Zane. The fact that he's been trying to reach me causes a warm sensation to rush over me. "I forgot to turn my ringer back on after the meeting at the law office."

He takes a deep breath, his chest rising and falling shakily. Is he anxious? Over us?

All I can think is *me too*. Is there still an us?

I squint in the face of the setting sun, trying to cover up the gloomy emotions taking over my features. "Why are you here, Zane?" It comes out much harsher than intended.

"To see you. I miss you like crazy."

Like crazy? That's good. That's so good. I love *like crazy*. "Have you been waiting long?" I ask with a peevish tone.

"A while. The truth is, I would've waited all day."

All day? For me? That's even better than *like crazy*. "Why now?" I whisper. "Why not three days ago? Two days ago?" I needed him so much.

"Life is finally calming down. Sorry I've been so swamped."

Swamped. My anger begins to deflate. He's right. He's been inundated with life changing events. He does look tired. I wonder if he's had much sleep. I don't know why tired looks good on him. So unfair. But he looks so good right now, I long to wrap my arms around him, to rest my head against his heart, to feel safe in his embrace.

"It's okay. I understand." I'm usually so independent. The Great Big Dark is really messing with me. I've been far too consumed with myself. I hate feeling so needy that I can't recognize his current responsibilities and give him space.

"No, it's not okay. I've left everything in Ryker's capable hands for the next while and I'm on leave from the military. I'm all yours."

"But . . ."

"You're more important to me than anything else, Mila."

I close my eyes, knowing it's exactly what I needed to hear. "Did Ryker send you?" My voice cracks, revealing my unsteady emotions. I need to know he's here of his own accord.

"He did pull me aside today, just before I left to go after you. He told me what he'd witnessed, said he was worried about you. It was what I'd already figured out after seeing you this morning. I came as soon as I could get away."

I let that sink in. "Hold up. Ryker is actually trying to help us?"

"Yep. Go figure. Life is changing. All around us, all the time. It's the way life works."

I look down at the ground. "Yes, it is."

"Mila, look at me. Please."

I do.

"Some of the life changes can be good. Really good. If you'll let them happen."

"Maybe." I swallow through a dry throat. "So, you're here to save the day? Is that it?"

I regret my words immediately. I'm not interested in a verbal sparring match. It's easy to toss around barbed comments with Ryker. He doesn't mean anything to me. Zane is different. Zane means the world to me. I only want tenderness between us.

He doesn't take offense. "I'm here for one reason and one reason only."

"Why?" I ask.

"Because I love you," he says with passion evident in every syllable. "I'm crazy in love with you."

Oh. He's not one to play games. If he feels it, he says it. It doesn't get any more tender than that. I absorb his words, let them enter my heart, hoping they'll chase away the darkness.

The darkness remains, but he just gave my anger a run for its money. How can I stay mad after that declaration?

"I can explain everything, Mila. Will you let me?"

"Yes, okay." I owe it to myself to give us a chance.

"I'm sorry I haven't been here for you," he says. "I

didn't know you were alone. I thought your parents were still here."

I shake my head in the negative. I'm going to start crying again. It doesn't matter. He already knows I couldn't stop crying this morning. If he truly loves me, he'll love me anyway, warts and all, nonstop crying and all.

"I didn't know you'd left the penthouse," he says.

"Haven't you been there?"

"No. After I returned home from my overseas mission, I grabbed myself a hotel. I knew Ryker wouldn't welcome me."

I cradle my hand to my chest. "After . . . everything, I stayed with my parents when I was released from the hospital. They helped me get set up here." I wipe away the stray tears that insist on falling.

Zane's already disturbed expression deepens even more. He doesn't ignore my random tears the way Ryker did.

"I thought you might return to Idaho with them while you recovered."

"That's my next step. I'll be returning to Idaho in a week or two," I say firmly. Not sure it comes across as firm when combined with my weepiness.

"Then why stay here at all?" he asks.

"I've been asking myself the same question." I press my sleeves to my face, solving the problem of having to constantly call attention to my tears. Sort of.

Zane doesn't politely avert his eyes. Oh no, he stares at me without apology.

"When did your parents leave?" he asks.

"They stayed for a little over a week. Mom came down with the flu, so Dad took her home. He has it now too. They're not doing too well. They've had a few complications, but they're going to be okay."

Surprise washes over his features and his entire body goes still, like his blood froze in his veins. "What?" he says in a harsh whisper. "You've been alone all this time?"

I look down at the ground again. "Yeah." My tears dot the sidewalk. I wish the ground would open up and swallow me whole. I feel so pathetic. I raise my chin, trying to put on a brave face.

"I'm so sorry, Mila. I had no idea."

I nod. "I know."

He studies me, his expression growing darker. He sees what I'm trying to hide, and I feel so vulnerable.

After a few moments of awkward silence, he asks, "How's your hand?"

"It hurts," I say bluntly. "All the time."

"But it's healing?"

"Yeah, I guess so. I see the doctor again in a couple of days." There goes my shaky voice. It's obvious I'm a mess, that I can't control my emotions. "You know what, Zane? I'm fine. I really am."

"I can see that," he says, deadpan. He doesn't say it sarcastically. Instead, his features are infused with worry.

"At least, I'm going to be fine. I might not be able to stop crying, but I have a path forward."

"I wouldn't expect anything different from you."

"Oh, Zane." I cover my face. "I don't want you to be here because you feel sorry for me, because you feel bad for the poor girl who lost everything. I want you to be here because you want to be here, not due to guilt or remorse."

His expression turns intense. "I'm here because I love you more than I've ever loved anyone in my entire life, more than you can possibly comprehend."

I stand there on the sidewalk, dumbfounded and blank, our second frozen encounter.

An older lady walks by with a tiny poodle on a leash. "Hey, if you don't want him, I'll take him."

Neither one of us laughs or responds.

"Will you join me on the patio? Please? We need to talk," Zane says with a pleading tone. "We need privacy."

He's right. Too much has been left unsaid. "Okay," I

say when I start breathing again.

This is it. The moment I've been waiting for.

Explanation time.

chapter thirty-six

♥

ZANE ESCORTS ME to my transformed patio, and closes the gate behind us. He puts my roses in a vase on the table, adding to the elegance of the décor and causing a sweet scent to waft around us.

He has me sit down, placing a pillow behind my back, and a light throw blanket over my lap, like I'm an invalid or something.

"Comfortable?" he asks.

I nod, dumbfounded by the royal treatment. I can't believe he's doing all this for me.

The sound of a barking dog at my patio door makes him pause. "Is that . . . Articus?"

"Yes, I'm sure he needs to be let outside." The door has a large window on it, but the blinds are closed.

"I'll do it." Zane holds out his hand. "Keys?"

He unlocks the door and Artie bursts outside to pee. Amazingly enough, he doesn't knock over a single candle. When he's done, he runs to Zane, jumping up and down in his excitement to see him.

Zane picks him up. "Hey, buddy." Artie is going nuts in his arms, hardly able to calm down. To me, he says, "Ryker's got you dog watching again, I see."

"No, he gave him to me."

"What? Articus is yours now?" Zane holds Artie up, so they're face to face. "You lucky dog, you."

Zane rubs Artie's neck while tucking him under one arm. He immediately closes his eyes and rests his head as though he's in a state of euphoria.

Maybe I just need Zane to do the same for me. If only that could cure me.

"Are you ready to eat?" Zane asks.

"Okay."

He lifts up the steel dome in front of me with a flourish. I look down and bite my lip. I want to laugh. So hard my stomach will ache. But I just don't have it in me. Instead, more tears spill down my cheeks at the memories his meal choice evokes.

Before me, is a heaping bowl of Lucky Charms.

"In memory of one of our first meals together," he says, subdued.

I don't think he expected tears to be my response.

He watches me with penetrating eyes, making heat rush to my face. Zane makes me feel *looked at*.

"You're not alone, Mila. I'm here and I'm not going anywhere."

He has no idea how much those words mean to me. I lower my head.

"Shoot, I forgot spoons. Mind if I borrow some?" he asks, trying to sound upbeat.

"No problem."

He steps inside my dark apartment. I think about what he's about to see, the conclusions he'll draw. He'll notice the pulled-tightly-closed drapes, the empty tubs of ice cream on the coffee table, my clothes piled around the room, and the makeshift bed on the couch. It screams *the person who lives here has given up on life*. He'll see and comprehend everything. A part of me wishes he didn't have to know about my struggles. But isn't that what love is all about? Loving someone during good times and bad.

When he returns, he places the spoons on the table. He grabs two small cartons of milk from a cooler tucked into a corner of the patio. I didn't notice it earlier. He takes his seat and settles Artie on his lap.

"Where's your baby grand?" he asks as he pours milk on his cereal.

"It's still at Ryker's. I don't want to see it."

"You still have one good hand. You could keep practicing."

I shake my head in the negative. "I don't want to.

Lately, I've just been . . . I mean, I'm really . . ."

"Having a hard time," he finishes for me.

"Yes." Why does it hurt to admit it? I feel so weak. It shouldn't be off-limits to admit to a bout with the Great Big Dark. Like the doctor said, a cry for help should be encouraged. It's the time when you need people to rally around you the most. I know that now. "My parents think you've been here with me. I didn't want to worry them, so I let them believe it was true."

"As a result, no one was here with you and you've been alone."

"Not completely alone. I have Artie."

He rests his forearms on the table. "I'm sorry I haven't been here for you. I should've known how down you would feel."

I shrug like it's no big deal. "You had your own problems."

"Mine were expected. Yours were not."

That's true. "I've lost everything. I literally don't know what to do with myself."

"And yet you stayed here in San Francisco. Why, Mila? Why stay here?" he asks again. "Tell me the truth this time."

"I stayed here for you."

His eyes blink heavily. "And I haven't been here."

"No."

"I'm here now. You're my priority, Mila. Nothing matters to me as much as you do."

"What about Debra and her accusations?"

He scoffs. "Debra's not an issue. Her irrefutable evidence is ridiculous. Everyone knows it. She skimmed nearly a million from Martel Investments over the past ten years. She needs to be happy with what she has."

"But the transition . . ."

"Is going smoothly. The hardest part is behind us. Stop worrying about me. Let's concentrate on you."

Even with Zane here professing his love, the Great Big

Dark hasn't lifted yet. But I think it will if I give it some time and allow people to help me. It's all about reaching out and admitting I need help. I can't keep this bottled up.

"Aren't you going to eat?" he asks.

"I can't open the milk carton."

His breath hisses between his teeth like he's disgusted with himself. "I'm sorry. I didn't even think of that."

He opens the carton and pours it on my cereal. We both begin to eat. I have to pinch myself to know this is really happening. I'm sitting in a beautifully romantic setting with Zane while eating Lucky Charms, of all things. There's something so perfect about this moment. It makes my heart squeeze in my chest.

"There's deli sandwiches, pasta salad, and fruit salad in the cooler, by the way. Lucky Charms are simply the appetizer."

They're not just an appetizer. They're a reminder of us. We both know it. In my emotional state, it's hard to tell if I'm pleased or not, so I say, "This is perfect, Zane. Thank you."

We polish off our cereal as darkness falls. My patio looks like something out of a storybook. Utterly charming.

Zane sits back in his chair, observing me thoughtfully. "You look gorgeous in the candlelight."

My expression must convey uncertainty, because he adds, "I think it's time for us to have a talk, to be brutally honest with each other."

"Okay." I look directly in his eyes, take a deep breath, and let it all out. "I needed you. And you weren't there."

"It won't happen again."

"You drove away from me. You left me standing on a curb with dust in my eyes."

"Biggest mistake of my life."

"Do you know how that made me feel?"

"I can imagine. I'm so sorry."

I shrug. "You can blame it on grief. I did."

"I could. But it's no excuse. The truth is I hated seeing

you with Ryker. I was angry."

"I was there for *you*. I thought you would need someone. I thought you would need *me*."

"I did. I needed you so much. Can you forgive me?"

"I already did." I hated that moment, but I also knew it stemmed from grief. I'm positive anger wasn't the driving force. "I saw a doctor today. That's where I was."

"And?"

"I . . . should be feeling better soon."

"Are you talking about your hand?" he probes.

"No." Why is it so hard to say? "I'm talking about how I've been feeling lately."

"How have you been feeling?"

"Um . . . pretty horrible." It comes out as a whisper.

"What did the doctor say?" When I'm quiet, he adds, "You can tell me, Mila."

It takes me a minute, but I finally blurt it out. "She said I have situational depression."

My announcement doesn't faze him. "Under the circumstances, it's not surprising. Have you struggled with depression in the past?"

"No. I mean, I've had ups and downs. Nothing like this, though."

"I'd like to take you home to Idaho as soon as possible, get you out of isolation. I'd like to stay with you, if you don't mind."

My face crumples with emotion. "I would like that." It's exactly what I need, to be surrounded by the people I love. "But, how can you . . ."

"I'll work it out. I'll stay with you for as long as you need me."

"That would be forever."

"Done," he says, his eyes intense.

I look down at my lap. A burst of happiness rushes through me. The sensation feels foreign, but very welcome. All I had to do was reach out. Help has always been there, waiting in the wings.

He hasn't moved from his chair or tried to approach me. "You're very far away." I long for physical comfort.

"If I move closer, we won't be talking anymore. And I know we need to talk right now."

I swallow and I'm pretty sure he hears it from across the table. "We do. I have so many questions."

"Ask them. Ask them all. I'll tell you everything."

I love those words. "But you didn't tell me anything about what was happening in your life. It was all a surprise to me."

"I'm used to keeping my dealings with Martel Investments secret. I've had to for quite some time. It was imperative that I do so. It's a hard habit to break."

"Do I know you, Zane? Who are you? The funny and casual man who loves to wear jeans and t-shirts and dance while he cooks? Or are you the stone-faced businessman who wears fancy suits?"

"Can I be both?"

"If that's who you are."

"That's who I am."

"And are you a man who wants to steal your brother's girl? Just to win? To spite him?"

"Do you think that's who I am?"

"No. It never felt like that."

"Trust your instincts. I promise, I don't play games when it comes to love. I would never do that to you."

"Is this love?" I ask, even though he's already told me he loves me twice. I want to hear it again, need to hear it again. And again and again.

"Are you ready to hear that answer? Because I won't hold back anything."

My heart starts to hurt because it's pounding so hard. I'm not sure what he means, but I think it means he has a lot more to say to me.

"Okay, we'll get back to that question. Tell me this, why didn't you say anything to me that night in Ryker's apartment? You wouldn't talk to me. I mean, now that I know everything that was revealed with your father's video, I understand why you couldn't say what was going on. But the rest . . . I don't understand."

"I realize how that must've looked to you and I'm sorry. I was so worried we weren't strong enough to survive Ryker's antics. The look on your face, the uncertainty from Ryker's accusations, it killed me."

"I just needed reassurance. I would've believed anything you said in that moment."

I swear his eyes glitter at me. "Thank you for that," he says in a raspy whisper. He leans forward. "You know what? The last thing I want to do right now is talk. I wanna kiss you senseless."

There's the Zane I know, saying the things I love to hear in his own way. I want his kiss, and his touch too. But he was right the first time. Once we start kissing, we won't be able to stop long enough to have a discussion. There are things I need to know before I can give myself to him in that manner.

"Talk first," I remind him.

He sits back in his chair, folding his arms across his chest, a picture of restraint. "Of course," he says in his business tone. "The thing is, I couldn't explain in front of Ryker. Anything I said would've been twisted around and thrown right back at me. Over the years, I've learned to respond with silence to Debra and Ryker. It's my way. It takes two to fight, and if I back away, the fun is over for them. Instead, I listen and learn as they reveal more than they realize. Every time."

He runs one hand through his hair and continues. "I'm sorry my silence hurt you. The truth is, I thought I had plenty of time to talk to you when Ryker was done with his tirade. He always fizzles out quickly. I knew I could explain everything in privacy later, but not right then, not with him watching and listening."

Zane gathers his thoughts before going on. "I didn't know that everything was about to change in a big way. I wasn't expecting what happened next. It was the worst moment of my life, seeing you hurt and in pain, and knowing what an injury to your hand meant. After that, everything caught up with us and spiraled out of our control. It feels like it's been that way ever since."

"Not anymore," I whisper.

"Not anymore," he repeats. "We're taking control now. I want this. I want you, Mila. I want to be here for your dark moments and your happy moments. That's what a relationship is all about; helping each other through hard times. As long as we're together, we can get through this."

My lips tremble as I'm overcome with emotion. But there's still one more question I need to ask, one more thing I have to know before we can move on.

"One more thing."

He exhales and looks down for a moment. "Go ahead."

"Is it true what Ryker said about you attending the symphony? You were there to see me? Several nights in a row? Before we ever met?"

He closes his eyes as though he's in pain. "I know how that sounds. But the answer is yes."

No. I cover my face with my good hand. "What does that mean?"

It should feel creepy. But it doesn't. It feels like the most romantic thing in the world. And yet I'm scared of his pending answer, because I don't want it to be creepy.

Zane approaches slowly and lets Artie jump onto my lap. He takes my hand away from my face and lowers it down.

With his eyes never leaving mine, he slowly removes his suit jacket and tie. I watch him with a greedy gaze. He kneels in front of me and holds my good hand.

"Is this okay? Because I can't stay away any longer."

I nod and curse my tears. Except they're happy tears now. I have a feeling what he's about to say is going to be good. So good I won't be able to bear the happiness that's about to enter my soul.

"What it means is that I'm exactly like my father," Zane says, in an emotion-filled whisper. "He knew my mom was the one for him long before he actually met her. He watched her for days before summoning up the courage to talk to her. I saw you perform for the first time, and I couldn't take my eyes off you. The way your fingers flew over the keys, the arch of your back, your smile when you were done performing. I've never felt so captivated in my life. I couldn't stop. I kept coming back for more. I simply wanted to see you. Just having my eyes on you was enough. This was right after Dad had his stroke. I needed something in the evenings, something to fill me. You became my obsession, the thing that brought me happiness during a dark time. I didn't even think about introducing myself. I was content to watch."

He gives my hand a squeeze. "Then I had to return to my military assignment. But I couldn't stop thinking about you. Every day, you were on my mind. I knew when I returned home, I had to try to meet you, and I planned to do just that." He shakes his head. "You could've knocked me over with a feather when I saw you in Ryker's penthouse that day. I couldn't believe Ryker went to the trouble of seeking you out. I was floored. I wondered how he could do that to me. And to you. My relationship with him is . . . messed up."

He reaches out, tracing my cheeks with his fingers, wiping away my tears. "Not only were you seeing Ryker, but you were practically engaged. I couldn't wrap my mind around it. When we started to click, I knew I was on dangerous ground. I tried to hold back, I really did. But when you told me your relationship with Ryker was over, I couldn't. I just couldn't anymore."

"I didn't want you to."

"I got that. Loud and clear, and I loved it. The thing is, there's a reason why I was so taken with you when I saw you at the symphony, that just seeing you in the flesh captivated me. I didn't know it then, but I know it now.

You were the one for me, my soulmate. Some inner voice was telling me you were the one from the very beginning. I fell in love with you long before I actually met you."

"And after you met me?" My voice shakes with emotion.

"Everything that's happened since has only confirmed what I've felt from the very beginning."

"And what's that?"

"That I'm knocked flat and turned upside down in love with you."

That's a Zane way of saying he loves me. I adore it.

"It's you, Mila, you. You're the love of my life, the one I want to marry, the one I want to have children with. I know you think your life is over, but you once told me you had another dream besides the piano. And I want to give you that dream. A houseful of children, made by me and you."

"Little urchins who get crumbs all over the place and call you dad?" I say, repeating what he said to me a while ago.

"You remember that?" He smiles. "Yep. That's what dreams are made of, right there." His face grows serious. "And if you can play the piano again, then wonderful. I believe you will, but if you can't, we can still find happiness in this life. More than you can comprehend. More than you can contain inside of you."

My entire body is shaking in response to his words. "I want that too. If I have that, I can be happy."

"You got it. I'm yours."

"But, Zane, we've known each other for about two seconds and . . ."

His fingers cover my lips. "I know. I know we need more time together. I'm fine with that. But when you're sure—because I already am—then I want to marry you and give you your dreams. I'm ready when you are."

I nod, because I can't speak.

Zane scoots closer and engulfs me in a tight hug. At

first, he just holds me. I rest my head on his shoulder and absorb his comfort, his strength. I wish an embrace could make the Great Big Dark disappear. If only it were that easy. Regardless, he infuses me with warmth. And warmth has the power to chase away the cold. The tiny pinpoints of light surrounding us make this moment entirely enchanting.

He leans back and cups my cheeks in his hands. And he finally kisses me. It's not a soft lackluster kiss. He presses his lips to mine and kisses me with all of his feelings evident in the forcefulness of his kiss, in the passionate nature of his kiss. I can feel his love in his actions.

I allow all of my insecurities to wash away, and I let confidence in our relationship take over. I encircle my arms around his neck.

Without breaking our kiss, Zane wraps one arm under my knees and one around my back and lifts me up, cradling me like a baby. Artie lets out a little whine at being disturbed, but repositions himself and remains on my lap. Zane holds me, swaying gently with the soft violin music. My head falls back as our kiss deepens and our mouths open to each other. He holds me so close, I don't know where he begins and I end. We're one, in our hearts, and in our minds, and in our love.

It's the moment when I know I'm going to be okay. The days ahead will be hard. But with Zane at my side, I can do it.

My dreams are not over. My life is not over.

This isn't the end.

It's the beginning.

This kiss, this amazing, heart-stopping kiss that is sending me into a realm of bliss I've never known, this is the tip of the iceberg.

I can't wait to delve deeper, to explore all aspects of my relationship with this man who has stolen my heart.

Something tells me I have a lot to look forward to.

epilogue
♡
Three years later

I SMILE AS I pull the piano keyboard cover closed, pleased with my progress.

I'm not quite back to where I was yet, but I'm close. My fingers on my left hand are still a bit stiff and can't hit the notes as fast as I'd like them to. Perhaps only the trained ear would notice. My doctor tells me to give it time. She believes I can do it and tells me the end goal is not to play the piano for recreation. Nor does it have to do with everyday mobility of my hand.

I've already achieved those milestones.

She wants more for me, and I want more too.

The end goal is to play for the symphony again. She won't quit until she sits in the audience to hear me play. Ryker wasn't kidding when he said he'd get me the best physical therapist money could buy. She's amazing and believes in me.

I believe in me too, and have every intention of making my new goal a reality. I will play with the San Francisco Symphony one day. Mark my words. It might be two years from now, or it might be five. But it'll happen.

However, other things are tugging on my time nowadays, and I don't practice as much as I should. I'm happy with the balance between my two dreams. I want both and I can have both. I'm surrounded by family members who support me.

I approach the stovetop and give the pot of spaghetti sauce a stir as the doorbell rings.

It's Ryker, joining us for dinner, as he always does on Tuesday nights.

I swing open the door. "Hi Ryker, come on in."

He's still in his suit, as usual, even though it's now

seven at night. He doesn't even look work-worn. Not a single hair is out of place. He catches the eyes of women all the time. He's dated about twelve more ladies since Zane and I married. He simply can't find The One. He's never sure and can never make a decision. Always falling, never the fallen. I know that side of him well.

"Is she already in bed?" he asks, without so much as a hello. He's holding a cute little pink bear.

"I'm not sure. Zane's putting her down."

"That means no. He can't resist playing with her."

He heads for the stairs, bounding up them quickly.

I take them slow and easy for the two-hundredth time today. While I love our three-story Victorian home, the stairs will be the death of me. They do keep me in shape, though. I barely found out I'm pregnant with our second child and I don't remember the stairs being this hard the last time I was dealing with early pregnancy symptoms.

During my last pregnancy, I was petrified of the postpartum stage. After my bout with the Great Big Dark, I feared feeling that way again. I knew it was common during the weeks after a baby was born and I wasted so much of my time worrying over it.

It didn't happen. I was fine. I don't have time to dwell on it this time around, but it does cross my mind now and again. Zane always says we'll face it together if it happens.

I love that man.

I hear giggling before I even reach the door of Ella's room. Sure enough, our angelic six-month old is wide awake, sitting on the floor next to her father and uncle while they play peek-a-boo with her, using the new pink bear as the BOO.

Ella's in her pajamas, freshly bathed. At least Zane has her halfway ready for bedtime.

Ryker's elegant suit jacket has been tossed aside in a crumpled pile, and he's distorting his face in the weirdest ways as he attempts to earn a giggle from Ella. She's sitting on the floor in her straight-back position, thoroughly entertained.

My little girl. She's brought me so much happiness. It's more than my heart can contain. Zane was right about that.

My eyes rest on Zane. He's already in his jeans and t-shirt for the evening, looking happy and relaxed. A warm tingle rushes through my body, a burst of love so strong it devours me. He's my person, the one who makes me happy, the one who animates me.

I took a chance and married him after dating for only six months. No regrets. It's the best decision I've ever made. No doubt about that. We had fifteen months together before we found out we were expecting our first baby. It was our honeymoon period, the time that grounded us as a couple. It was a time of healing, a time filled with lots of love and laughter. It was exactly what I needed.

When Ella giggles so hard, her face turns red, he laughs aloud, his smile huge. I never tire of watching him with her.

That man is captivated with his daughter. Our little girl is going to be able to sweet talk her daddy into whatever her heart pleases. We're in so much trouble.

I'm going to have to be the bad guy in her life, the one who sets all the rules. I can see it coming.

But I'm not worried. I love how much Zane loves our daughter. It makes me love him even more.

When he's not obsessed with Ella, he's obsessed with me. I believe that's why I'm prego again already. Go figure. That's how the birds and the bees work. There are consequences.

That's okay. We love our cute little consequences, born and unborn. I also love the birds and the bees. We both do. A little too much.

Zane's eyes catch me standing in the doorway and I swear his brown eyes turn into melted chocolate at the sight of me. I love it.

Or maybe that's me craving chocolate. Never can tell nowadays.

His attention quickly shifts to the other love of his life. Both Ryker and Zane are enraptured.

"Hey guys, dinner will be ready soon."

No response. It's like I'm not even there.

"We're having mud cakes with a few rocks on the side."

"Okay," Zane says, tickling Ella. "Sounds great. Be down in a few."

A few means thirty minutes when it comes to his playtime with Ella.

Ryker shoots me a worried frown. He was paying attention, after all.

"Just kidding. Spaghetti and meatballs."

He sends me a thumbs up.

"Okay, I'm gonna take Artie for a quick walk. I think I'll rob the corner market while I'm out. Would you like me to steal anything for you?"

"I'm good. Thanks, sweetheart."

Zane is now flat on his back, taking Ella for an airplane ride on his bent legs. She giggles whenever she flies toward Uncle Ryker, especially when he makes a show of acting like she's crashing into him. She smiles at me when she sees me, her chubby hand reaching out in an attempt to wave. But she doesn't cry for me. She's such a Daddy's girl.

"I'll take a few twenties," Ryker tells me.

He's working on his humor. Go, Ryker. "You got it. The rest is mine though. Steal your own loot."

Ryker snaps his fingers and swings his arm in a gosh-darn-it way. Hey, he's trying. Even his temper has mellowed. We rarely see cruel-humored Ryker anymore. Although, I wouldn't want to work for him in the business world. His nickname at Martel Investments is *The Shark*.

I can't help but smile as I head downstairs. My distracted man is busy having playtime with his daughter.

I won't disturb him again.

The decision to invite Ryker over for dinner was a tough one at first. Zane has always wanted a relationship with his brother. Naturally, he felt wary, after everything that went down between them. I was too. And I'm not going to lie, the first few dinners were phenomenally awkward. Zane always asked me to check his back after Ryker left, to make sure there wasn't a knife sticking in it. He was joking, of course. But there was an element of truth to the fear. We both knew we couldn't trust him. It had to be earned.

The more we tried to keep up good relations, the more the two relaxed in each other's company. It had a twofold effect. It improved their sibling relationship and it improved their working relationship. Win-win.

The arrival of Ella sealed the deal. Ryker is now the doting uncle and the relationship between the two brothers is undergoing a metamorphosis. I don't think they'll ever be best buddies. But they're both trying and that's the best they can do after a lifetime of being poisoned by their mother/stepmother toward each other.

Ryker finally admitted to us that he'd been told all of his life that Zane wanted what he had, that he had to protect himself, to fight back. It was so ingrained into his subconscious, it took him a while to realize how untrue it was. He even apologized to Zane. The damage is slowly being undone. Their father would be pleased.

I take Artie out for a quick walk, but decide to linger in the warm sunshine for a bit. Zane and Ryker need their time with Ella, and I won't hurry them.

When I return thirty or so minutes later, the house is quiet. I check on the spaghetti sauce and head upstairs again. I find Zane holding Ella, rocking her up and down in outstretched arms, one hand supporting her neck, the other her bum. It's like he's a human swing. He calls it his magic bounce. Since she was a newborn, he's been able to get her to sleep in no time with this method. Nothing's changed now, except she's six months and weighs a lot more. He says it's a better workout than weights. His bulging biceps don't lie. Or ever stop staring at me.

Ryker's standing next to him. They're both watching her eyelids get heavier and heavier. They mimic silent cheers when the blink gets longer. I won't use the word adorable to their faces, because men don't want to be called adorable. But it is. It's stinkin' adorable. Just saying.

Ryker leaves the room, pounding his heart with his fist twice as he exits. I watch Zane slowly set Ella in her crib. She's one lucky little girl. She gets rocked to sleep every single night by her daddy.

I'm even luckier. I get to be held all night in his arms.

When he turns and sees me watching him, he imitates my happy dance, which always makes me dissolve into laughter.

"For the record, that's not how I look when I do my happy dance."

"Oh, it's dead on. I practiced in front of the mirror to get it right."

We leave the room and Zane closes the door. He holds me tight for a few minutes. "Mmm, I missed you today." He nuzzles my neck. "I'm so jealous. You get all day with Ella and she gets all day with you."

"At least me and you get all night."

"Good point." He gently massages my back.

"It's fun to be with her all day. I love my life. She's a happy little thing."

"Right?" He pats my belly. "I hope Ella Two will be just as happy."

"No guarantees. Colic is a thing. And Ella could be a fella this time around."

He laughs at my silly rhyme. "No worries. My magic bounce will beat colic every time."

"You do have the magic touch, Mr. Martel."

"Yeah?" he says, raising his eyebrows. "How would you like to enjoy that magic touch this evening?"

"I'm counting on it."

He presses his lips to mine, and we get lost in each other for a moment or two. "I love you," he whispers.

"I love you too."

So much love. Truly more than my heart can contain.

We hear Ryker say from downstairs, "I can hear you guys. Knock it off."

Zane and I join Ryker downstairs, unapologetic for our actions. I serve dinner and we settle at the table, making fast work of our meal amidst light conversation.

"Delicious as always, Mila."

"Thank you, Ryker."

Ryker clears his throat. "So, I spent the early evening with my mother. Trying to teach her to budget her money is highly frustrating."

"She should be set for life, shouldn't she?" Zane asks.

"You would think. You gave her the house and she has a healthy bank account. I helped her invest her money. Technically, she can live off the money she earns from her investments."

"So, what's the problem?" Zane says, sneaking one more piece of French bread.

"Spending. She can't avoid three little words."

"What words are those?" I ask.

"Add To Cart."

"Ryker," I say, holding out my fist for him to bump. "You made a funny. That was a good one."

"I know. I've been waiting all night to say it."

"I'm so proud of you," I tell him.

Zane shakes his head at our banter. "Seriously, are you worried about her, Ryker?"

"If she runs out of money, she'll expect me to support her. So, yes."

Zane and Ryker discuss different methods of helping her budget her money while we clear our plates and load the dishwasher together.

I feel for Ryker. Debra's not an easy woman. She's been

given much more than she deserves. Zane felt at peace with giving her the family home. He promised his father he would help look after her. It was his way of honoring that promise. He now feels absolved of any and all responsibility towards her, however. As a matter of fact, he's done with her.

She gave up on trying to frame Zane for embezzlement. I think her lawyers finally talked some sense into her and made her realize she was lucky she wasn't in jail, and if she pursued her ridiculous case, that's exactly where she'd find herself.

Other than giving her the house, we keep our distance and let Ryker handle his mother. Every once in a while, he vents about his frustrations. He used to be such a momma's boy. The transition has been tough on him, but he stands up to her and doesn't put up with any guff.

"By the way, are you still seeing Evie?" Zane asks as we settle on the couch, each with a mug of herb tea, and enjoying the plate of cookies on the coffee table.

Good time for a subject change.

Ryker's face clouds. "Yeah. It's going well, but she wants me to take her dancing Friday night." He sighs heavily.

Zane guffaws. "Uh-oh. That's right up there with Indiana Jones' fear of snakes."

"Exactly. Do you think . . . do you think maybe you could give me a few tips, Mila? Do you mind, Zane? I don't want to blow it."

"Whoa," I say. "If you're willing to dance, that means you really like this girl."

"I do." A deer in the headlight's expression takes over his face. "And I'm petrified."

Zane jumps to his feet. "Watch and learn, Ryker. You got this." He pulls out his phone and clicks on a song. It's *Next to Me* by Imagine Dragons. It has a great beat for waltzing around the room and I admit, we've danced to it plenty of times in the privacy of our own home. He uses it as foreplay. Because Zane is romantic like that. And I love it. And him. So much.

Zane holds out his hand to me. "Dance with me, baby. I wanna hold you in my arms."

I look at Ryker. "No, don't say that."

Ryker shakes his head. "I won't. No way."

Zane leans closer to me. "It's worked in the past. Like a charm."

I bite my lip. "True."

Zane gives me his seductive smile, the one that's only for me, the one that makes me melt.

I take his hand and he pulls me to my feet. Dramatically, in time to the beat of the music, he pushes my lower back and snaps our bodies together.

"Don't do that either unless you want to get slapped," I tell Ryker.

"Nope, nope, nope," Ryker mumbles to himself.

Zane waltzes me around the room, holding me so close, it's scandalous. I forget we have an audience and get lost in the moment.

When the music ends, Zane whispers in my ear, "To be continued."

We share a smile as he steps away, holding my hands. I am putty in his. He gets me. Every time. "That's how it's done, bro."

I turn to Ryker. "It is. Listen to him. He knows what he's talking about."

Ryker's face is ashen. "I can't do that. There's no way."

"Yes, you can." Zane walks over to Ryker, restarts the music, and holds his hand out to him. "C'mon, I'll teach you."

"No freakin' way. I'm not dancing with you."

"Yes, you are. You gotta practice your moves."

"Do it, Ryker. You don't want to step on her toes. It'll ruin the moment."

I stand back as Ryker gives in and stands stiffly in Zane's arms. "This is stupid."

"Now, just move in a circle and let the beat carry you away. Hold her tight and look in her eyes. This isn't a dance contest, it's all about you and her. That's all you gotta know."

They start moving around the room and I head for the stairs.

"I'm out, guys. You're on your own."

Early pregnancy fatigue has me beat. I pause halfway up and watch Zane and his brother dancing awkwardly together.

"Is this right?" Ryker asks.

"Yep. You're doing great."

I can't hide a smile and a burst of laughter at the sight.

At the same time, warmth fills my soul. Zane has a family, a family that adores him.

The prince has become a king.

A Note from Taylor Dean

You might be wondering why I decided to include a small snippet about situational depression toward the end of this book.

After all, it's . . . depressing. And no one wants to read something that makes them feel depressed.

While I tried to keep it light, I believe it's an important topic that should be discussed. People should be encouraged to talk about their mental health. It shouldn't be taboo, and no one should feel shame over it. Keeping it to ourselves is the worst thing we can do.

Two years ago, I found myself facing a health issue that left me very depressed and wondering what was wrong with me.

In HEART THIEF, I write about situational depression from my point of view, from my experience with it. I didn't try to portray a technically accurate depiction of textbook depression. Just my truth, pure and simple. I can't speak to anyone else's experience, nor was it my intention to provide medical advice or easy answers.

Everyone is different, and every situation should be handled differently. It's not a simple issue with a simple cure.

My only hope is that the overriding message the reader is left with is to reach out, seek help, and don't keep it to yourself. That's what helped me get through it.

If reading this book helps just one person survive it, then I will be happy.

Life changes are tough. Know that you're not alone.

-Taylor

Thank you for reading Heart Thief.
If you enjoyed this book, you'll also enjoy the
other two standalone books in the *Love Under
Wraps* series.

December 2019: Rules are made to be Broken

*I've loved Will Henderson from the first day I laid eyes on him.
But I made a solemn promise that same day. I would never, ever
date Will Henderson.*

For almost a decade, Charlotte Dubois has loved Will Henderson
from afar, squelching her heart's silent yearnings. But no way
could she date her best friend Kelsey's brother. Their whole
friendship is based on one rule: No friend of Kelsey can ever date
Will. Instead, Charlotte has watched him date and break more
hearts than should be legal.

Will Henderson never got over that stolen kiss he shared with
Charlotte years ago — though he's tried valiantly to rid his system
of his sister's best friend.

When circumstances bring the two into each other's arms again,
Will wants to convince Charlotte to break the rules and take a
chance on him. But to do so, they will have to hide their
relationship from the ones they love most.

Can true love triumph, or will they both end up losing?

January 2020: A Wrinkle in Forever

What do you do when forever unravels?

Ever since Laurel Tremain kicked Everett Montgomery out of student council her sophomore year of high school, she lost her heart to the arrogant, but oh-so-charming jock. That was the moment their love story began, and once it started, it flourished into a forever kind of love.

But a tragic accident the night before their wedding leaves Laurel broken, unable to give Rett what he most desires.

When she realizes Rett will never be the one to walk away, she runs, placing a permanent wrinkle in the fabric of their lives.

Years later, a twist of fate brings Laurel into Everett's orbit once again. He's tried to move on since she stole a piece of his soul and disappeared, but life hasn't turned out the way he hoped. His forever has diverged far off course.

One thing he knows: Time hasn't erased his love for Laurel. And he wants her back.

However, reality brings them both crashing down to earth when they discover their second chance lies squarely in the forbidden zone. Will Laurel and Rett be doomed to turn their backs on their hearts and love each other from afar?

Find out in this modern twist on the Jane Eyre love story.

Other books by Taylor Dean
I'm With You

Can three little words irrevocably change your life?

When the doctors inform Chloe Brennan that her pregnancy is *"incompatible with life,"* her subsequent choices will change her path forever. She becomes one of the quiet, unsung heroes of this world, incredibly strong, yet somehow wrongly looked upon as damaged.

Three people will pierce Chloe's existence: her husband, a stranger, and a precious baby. One will say goodbye, one will say hello, and one will say both at the same time.

I'm With You is a novel about selfless love and the sacredness of life.

Stone Silence
Spencer's Story
(Sound of Silence Series, Book One)

Great big beautiful love.

Does it really exist?

Everyone tells me it does. They say, "Spencer Elliott, don't worry, you'll find it one day. You just have to find the right man and when you do, it will surprise the heck out of you."

I'm still waiting for that heck of a surprise to hit. It has proven to be elusive thus far. I'm pretty sure the entire world is lying about love and the joke is on me.

I know I want a man in my heart and in my life. Unfortunately, most men immediately push my OFF button and I lose interest quickly.

Feeling pressure to prove I'm trying to find my soulmate, I finally give in and agree to a date. Huge mistake. Afterward I find myself abandoned in the middle of nowhere, in desperate need of help.

That's when I meet Stony by chance. He's a silent and unsmiling man who intrigues me with his ability to keep going after life has knocked him down. Suddenly the abstract notion of love becomes tangible and within my reach. Once I experience it, I wonder how I ever lived without it.

That's when I stay with Stony by choice. But when Stony's hidden past and present-day reality collide, his silence is broken. And the truth about his life nearly brings me to my knees. I can't compete with ghosts from the past.

I refuse to fight for a man's love. He either loves me or he doesn't. It's as simple and as complicated as that. My only hope is . . . he does.

Jailbird
Mia's Story
(Sound of Silence Series, Book Two)

My hometown decided to rename me Jailbird.

Every day I silently scream out, "*My name is Mia Faraday!*" My time in jail does not define me. I am so much more than one heated mistake.

And yet, my slip-up weighs on me. There's so much more to the story than anyone realizes. I must face Stony, my ex, and confess everything.

I don't want to. I'd rather have five teeth pulled. While I'm awake. Without anesthesia.

But this is something I have to do, something I need to do. Not just for Stony. I need to do it for me. Especially for me. I can't move forward with my life until I gain closure from the past.

When I meet Grayson Elliott, I am easily pulled into his orbit and it's exactly where I'd love to stay. He makes me laugh and not take life so seriously. He makes me want to live again.

But I don't love me right now, and that healing needs to come first. I'm not relationship-ready or marriage material. My mind is focused on redemption. *I want it. I need it.*

Besides, when Grayson hears about my colorful past, I'm sure he'll be gone before I have time to utter the word *goodbye*.

After all, who could ever love a jailbird?

TAYLOR DEAN

Hothouse Flower
Shay's Story
(Sound of Silence Series, Book Three)

I loved Jace Faraday with all my heart.

I loved everything about him, from his huge smile to his fabulous laugh. Another man never caught my eye. It was always Jace and Shay, together forever.

Until it wasn't. He devastated me, he ruined me. I've never gotten over it.

But, I'm a survivor. I'm not a precious flower that can only thrive if kept safe from the perils of the outside world.

Except now Jace has returned home. He's just across the street from me, so close I swear I can actually feel his presence.

I can't avoid him forever. At some point I have to face him. And when I do, I know sparks will fly.

To redeem himself for his past actions, I need major remorse. I need a profuse apology and maybe even a little begging for forgiveness. I won't settle for anything less.

However, when the truth behind our break-up is revealed, I'm stunned. It leaves me reeling—and yearning for the five years that have been lost to us.

The thing is, once the truth is known, there's nothing to keep us apart.

Absolutely nothing.

Chasing Fireflies

A Power of the Matchmaker standalone Story

My sisters think I'm crazy.

But, I've never forgotten the mysterious woman from my childhood who told me Paul is the name of my one true love.

She told me to search far and wide for him.

I haven't stopped looking ever since.

When I stumble across an article about a successful American entrepreneur named Paul who lives and works in China, I'm intrigued. When the opportunity to teach English in China presents itself on the same day, I know it's not a coincidence.

It's destiny.

My sisters say I'm chasing a dream.

Just like the fireflies we tried to catch on the warm summer evenings of our youth, the dream seems beyond my grasp. Will my quest for the elusive Paul always be just short of fulfillment?

My sisters tell me it's a fool's errand.

Until I remind them of the day we saw the Red Bird.

The memory silences them.

The *Red Bird Incident* remains inarguable—and proves my search for Paul is not a silly fantasy.

I will find Paul . . . I will.

Violin Words
A Christmas Romance

WHO IS THE AUTHOR?

When Jade Lockwood begins to receive anonymous love letters, she becomes a woman on a mission.

She's determined to figure out who wrote the flowery, over-the-top letters filled with the sweetest violin words she's ever heard.

She's neglected her love life, concentrating on Lockwood Cabins, the business her father built from the ground up. But her sweet letters have awakened something inside of her, something that can't be ignored.

Facing Christmas alone this year, her emotions are already fragile. Add in a mysterious burglary, a handsome stranger, and a little deceit, and it just might be the most eventful Christmas she's ever endured.

Will Jade find her happy ending? Or will her love letters prove to be nothing more than a sinister ploy?

Find out in this charming Christmas novel.

I Have People

Missing any memories?

Holly Sinclair is happily married to the love of her life, Gabriel.

Young and in love, Holly hopes to have their first child soon. Of course, Gabriel wants to wait till Holly's health is restored, much to her dismay.

She feels perfectly fine. So what if she just woke up from an eight-month coma? So what if some of her memories are missing? She remembers Gabe and that's all that matters, right?

That is, until HE enters her life again . . . she forgot about HIM.

For Nick

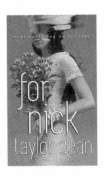

What would you do for love?

Zachary Drake had love in his life—and tragically lost it. He knows it won't come his way again. Andie Parker would do anything for the love of her life. Even marry a total stranger.

In spite of the unorthodox manner in which Zach and Andie come together, there is no denying that things are unexpectedly good between them, taking them both by surprise.

However, when secrets come between them—and trust does not—Andie soon finds herself vowing to never make the same mistake again. But, she'd do it again in a heartbeat and she knows it. She'd marry a hundred strangers if it helped Nick.

She'd do anything for Nick . . . anything.

Sierra

Named a Top Five Finalist by the Kindle Book Review for Best Indie Book of 2013 in the Romance Category

Have you ever been lost in the woods?

Alyssa Fontaine's life, loved ones — everything familiar and dear — are brutally taken from her. Taken captive by two men, she endures a horrific nightmare. A new life is forced upon her and even a new name. Just when it appears that no hope is in sight, she is saved by an unlikely twist of fate. Trapped in the beautiful Sierra Nevada Mountains, life will open its arms to her again and she will embrace it.

She will find love such as she never knew existed. Sierra is a heart-wrenching story of the power of the human spirit to survive amidst impossible circumstance and severe losses. It is a story of survival . . . and hope.

Lancaster House

A paranormal romance
Are you ever really alone?

Zoe Grayson needs a change. So, she moves to another state, purchases an old, dilapidated 1920s Victorian Mansion, and sets out to restore it to its former glory. As she begins the restoration, she finds herself falling in love with the old house . . . not to mention its illustrious builder, Mr. Lancaster. Zoe becomes obsessed with the house as she discovers its secrets; hidden rooms, secret passageways . . . and a mysterious man who seems to think the house is his. Who is he? More importantly, how does he live in her home unseen and unheard? The unexpected answers leave her reeling—and questioning everything she's ever known. To her dismay, Zoe's actions land her in the local psychiatric hospital, scheming for ways to return to Lancaster House . . . and the love of her life.

The Middle Aisle

A sequel to Lancaster House

Zoe Grayson is back in Lancaster House, ordered to bed rest for the duration of her unexpected pregnancy.

Doctor Wade Channing, her overzealous psychiatrist, is living in Lancaster House, taking care of her, waiting on her, and tending to her every need. It seems to be the perfect arrangement.

There's just one catch. She has to tell him her story—everything that has happened in her life since the moment she escaped from Serenity Hills. It's been quite an adventure to include renovating another home and a walk down the middle aisle. But, that's all over now. Nothing is real. It never was. How did she end up in this miserable situation?

Joshua's Folly

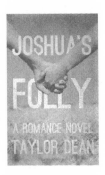

Can you fall in love with a picture?

After Marisa survives a traumatic experience in her youth, she finds comfort in the form of a photograph of Joshua, her foster mother's nephew. She falls in love with him, creating and refining an image of the man of her dreams.

When Marisa has the opportunity to visit Texas for the summer, staying at Joshua's cattle ranch outside of Amarillo, she meets Joshua in person for the first time. She quickly realizes he is someone she could really fall in love with, not just a silly childhood crush. Life is seemingly perfect for Josh and Marisa, with endless possibilities before them. That is, until Josh's reservations take a toll on their relationship and their summertime romance ends rather unexpectedly. Will Marisa be able to forgive Josh for his folly?

Girl of Mine

HE CAME HOME

The year is 2003 and Captain Lucas Graham is at Fort Bragg, North Carolina, about to be deployed to Iraq. A few weeks ago, he broke his engagement with Jillian Barrett, leaving her stunned and heartbroken. Knowing he can't leave for war without putting his affairs in order, Luke obtains a four-day pass with only one goal in mind: explain his life story to his former fiancée.

The problem: Jill is now engaged to another man. But Luke isn't giving up. He only has four days to gain an audience with Jill, even if he has to resort to drastic measures to do so. And he will . . .

𝒜 Me and You Thing

THE DEEPEST HEARTACHE IS THE ONE YOU DON'T SEE COMING.

Golden couple, Sawyer and Quinn Denali, have an amazing love story. A match in every way, their happiness is evident to all who spend time with them. The arrival of twin baby girls completes their picture-perfect family.

When Quinn has the opportunity to help others on a two-week volunteer trip, she reluctantly leaves her family, knowing a short break from the demands of motherhood will be good for her. She doesn't expect the trip to change her life forever. But it does. It changes everything.

Struggling from day to day, the young family moves forward, finding happiness . . . and love.

But fate isn't done mixing things up in their lives. When an unexpected event leaves them all reeling, the unspoken question rings loudly and can't be ignored: "What happens now?"

A Me and You Thing is a novel that explores the strength of enduring love and friendship.

Taylor Dean lives in Texas and is the mother of four grown children. Upon finding herself with an empty nest, she began to write the stories that were always wandering around in her head, quickly finding she had a passion for writing, specifically romance. Whether it's paranormal, contemporary, or suspense—you'll find all sub-genres of clean romance in her line-up. Connect with Taylor at www.taylordeanbooks.com

Made in the USA
Lexington, KY
04 December 2019